The BBC Hunters

James Ward

COOL MILLENNIUM BOOKS

3

Published in the United Kingdom. All rights reserved. No part of this publication may be
reproduced, distributed or transmitted in any form or means, without written permission.

Copyright © James Ward 2019

First published 2019.
This edition published 2021.

A CIP catalogue record for this book is available from the British Library.

ISBN: 978-1-913851-36-1

Cover picture shows BBC Broadcasting House.

This novel was produced in the UK and uses British-English language conventions ('authorise'
instead of 'authorize', 'The government are' instead of 'the government is', etc.)

To my wife

Chapter 1: The Strange, Sad Tale of a Dream Team

The consensus just about everywhere (even, reluctantly, in the Kremlin) was that the so-called Web Brigades had failed. New US sanctions, Bellingcat, travel bans, asset freezes, the OPCW fiasco: not exactly an endless list, but far too long for comfort. In any case, the west was clued-up. Everything was set to get harder now.

But where others saw diminishing returns (failure in a *positive* sense was the official line: it hadn't been a catastrophe), Stanislav Viktorovich Kuznetsov, the FSB's Director of Overseas Strategic Affairs, saw opportunity. A house-shaped man with a grey walrus moustache and rheumy eyes, this was his retirement year, and fate had presented him with a rare chance to put something new and exciting forward. Play all his cards in roughly the correct order and he could well go out in triumph.

Delegation, he realised, was key. He painstakingly set about assembling a team of what he called 'lateral thinkers': a dozen men and women to reboot the offensive on western culture. He raided marketing firms, strategic management companies, advertising corporations, the creative industries. He put a select team of four high-ranking FSB officers in charge of the vetting process: every 'applicant' hand-picked by Kuznetsov was invited - no one was forced - to attend an interview at Lubyanka Square, where he or she was wired to a lie detector and cross-examined for an hour. All expressed roughly the same views. Putin had restored Russian pride (crushed the Chechens, taken back Crimea, revitalised the church), and he was a 'real' man (played ice-hockey and practised judo, went diving and fishing and horse-riding). He might be reviled in the west, but then 'western' countries were in thrall to the LGBT+ delusion, the progeny of 'human rights', the West's trump card against Soviet Communism in the nineteen-seventies and eighties, and which had finally come back to bite it with a vengeance.

All looked rosy for a time. An emerging dream team. But, as subsequent events demonstrated, Kuznetsov wasn't as good at assembling working groups as he'd always made out. His chief preoccupation was always to claim sole credit afterwards, and, in this case, he made two fatal mistakes.

The first was introducing each group member to the others before informing the group as a whole of its *raison d'être*. For six whole months, its members had no idea why it was being convened. In the interval between the arrival of the first participant, in September, and the day it began work in March, the team bonded unexpectedly strongly in the social sense. There was even a romance. By mid-April, it was meeting twice weekly, in the evening, for dinners, discussions of literary matters and the odd drunken city walking tour.

Kuznetsov's second mistake lay in arranging for the screening interviews to be conducted by uniformed officers (which was intimidating), none of whom were experienced, or even qualified, interrogators (making them relatively oblivious to the fact that they were intimidating, and the likely distorting effects of that). So in retrospect, it was probably obvious the candidates' answers would have a patriotic twang. The problem was not in what they said – the lie detector never wavered – but in what was never asked. Because it later transpired that the respondents' patriotism, though genuine, was qualified. The President and his buddies, they thought, *were* corrupt (but no more so than western politicians); the country *had* become poorer under the United Russia Party (but maybe that was the deliberate fault of the west and their sanctions - and, hey, you should have seen poverty under Yeltsin!); and yes, government censorship *was* tightening (but Russia was a big country and, sadly, only a strong centre could stop it flying apart). Like creatives everywhere, they possessed a healthy quota of anti-statism. But this passed completely beneath the FSB's radar.

In June, six months after the first members were recruited, Kuznetsov invited Pasha Domogarov, the man he'd appointed team leader, to his home in Patriarshiye Ponds. He plied him with vintage wine, introduced him to his family, spoke intelligently about current affairs, and announced that he expected his new twelve-person group to help devise the next phase in the disruption of Russia's enemies abroad.

Two days afterwards, Domogarov summoned what he still thought of primarily as *his eleven best friends* to an urgent meeting at his tenth-floor flat in Kapotnya. He explained self-consciously what the Director required while the others sat in glum silence. Although they all knew nothing really good lasts for ever, they unanimously wanted to continue as they were. They definitely didn't want to plot international subterfuge. A general discussion ensued, which, since it was accompanied by free drinks and takeaway meals, and since everyone assumed it was being recorded, began and ended with the pretence of enthusiasm.

After just fourteen days, with the FSB's research facility at its complete disposal, the team came up with the outline of a workable plan. They squared it with their consciences by telling themselves that, if it succeeded, it would be good for humanity. Western liberalism was a snake that ate its own tail and something the world could do without.

But during that fortnight, one member committed suicide; another 'disappeared', apparently having suddenly left the country. None of the others remarked at length on these facts. From the outset, it was as if they were half anticipated.

But from Kuznetsov's point of view, they were terrifying: the sort of things scandals are made of. He quietly resolved to bury the whole project as soon as possible. Thank God, it didn't yet have so much as an official name.

On the other hand, he'd come a long way. He'd gone to a lot of effort. He could be forgiven for wanting *something* back.

Thankfully, just as he was about to permanently pull the plug, Domogarov told him the group had come up with 'an idea of genius'.

Hearing is believing. The next day, Domogarov climbed the two wide flights of stairs to the Director's office. He wore a new suit and fashionable brogues, and carried a bespoke paper bag with a pile of books inside. The Director's secretary – his wife, a twenty-something ex-fashion model in a Cartier suit – greeted him as a friend, enquired after his health and ushered him into her husband's office: small with an unpretentious desk, sofa, armchair, a gilt-framed portrait of Nicholas II and another – curiously - of Rasputin.

The Director himself advanced, shook Domogarov's hand warmly, said 'Sit down!' several times in a gushing tone, and pushed the armchair forward an inch. He grimaced fleetingly at the carrier bag as if this wasn't the occasion to be giving gifts, then seemed to regain his bonhomie. He sat down at his desk mainly as way of putting a formal barrier between himself and his visitor.

"So fire away," he said.

Domogarov folded his hands. "What we're attempting shouldn't be too difficult," he began. "We're not Communists any more. We don't believe in some never-to-be-realised Utopia of workers owning 'the means of production', whatever that even signifies nowadays." He switched to a different, and less natural rhythm of speech, as if reading from a collection of prompt-cards. "We're simply ordinary people, upholders of values and traditions all Europeans hold dear, or used to. We believe in the primacy of the family, the absolute truth of the Christian creeds, the essential and irreducible difference between the genders, pragmatism in politics, the desirability of nationalism, the superiority of the West – which fully includes Russia, or used to – over every other culture in the world, and the debilitating effects of mass immigration and the LBGT ideology. We're not racist; we're not sexist; we're not even anti-gay, providing the gays don't try to pass their life-style off as morally equivalent to ours. We're just normal. We're a bastion of traditional values in a Europe gone radic-ally wrong."

The Director's expression grew increasingly sour. "That sounds suspiciously like something you learned by heart. Are you nervous?"

"Of course, but - "

"Listen, Pasha. This always happens. I invite someone to come up with an idea for me. Then I get them into my office to talk about it. If it's a bad idea, they usually start by making a speech, telling me all sorts of things I already know. It's as if they think they're establishing common ground with me on the assumption that things are likely to go downhill later. From my point of view, they're building a wall to protect them from what they perceive is going to be a well-deserved rub-bishing of what they're going to propose. It rarely has the effect they desire, because – I'm sure you can see this - it's ever so slightly cowardly. Just tell me what you're suggesting. If I don't like it, we'll wrap things up now."

"The next step in our campaign against the west," Domog-arov said, "is to take over the UK's 'BBC'. *The British Broadcast-ing Corporation*," he said in English.

Silence. Their eyes locked. The Director looked even less pleased than a moment ago. "I see," he said morosely. He scratched his temple. "I must admit, I wasn't expecting that."

"I didn't think you would be."

"I'm disappointed, Pasha."

"There's no need to be. Let me - "

"*That's* your big idea? *That's* what you've been working on for the last fortnight?"

"Let me show you something." Domogarov stood up, reached into his carrier bag and lifted out six English-language paperbacks. He laid them slowly and methodically on the desk. He added a sealed B5 envelope at the bottom of the arrangement, right in front of Kuznetsov, as if it were the *coup de grâce*.

"What are these?" the Director said, pushing the envelope out of the way. "I mean, for God's sake don't state the obvious: I can see they're books. But I can't read English. What precisely are you trying to show me?"

Domogarov pointed to each in turn. "This one's called, *The BBC's Liberal Assault on the British Mind*; this is, *How and Why the BBC is Trying to Change the Way You Think*; this is, *The BBC's Cultural Marxism Exposed*; here we have *The BBC's True Agenda: Identity Politics, Doublethink and the End of Britain*; this is, *Metropolitan Liberal Elitism: The Decline and Fall of the BBC*, and finally, *Why the BBC is Destroying British Culture*."

"I see," the Director said again. He looked more interested now – just slightly. "And they come from…? Where did you get them?"

"They were all published in Britain by native British authors within the last ten years. They all push broadly the same message."

"That being?"

"The BBC's leading us in a direction we don't want to go. We're simply ordinary people, upholders of values and traditions all Europeans hold dear, or used to. We believe in the primacy of the family, the truth of the Christian creeds, the essential difference between the genders, pragmatism in politics, the desirability of nationalism, the superiority of the West over every other culture in the world, and the debilitating effects of mass immigration and the LBGT ideology. We're not racist; we're not sexist; we're not even anti-gay, providing the gays don't try to pass their lifestyle off as morally equivalent to ours. We're just normal. We're a bastion of traditional values." He paused for breath, beamed happily, and only just stopped himself performing a pirouette. "Now you can see, Director, why I learned what I said earlier by heart!"

"And are there *lots* of people in Britain who see the BBC in this way?" His tone was definitely interested now.

"More than enough to make our plan workable."

"By 'our' you mean you and your team. You want to take over the BBC. You think we can. By 'we': Russia."

"Not 'take over', but reinvent. The beauty of it is, we don't even have to co-opt anyone. There are high-ranking people in Britain eminently suited to senior positions in the BBC, all of whom share the views outlined in these six books. It's just a question of getting them into place. Once they're there, they'll create a Britain much more in tune with Russian values and hence interests. In the meantime, no need for clandestine meetings on oligarchs' yachts, no requirement for secret rendezvous in Hyde Park, no coercion whatsoever. The people we're targeting don't even need to know we're using them. And in a way, we're *not*. But once established, they'll be talkable-to. And they'll change the way the whole UK thinks. Because that's what the BBC does. People trust it. It forms people's opinions, not just in Britain, but globally. It's what's sometimes called an 'influencer', Director, but a colossal one, an all-powerful one. With the right people in charge, it'll start marching to our tune. Because if you think about it, we're only marching to the tune of traditional common sense."

"'Talkable-to.'" The Director was clearly doing his best to maintain a cautious demeanour, but he was equally obviously excited.

"It's partly about reassigning the web brigades," Pasha went on. "Putting them to work in different vicinities to the past. 'Nudging' the right individuals. 'Nudging' certain people in Britain to think of applying for certain jobs, 'nudging' others to support them, 'nudging' yet others to wave them through. It's all about *nudging*. Richard Thaler and Cass Sunstein, they're Americans, of course - "

The Director held his hand up. "I've heard enough. Sit down, Pasha."

Domogarov returned to his armchair like a dog scurrying to its basket. Once there, he seemed to shrink slightly.

The Director sighed. "So we've got to identify the right people in at least three different areas, then we've got to 'nudge' them, as you put it. How long do you think that's going to take?"

Domogarov felt the first drops of a bucket of icy water being poured over him. "I, er, admit it's a long-term project, Director. Five, ten years?"

"You haven't come up with any way of *accelerating* it?"

"It's – it's in the envelope. I've worked on it entirely by myself. I mean, it's all my own work. Best to keep the circle of those in the know, so to speak, as limited as possible when - "

"Okay, Pasha, enough. You all seem to have worked to the best of your abilities, but it's obviously not fully there yet as an idea."

"But, sir, look in the envelope!"

"And I can't give you any more time," the Director continued. "I'm afraid, given what happened to Yuliyr and Elizaveta, I've no choice but to call it a day. You probably expected such a thing."

Domogarov felt himself deflate even more. "Half-expected, yes. Do we know where Elizaveta is yet?"

The Director scowled. "I, er... No. Not yet."

An awkward silence, no more than half a second, during which the Director showed no inclination to elucidate, and even less concern for the missing woman; in which he merely seemed annoyed at being wrong footed.

In a flash, Domogarov saw what had happened, or thought he did. Elizaveta was dead. She'd been located by the state, somewhere far away, and she'd been killed.

The Director chuckled self-consciously. "Honestly, Pasha, I never realised you creatives were *such a sensitive bunch!* Fancy Yuliyr and Elizaveta being unable to cope with pressure to *that* extent! If I'd known, I'd never have started on all this! In any case, my friend, we can't risk any more collateral. Obviously, for the sake of your mental wellbeing, we'll be watching all ten of you very carefully from now. Like I say, your own good, that's all it is. Such a tragic conclusion. Nevertheless, you did your best and no one's going to stop you applying for better jobs. Meanwhile, you'll go back to what you were doing before all this started."

Domogarov stood up. He went to collect his books and the envelope from the desk, while the Director strode across the room and held the door open.

"*Leave* those," the Director said. "I'll take care of them, or I'll get my secretary to. And, er, good luck, Pasha." He smiled. "You can go now," he added as if the meaning of him holding open the door, insisting his wife could deal with everything, and wishing Pasha good luck wasn't sufficiently clear.

Domogarov felt he'd been booted out, and in a sense, he had. As he descended the wide staircase towards the exit, he realised the Director was going to steal his idea.

Which had probably been the intention all along.

But that didn't matter. More importantly, he saw his own fate. He was going the same way as Elizaveta. The Director would come after him.

And if not the Director, someone. Not necessarily even the government; more likely its 'friends': unofficial sycophants-cum-thugs who specialised in meting out rough justice to inconvenient persons, and who expected to be rewarded for 'services rendered'. Gangsters.

A few seconds' thought convinced the Director that Domogarov's idea was viable. Sufficiently to approach the Assistant to the Secretary, a day later, where he passed it off as his own.

The Assistant nodded sagely, pretending to be sceptical. He knew all about the Director's little twelve person committee; nevertheless, twenty-four hours later, he took the plan to the Secretary where he passed it off as his own. The Secretary also knew about the Director's team, but assumed he was alone in this, so said nothing. He then took the idea to the Deputy Minister, where he passed it off as his own. And so the process continued, each higher official claiming to have thought of it him or herself, yet also knowing its true origin, until it reached the President, who was too exalted to bother himself with anything as insignificant as an FSB Director's working group, and who considered the idea - whilst eating ramen noodles and watching football on TV - as if it had appeared from the ether. He then brought it to a committee which included all those who'd passed it up the chain (with the obvious exception of Domogarov and his team), where he passed it off as his own. It was approved unanimously, and received a standing ovation.

But by now, virtually everyone in the sequence feared losing face. It could never become common knowledge whose idea this really was.

The fate of Domogarov and his team was thus sealed from at least ten different directions.

And then something astonishing occurred. On the same day, at exactly the same time in the evening, all ten government surveillance squads suddenly found themselves looking at … precisely nothing. To all intents and purposes, Domogarov and his former crew had disappeared into thin air.

In the highest echelons of the Kremlin, officials quietly panicked. They cancelled appointments, made urgent phone calls, transferred large amounts of money between secret bank accounts. They despatched detectives and assassins and bounty-hunters to make sure the missing individuals disappeared in a more fitting manner.

They tried to keep all this to themselves. But the Foreign Intelligence Service of the Russian Federation, the SVR, also had a critical interest, and it launched a more thorough investigation of its own under conditions of absolute secrecy. It began with the flats, bedsits and rooms of the missing ten. A painstaking search - in which, in at least four cases, floorboards were taken up and furniture overturned - uncovered no clue as to how the wondrous disappearance had been effected.

But it turned out that Domogarov and his girlfriend owned several photographs of an unknown man who – as far as could be discovered - was neither a relative, nor a colleague, nor a friend; and who wasn't even particularly Russian-looking. Moreover, three other members of the missing team possessed portrait pictures of the same male, apparently all taken at different times, and quite possibly without the subject's knowledge. He was in his early thirties by the look of him, clean-shaven, blond curly hair, probably a little under two metres tall, handsome in a rugged sort of way (could he be any one of the team's boyfriend or former boyfriend?).

The result, when face recognition programs were applied, was even more bewildering than the team's sudden disappearance. For the software verified conclusively what a few high-ranking officials already suspected, but no one could quite bring themselves to believe: that this man was the British secret agent, John Mordred. Physical copies of his dossier were stored, as an insurance policy, in four different filing cabinets at separate locations in Moscow, each duplicate being at least twice the size of any comparable report on any other foreign agent.

An hour after the discovery, four senior SVR officers climbed the two wide flights of stairs to the office of the FSB's Director of Overseas Strategic Affairs. They found Stanislav Kuznetsov already waiting for them with a written confession. Since he loved his country, he said, and since his intentions had been consistently noble, he had nothing to hide. Everything he'd done was logged in there, every bit of it.

From the authorities' point of view, whether his statement gave enough detail and was verifiable enough to put him morally in the clear remained an open question, but procedurally it certainly didn't. He was what the Americans called 'a loose cannon'. He'd acted well above his pay grade, making no verifiable attempt to obtain the necessary permissions. As a result, he was given twenty-four hours to clear his desk, and formally notified that his pension was under review.

The SVR's overall verdict: this was bad. Heads had already been scheduled to roll, but they'd been Russian heads, and it was arguably one of the legitimate rights of the state to deal with its own citizens as it reasonably saw fit if they turned traitor.

Someone else's citizens? Pragmatically, at least, that was a different matter.

At this point, it became a matter for the highest authority in the land.

The President considered the problem whilst eating a pretzel and watching football on Channel 5. His conclusion - after FC Rubin Kazan won 4-1 on penalties - was that anyone who aided and abetted a traitor was an enemy, and therefore a legitimate target. But killing a foreign national could only be an absolute last resort. Given the enormity of what was at stake, these so-called Novelists had to be stopped from ever making contact with 'John Mordred'. If that meant the security services discharging every weapon in their arsenal, then so be it.

The SVR interpreted this as a mandate to link hands with Russia's Main Directorate of the General Staff of the Armed Forces of the Russian Federation, the GU. Together, they embarked on what some of the Kremlin's more erudite officials claimed was perhaps the biggest incursion of Russian forces

into the European continent west of Berlin since the Sixth Co-
alition of 1814.

Chapter 2: One Guy Named Mobe

Two months later

"You're John Mordred, aren't you?"

Mordred turned: a man of about his own age, thin, Asian-descent, short black beard, gelled hair, expensive overcoat, holding a glass of lager. It wasn't a hostile question. Just the sort you might ask a minor celebrity if you found yourself in close proximity to one, somewhere unusual: *Excuse me, but just out of curiosity, would you mind confirming...?*

"I might be," Mordred said wearily.

Tuesday 11am in the White Horse & Bower. Apart from the landlord and three old women huddled in the corner, the bar was empty. Mordred was - had been - sitting alone by the window. He'd come in because he'd had the distinct sensation of being followed and he'd learned never to ignore it. An empty pub wouldn't necessarily flush the problem out, but it was a good place to do a recce. And if your tail was alone, it usually gave him or her a few moments of anxiety: what if you left by the back entrance?

The man grinned and sat down. "I expect you're wondering how I know you," he said in a semi-whisper. "You're a spy, aren't you?"

Mordred grimaced. "I used to be."

"Right. What are you drinking? I'd like to get you another."

"I've a meeting to get to so - "

"At Thames House? Sorry, sorry," he said, apparently registering Mordred's sour expression for the first time. "I'm a journalist. I take an interest in these sorts of things. Let's face it, John, you're pretty famous nowadays – for a spy, I mean. The closest thing MI5's got to a star. The Ultimate Londoner, yes?" He laughed. "Hey, don't worry, I won't tell anyone I know all about you. Although it is in the public domain, most of it." He offered a handshake. "Mobeen," he said. "You can call me Mobe. Last name: Dhanial. Just so we're on an equal footing, I was born in Blackpool and I work freelance for *The Daily Mail.*"

Mordred ignored the hand. He stood up. "I've really got to go."

"I've got information for you," Mobe said. "I'm not here by accident."

"I only came in here by chance, so you can hardly have been waiting for me."

"Stop! Look, here's what I came to tell you. *Panorama.* You know *Panorama,* yeah? The BBC TV documentary programme? It's conducting a major investigation into government policy. I mean, *major.* No one knows what aspect even, except that it's got the potential to blow the government sky-high. Force a general election: that sky-high. They're keeping the tightest of mega-tight lids on it. But I know things. I've got entry. And by the way, you're not helping yourself, being so eager to shake me off. If you'd really given up spying, you wouldn't be like that. You'd be, 'Well, buy me another drink if you like. It's your loss.'"

"Like I said - "

"We're just around the corner from Thames House. There's no law against me following you, John. Two things could happen after that. One: you go into Thames House because, as you say, you've 'got a meeting'. In that case, I'll know you for a liar, and I'll be back. Or two: you've no choice but to wander round for a few hours with me two paces behind. In that case, you'll miss your meeting."

They were on their way out of the pub now.

"Maybe the meeting's just an excuse to get rid of you," Mordred said.

"We'll see, shall we?"

"What do you actually want?"

"I want us to work together."

"No, thanks."

"Please. To get the BBC." He apparently realised this required explanation. "Because it's run by a bunch of liberal milksops who are trying to force a left-wing ideology on the population."

Mordred laughed. "If you knew anything about me - "

"I've actually written a book about it, John. *The BBC's True Agenda: Identity Politics, Doublethink and the End of Britain.* You should read it. Twelve pounds ninety-nine. But you can get the ebook - "

" - you'd know that's actually a pretty good description of me too. Milksop. Bleeding heart, PC, SJW, snowflake. I doubt we'd get on."

"Opposites attract. Not that I'm gay. Or maybe I am. I don't trumpet the fact. Wouldn't ever attend a Pride event, for example."

"You're missing out, big time. In any case, I'm married."

"I know. The beautiful Phyllis Mordred *née* Robinson, ex-model. You landed on your feet there, Johnny."

Mordred laughed again, despite himself. Weird. A fairly repugnant kind of guy – probably - yet for reasons completely unknown, one to whom he couldn't stop talking. "So it's 'Johnny' now, is it?"

"Yep. I see us being a bit like Stefan and Rash in *New Blood.* Remember that? Typical BBC EU-phile fare, but still quite good. Wouldn't work now, obviously. A lot of water's passed under the bridge since 2016, thank God."

Mordred stopped dead and turned to face his interlocutor. "Look, Mobeen, don't take this the wrong way, but I don't want to work with you, and I can't imagine any basis on which it would be possible. You can keep pestering me if you like, but in that case – let's assume I *am* still a spy here, just for the sake of argument – I could easily compel you to desist. A simple phone call from my boss to yours, a hastily processed restraining order preventing you coming within a hundred yards of me, with a shadow permanently on your tail to ensure you comply, anything. You're not the first journalist in recent years who's had the bright idea of trying to join at the hip with me for the sake of a few inches of copy, and I'm sure you won't be the last. In the past, it's never taken any of them longer than a few days to twig that it's simply not worth the effort. So I think you'd better go now, don't you?"

"I love you too, John." He reached into the inside pocket of his overcoat and pulled out a business card. "Call me when you've changed your mind. Tomorrow, maybe."

Mordred took the card, folded it in two – tearing it somehow seemed too brutal - and handed it back. "Go to a Pride march."

"If I do, will you change your mind?"

"No. It's for your own good." He walked away.

This time, 'Mobe' didn't follow. "Remember my name!" he shouted. "It's Mobe Dhanial! MD! Like in a doctor's qualification! Call *The Daily Mail* when you've changed your mind! *Call Britain's number one newspaper! I love you, John!*"

Mordred sped up and crossed Horseferry Road without breaking stride. He didn't turn to look back until he was just about to round the corner into Millbank.

He wasn't being followed.

'Mobe' had something of the deranged person about him, and that's what had made him relatively likeable. Mystery solved. Those sorts of people might be bigots, and sometimes even crypto-fascists, but on one level, you couldn't help feeling sorry for them.

Which might be patronising, but that's how it was. You couldn't choose whether you thought someone was just a little too stupid for their own good. You couldn't help feeling that some day, they'd come to grief, and it would be as a result of the very things that made them so objectionable; that, in the long-term, they were far more likely to hurt themselves than others; that when it finally happened, there'd be no one around to feel sorry for them, just their own wretched solitariness and tears.

Poor Mobeen. He should really go on a Pride March.

A minute later, he strode across the reception of Thames House to where Colin Bale, - bald, forty, slightly apple-shaped, in a single-breasted wool suit - stood looking grim. He was late now. Just by a minute, but still. He signed in and took the lift to the third floor.

Seminar room E17 resembled a small classroom. Desks arranged in a large square, facing a projector screen, with most of one side occupied by rain-smeared windows in Victorian-looking frames with slightly peeling paint. At the front, Ruby Parker, the boss, a small black woman with a laptop, sat waiting to begin. Beside her, a middle-aged woman in a trouser suit sat poised to take the minutes. Sitting in silence, but without obviously doing anything useful like reading: Edna Watson, Alec Cunningham, Annabel Gould al-Banna, Phyllis Mordred, Ian Leonard, five men and women of roughly John's age and job description, one of whom was his wife. They didn't look pleased, even though he was only two and a half minutes overdue.

"Sorry I'm late," he said, pulling out the chair next to Ian and sitting down. "I was waylaid by a guy from *The Daily Mail*. He wanted us to work together on some project he's got. I had to be forceful in the end."

Ruby Parker clicked her tongue. She picked up the remote and switched on the projector. There was a slight purr. "And did you get his name?"

"Mobeen Dhanial."

She sighed, said 'excuse me a moment', and took out her phone. "Yes hello, Suki, I'd like you to find out everything you can about a *Daily Mail* journalist called *Mobeen Dhanial*. Put together a short profile, please, and have it on my desk in twenty minutes."

She pressed 'end call' and half-turned to face the screen. "Moving on," she said. The PowerPoint was apparently ready, but the screen was still blank.

"John and Phyllis," she said, apparently by way of pre-amble. "I stipulated a while ago that I didn't want you working together any more. That still stands, obviously. Phyllis, I'm going to be keeping you in London. I'll come to what I want you to do here presently. The rest of you are going abroad on what may be a long shot, but worth a try." She keyed the laptop. "I want you all to take a look at this photograph."

Slide number one. Twelve white men and women crowding in for a group shot on what was obviously a good night out. All smiled broadly, all were attractive, so Mordred's first impression was of a screengrab from boohoo.com or ASOS. The oldest looked to be in her early forties, but the others were at least a decade younger. Presumably, wherever it was taken was cold: they wore heavy coats and all but two had hats. The headgear alone – woollen papakhas, bearskin ushankas - gave them away as north-eastern European, probably Russian. The background was dark and featureless.

Ruby Parker didn't comment. She went straight to the next slide. The same group of twelve on what could have been the same occasion, but clearly wasn't: the clothes and hats were subtly different, although still designed for extreme cold. There were another six slides of the same group, always looking happy, photogenic, and consistently in winter garb.

Alec put his hand up. "So who are they?"

"I want you to remember their faces," she replied. "That's best achieved if I don't talk over the visuals for the first few seconds. Have patience." She let the silence run on, then turned to the room and folded her hands. "From the information we've gathered, they're twelve members of a working group assembled recently – over the last eight months or so - by the FSB's Director of Overseas Strategic Affairs, Stanislav Kuznetsov. We don't know what they were working on, but we do know it was important. Two of the women in the photos were in trouble even before the group concluded its work: this one" – she used a laser pointer - "committed suicide; while this one went inexplicably missing about nine weeks ago. The others all disappeared in Moscow – by that, I mean they probably went on the run, although the Moscow authorities apparently have difficulties acknowledging that explicitly, because it entails that they simply slipped through the fingers of whoever was watching them. Amazingly, they all seem to have 'disappeared' at the same time."

"I'm assuming they upset someone," Annabel said.

"Or someone upset *them*," Edna said.

"How do we know about them at all?" John asked. "Who told us?"

Ruby Parker smiled darkly. "Believe it or not, Grey department has an international assassin on retainer. He was called out as a matter of urgency on the night of the disappearances and paid to start searching for them. That's where we got these photos. He's one of several individuals charged with the same thing: finding the absentees, killing them, disposing of the bodies as completely as possible. Once they've been despatched, no one's supposed to know. Which is, of course, a tall order. If someone suspects they're being hunted by killers, their natural strategy is to hug public places. Murdering them and getting away at all is usually difficult enough. Add making the corpse disappear, and you've got a significant challenge. Which brings me to Fydor Nikolayevich Golovin." She used the laser pointer to indicate the man second from the left: wire-rimmed spectacles, sparkling teeth, in his twenties. "Golovin was killed getting off a train in Cologne, yesterday, at eleven at night. His attacker put one arm round the corpse in an attempt to suggest he might be drunk. But of course, it was a pretty inept performance, especially given the amount of blood. Further proof that 'international assassins', as spy novelists like to call them, are nearly always dim-witted."

"So that leaves – what? – nine?" Alec said. "Since the order was to make them vanish, how do we know any of the even exist any more?"

"Because Grey's man hasn't received new instructions," Ruby Parker said. "Given that he's being paid in the region of twenty thousand pounds a day, that's significant. In fact, it probably means all nine are alive."

Alec hooted. "Twenty thousand pounds *a day?*" He shook his head. "I'm in the wrong job."

"It might mean that communications between the different killers and their clients aren't very effective," Phyllis said. "I'm assuming Grey's man isn't the only assassin … Although … wait a minute: why are the GU even sending out hired 'international assassins'? Don't they have their own personnel?"

"Good question," Ruby Parker said. "Grey's man isn't working for the GU. He's working for Valery Yatzov, one of the Russian Federation's several Deputy Ministers of Defence. Which of course is a mystery in itself. Why are so many people not only categorically determined to see these ten dead, but also too jumpy to trust all the others to do it? Why do they feel the need to put their own highly-paid representatives into the fray?"

"Why do *we* want to find them?" Ian asked.

"Because the Russians clearly don't want us to," Ruby Parker said. "What other reason do we need?"

"Maybe it's a set-up," Mordred said.

"The Russians would have to know Grey's man is working for us," Ruby Parker replied, "since he's the only person who's brought us the message. Which we're pretty sure they don't."

"I don't want to seem negative," John continued, "but if the entire GU and any number of international assassins can't find them, what chance do we have? Five of us?"

"You won't be working alone," Ruby Parker said, "you'll be working with the Germans and the French. Grey's decided on Berlin and Paris as likely destinations for at least some of the ten. The French and German security services think we've got more information than we have, and they're eager to access it. In return, Brexit notwithstanding, they're prepared to cooperate with us. They've got the whole of their city police forces briefed to recognise the absconders and apprehend them on sight. They've also got CCTV, of course. The GU have to operate clandestinely, and they won't have boots on the ground in any great number. So in fact, the odds are heavily in our favour."

"There's still the question of whether they'll be prepared to tell us anything if we find them," John said. "If they've been working for the FSB, it's likely they'll have at least some residual patriotism. Just because they want to get away from Russia, it doesn't mean they want to help its supposed enemies. If they did, presumably they'd already have handed themselves in at some western embassy somewhere."

"That's a good point," Ruby Parker said. "That's why finding them is only the first stage. Then we've got to persuade them. You, Ian and Alec are going to Berlin. Edna and Annabel, you're going to Paris. I'll explain why there in a moment."

"Have the British police been informed?" Phyllis asked. "Presumably, that's why I'm staying here."

"Grey will cover this end," Ruby Parker said. "They're only letting us in at all because they're of the opinion that we've probably got a better bedside manner than they have, and that's likely what's going to be required here. No, Phyllis, I'd like you to take care of something else. I had a phone call from the Home Secretary this afternoon. He's convinced BBC's *Panorama* has some fairly devastating story about the government in the pipeline, and he'd like us to give him a heads-up concerning its broad focus. I told him we don't do that sort of thing, but he did raise the possibility – which may have been a ruse, I admit - that it could have national security implications, thus the sort of thing we need to know about. In any case, I need someone to take a look."

John felt himself involuntarily sit up. "Er, hang on."

They all turned to face him.

"That's exactly what the guy I just shook off said. Mobeen Dhanial. He claimed *Panorama* were making a documentary about the government. It's 'got the potential to blow the government sky-high.' His actual words."

Ruby Parker sat back in her chair as if there was something minutely droll about what he'd said. "And he wanted to work with you, you said?"

"That's what he proposed, yes," Mordred replied. "He said he thought we'd be like Stefan and Rash in *New Blood*."

"Bloody good series," Alec said. "I don't know why they never made any more."

"Typical pre-referendum, though," Ian said. "That bit where the Polish woman hands over the gold plate, and she's like, *You don't know what it's like being us, how awful it is.* I mean, like Poland's Ethiopia or something."

"That's roughly what Mobeen said," John told him. "Not that specific."

"What 'Polish woman'?" Alec said. "What are you even talking about, Ian?"

"One of the episodes," Ian said.

"Maybe Ian should go and work with Mobeen," John said.

Ruby Parker held up both hands. All speech stopped. She asked, "How did 'Mobeen Dhanial' find out about *Panorama*? *I* didn't know, and I'm pretty sure the Home Secretary's only just found out."

"I've no idea," John said. "I was too busy trying to get away from him. But I do recall him saying he had a way in. 'Entry', he called it."

"That's a way in," Alec said. "That's what the word means. Just to clarify matters."

Edna grinned. "So educational."

Ruby Parker looked at John. "And you say he wanted to work with you?"

"Yep."

"In that case, you've just talked yourself out of a trip to Berlin. Not that it would have been any sort of holiday, obviously. Phyllis, I want you to accompany Ian and Alec. John, you're staying here."

Alec laughed. "Idiot."

"Meeting closed," Ruby Parker said. "Collect your plane tickets downstairs in an hour's time. You'll leave tomorrow morning. John, stay here a moment: I'd like more details about Mobeen Dhanial. Then we'll see what Suki's dug up about him."

Chapter 3: Murder Comes from Maunsel Street

Mobeen Dhanial watched Mordred disappear round the corner into Millbank, then turned towards Westminster. Best not to push his luck. John would be back. He'd hear about the *Panorama* thing from somewhere else, and the word 'entry' would drive him nuts.

He hoped.

Bloody hell, John had been difficult!

But then, he'd expected that. Secret agents weren't like private detectives: they weren't on the lookout for customers, quite the reverse. Right now, John – if he wasn't actually in a meeting, which he probably wasn't – would be asking himself several questions.

Uppermost probably: how could he guarantee that Mobeen wouldn't resurface somewhere, sometime in the near future?

He wouldn't take anything for granted, which meant the *Mail* would probably get a phone call tomorrow morning.

To which they'd say *yeah, yeah* and hang up. They couldn't do anything much about their freelancers, and mostly, they didn't want to. The received wisdom was that interceding stymied creativity. And they didn't think it was their job.

At most, someone might mention it to him next time he checked in at base, but only in a *you'll never guess what* kind of way.

The second question John would ask was, Why does Mobeen think we can work together? He'd said it out loud already, of course, but it would hit him again with renewed force once he was alone. Why would any freelance journalist ever think he'd get an affirmative answer to *that* kind of offer?

Good question! Talk about an odd couple!

Mobeen turned left at the end of Horseferry Road. He needed to keep well within sight of people. It was like being in some sort of horror story, actually – *Casting the Runes*, by MR James, that one, yes: the continual sense you were being followed.

Which is really what he'd met John for, of course. *Obviously* they were never going to work together. But that wasn't the point. Truth be told, he couldn't imagine anything worse than working with bloody John-Milksop-SJW-bleeding-heart-Mordred: God help the guy, you couldn't fault him in terms of self-knowledge.

No, the point was that once the folk from *Panorama* saw Mobeen Dhanial in company with a *bona fide* secret agent, they'd scarper, and possibly never come back.

Because they'd definitely know who he was. Everyone in the media did. The Ultimate Londoner might have been forgotten in some quarters, but it had a bloody big Wikipedia page. And it still yielded well over 30,000 hits on Google, if you could be bothered.

Which – true – virtually no one could any more.

Anyway, in the highly unlikely event that *Panorama* didn't know who John Mordred was, they'd ask around. And someone would know. These were media folk, after all.

Mobeen suddenly caught sight of his face in a shop window. He didn't look scared any more.

Not that he'd ever been. No one knew the BBC was like this; that it employed burly guys to scare rival journalists off.

Which of course, it 'didn't'. Not officially, and certainly not to the knowledge of ninety-nine per cent of its employees. More in the way that it employed the Jimmy Saviles and Stuart Halls of this world. In the sense that *someone* in the organisation knew what was going on. *Someone* was responsible. Others turned a blind eye. In the present case, because the burly-scary guys were probably immigrants and it wasn't very 'liberal' to start probing.

But they wouldn't inflict anything serious on him. The BBC couldn't afford that sort of risk. For all it knew, he might have a recording device. Everyone's traceable. A couple of heavies threatening you, you video them, trace them back to some agency, find out who's employing them, and, whoops, those employers? They're *high-ranking execs in the British Broadcasting Corporation!?* Pop goes the weasel. Nothing was worth that kind of publicity.

In a strange sort of way, though, it might even be desirable. Maybe he *shouldn't* have gone to John. He might have been better advised to keep drawing them in. To the point where they struck out because they were at the end of their tether. With a bit of luck, that tactic might nail them.

What a story it'd be. Bigger than bloody *Panorama*, almost certainly. And he didn't even know what *Panorama* had yet.

The BBC employs heavies story vs. the story of whatever *Panorama* had. A difficult choice, but since the former probably involved getting his head kicked in, he didn't mind admitting he preferred the latter.

He'd call into a café for something to eat in a minute. Mc-Donald's? It'd been a while since he'd had a decent burger.

He stopped on the corner of Vincent Square and looked both ways. No cars, only

- oh, shit -

two guys approaching fast from Maunsel Street: young, hoodies, baseball caps

And it was clearly him they were after.

He'd half expected something like this all week.

He could stand or run. He wasn't much of a sprinter, so it was unlikely he'd outpace them, and, if they had a message to deliver, they'd be back anyway.

Might as well find out what they wanted.

Adrenalin flooded his system and he felt light-headed but as if he might be capable of great feats of strength. He wasn't scared.

Then, just as suddenly, yes, he was.

The men closed. They stood one in front, the other behind, as if this was something they did all the time, and nothing personal, stay cool, it'll be over in a few seconds, don't panic and you needn't get hurt, yeah? One held a knife. Both looked robust – not your usual stringy teenagers – and probably in their early thirties. *Panorama's* men.

"What do you want?" he asked, as aggressively as he could.

"Your cash," the first said.

A foreign accent, but that was what he'd expected. Immigrants, therefore beyond reproach, BBC-wise.

Mobeen took out his wallet – he'd recently emptied it of all but the essentials in preparation for something much like this – and glumly handed it over.

A formality, of course. The *hors d'oeuvre*. The main course was yet to arrive. A clichéd *back off* message. He wouldn't argue. No point.

The guy behind suddenly grabbed his shoulders. The guy in front thrust his blade upwards and beneath Mobeen's rib cage, then removed it. Again, a kind of *don't take this personally* about them. *There, now that wasn't too bad, was it?*

Mobeen gasped, partly in pain, but also in surprise. Why had they *knifed* him? My God, what the hell was the *point?*

Too late to ask. Wooziness supplanted indignation. But it hurt – a *lot!* - and the two men were walking away, and he was on his knees now, feeling sick, and there was blood everywhere, really everywhere, and his hands and the pavement were soaked - and someone was screaming, and so - maybe an ambulance was in order? Right this very second? Yes?

Yes?

Chapter 4: Berlin or Paris or Wherever

Edna, Alec, Annabel, Phyllis, Ian and the minute-taker exited Seminar room E17 in no particular hurry but without conversing. Ian was last out. He closed the door behind him leaving John Mordred and Ruby Parker alone.

"Let's begin with Mobeen Dhanial," she said.

"There's really not much to tell. I went in to the White Horse and Bower for a non-alcoholic drink – I thought I was being followed – when he came in. He pretended he'd been waiting for me. Since he had an agenda, I assume he'd been following me for some time. Why he didn't approach me in the street, I don't know."

"He was looking for you to open up a bit. That's probably more easily done over drinks."

"But he couldn't have known I'd go into the White Horse. It wasn't planned."

"Today is his lucky day maybe. I assume he offered to buy you another drink?"

"More or less straight away. He's written a book, incidentally. I can't recall the title, but I'm sure Suki will have located it. Some kind of attack on the BBC. He wants to bring it down. That's why he's looking into *Panorama*."

"A BBC hunter, you mean. He's chosen a strange bedfellow in you, John."

"By 'BBC hunter' ...?"

She chuckled. "The country's full of intellectuals who want to dismantle the BBC, John, you must have noticed that. They distrust it for all sorts of reasons. Some believe it's too pro-establishment; some think it's too politically correct; for some, it's too right-wing, others, too socialist. You only need pick up the tabloids to realise its denigration's a kind of national cottage industry. Here in MI7, we call such individuals and

33

pressure groups 'the BBC hunters', which lends them at least a veneer of respectability. Almost all of them want it reconstituted on a more commercial basis; mostly because they think that would sound its death-knell. Beware of being sucked in by them."

"Understood."

"Anyway, Mobeen Dhanial wasn't primarily what I wanted to talk to you about. Rather, the missing twelve Russians. We're not at all sure about this, but we've a contact in the GU, and we think their disappearance is in some mysterious way connected to you, John."

"Me?"

"Some of them owned pictures of you, which they left behind when they 'disappeared'."

"Er, what sort of 'pictures'?"

"Just ordinary photographs, I believe, in mundane settings. Our best guess is that they've identified you as someone on the 'other side' whom they feel they can trust to get a fair deal. They found out about you in the same way Mobeen Dhanial did; in the same way anyone determined enough can. You're not a part of MI7 because of your anonymity any more. Rather, the reverse. And this is exactly the kind of scenario in which your usefulness – if it were ever in doubt - is confirmed."

"So let me get this straight: you think they're on their way to *find* me?"

"Like I say, it's only our best guess. At first, we thought it might be a trap of some kind, just as you suggested earlier. Send a few people over here to suborn you, make them look like victims to appeal to your possibly overdeveloped humanitarian side. But we dismissed that idea. If that was the plan, there'd be far easier ways."

"So why did you want to send me to Berlin a moment ago? Surely, if these twelve men and women... Do we have a name for them? It seems unwieldy to keep calling them 'the twelve men and women' all the time."

"The Russians themselves are apparently calling them 'the Novelists'. Which sounds like a pastiche of John le Carré, but in its favour, apparently six of them had literary ambitions. In any case, go on."

"If they're coming to see me, they'll be on their way to Thames House. Wouldn't it be better for me to sit outside the front door holding a 'Welcome to Britain' sign?"

"The GU are working on the same assumption we are. Which is why you're currently being observed by four Russian agents, two French ones, two or three Americans, a German and four of our very own Grey department. Eleven people in all. And they're just the ones we know about."

"Bloody hell. No wonder I had the sense of being watched. Mobeen Dhanial doesn't even begin to account for that level of surveillance."

"Quite."

"On the plus side, they'll be easy to shake off. Say if I get into a lift, or break into a run, or get an Uber."

"They probably know where you live. And they must know that you work here."

"Mobeen Dhanial seems quite benign by comparison. Anyway, they must be capable. I didn't see anyone."

"They're professional spies."

Mordred chuckled. "If they're so good, how come we know about them?"

"Because we're better. The answer to your earlier question – why did I want to send you to Berlin – is, because it'll make them think that's where we expect the Novelists. They don't know that you're not in on it, and, although they probably don't *think* you are, they almost certainly won't risk taking it for granted. Unless they get reinforcements, sending you to Germany would have the effect of dispersing their manpower."

"Even if I wasn't in on it at the beginning, I am now."

"You can probably find out fairly quickly what Mobeen Dhanial wants, and what sort of 'entry' he's got. That means going back to him, of course. I'm pretty sure this *Panorama* matter of his will be a complete waste of time. Once we've established that, you can go to Paris."

"I thought it was Berlin."

"Phyllis is going to Berlin now. Remember what I said about you and her working together?"

"I don't want to ruin my prospects, but you do realise that, as a married couple, we'll almost inevitably talk to each other about work at some point?"

"That's just sharing information. It's what we do all the time. Providing it doesn't spill over into close formal cooperation, I can't see why it would be a problem."

There was a knock at the door. Suki put her head round. She held a sheaf of papers against her chest and looked apologetic.

"I didn't ask you to bring me the report in person," Ruby Parker said. "Is there a problem?"

"You asked me to find out about Mobeen Dhanial," she said. "There's just been a murder two streets away from here. We're pretty sure he's the victim."

Chapter 5: When a Conference Goes from Bad to Worse

Much of the fortnight the Novelists had worked on Kuznetsov's pet project they'd also been secretly researching how to exit the country. The best way, it seemed, was to don an effective disguise, avoid all major roads, and hitch lifts, ideally from long-distance lorry drivers headed anywhere west. They split up as soon as they left Moscow. Domogarov and his two companions selected Crimea as their initial destination. That way, they could present themselves as uber-patriots journeying to cheer on the occupation. From Armyansk, they could slip quietly into Ukraine where the FSB had no traction.

The group bankrolled its escape after one of its members stumbled on compromising information about a senior Moscow police officer. She used the leverage, and an uncharacteristic display of bravado, to demand twenty thousand US dollars. What she got instead was a large cache of recently impounded gold coins from the Lubyanka Building's 'evidence for ongoing cases' room. At the time of the group's departure, the theft hadn't yet been discovered. Another reason to leave the country, if such a thing were needed.

Obviously, they'd be frantically looked for, they realised that, but they also knew Russia's huge police force wouldn't necessarily work to the authorities' advantage. In fact, the opposite: the average Russian's relative indifference to prosecuting state interests (relative to taking home a decent pay packet and living a quiet life, both of which the FSB offered in adequate amounts) meant that everyone in the service would likely assume that hunting down fugitives from Moscow was some other colleague's business. Those who didn't – the enthusiastic, the ambitious and the plain zealous – were needles in a haystack, and because of Russia's size, they'd also be looking for needles in a haystack.

Pasha Domogarov and his ex-girlfriend, Valentina Leontievna Morozova, couldn't bring themselves to travel separ-
ately, so they resolved to go as a couple. When at the last
minute, Kseniya Yumasheva was too scared to embark alone,
they adjusted to become a trio.

The two women wore double thick hair extensions. They
calculated that with long hair and summer dresses, they were
more likely to get lifts, even with a man in tow. But given that
Pasha could talk knowledgeably about ice-hockey and football, once they were picked up most lorry drivers preferred
him to the women. On one memorable occasion, an in-depth
discussion of the FC Zenit Saint Petersburg vs Lokomotiv Moscow match got them two hundred miles farther than they'd
been promised. Within a week, all three were in Crimea. Four
days afterwards, they were in Kiev.

From there, they were able to follow the refugee trail to Calais. They didn't know what had, or would, become of their
seven friends, but the idea was that, once they reached Britain,
they would meet up in London's Trafalgar Square. They'd go
there at ten o'clock each morning, stay thirty minutes, and
only abandon hope after six months. It wasn't much of a plan,
and any one of their number being captured and tortured
might expose it, but, at short notice, and a hundred other
things to worry about, they couldn't think of a better one.

Pasha was a tall, thin, thirty-two-year-old with a close
cropped black beard, a strong jawline and feminine-looking
brown eyes. Valentina was ten years older, long limbed,
strong, and thoughtful. She liked to consider a problem from
every angle before committing to anything practical. Kseniya,
the youngest, was in her early twenties. She had rings beneath
her eyes, wavy blonde hair with a fringe, pallid skin, and the
small, delicate hands of a poet. She'd lost both her parents recently in a traffic accident, and she had a habit of weeping
quietly at four o'clock in the morning.

In some ways, though, she had it easy. If you left Russia as an enemy of the state (or more precisely, of the President), your family was likely to suffer. Not too overtly; nothing like the bad old days of cancer wards and gulags. But even so. They'd be questioned. Their neighbours would mysteriously come to know. They'd be watched. They'd be marked out for future subtle impediments. Pasha's parents were good citizens, both in their seventies now. He loved them, and leaving them behind in Russia wasn't easy. Valentina hadn't spoken to hers since her divorce ten years ago. She still cared for them, but long absence had desensitised her to what fate ultimately had in store for them. Anyway, both sets of parents were old. It seemed brutal to think it, but they had little to lose nowadays.

After seven weeks, the fugitive trio reached the harbour at Calais. They bought champagne and vodka, luxury biscuits, four cigars and imitation designer clothes. Valentina took three days to select their victim, an elderly Englishman with a motor launch. On the fourth day, they strode along the jetty at 10pm, introduced themselves to their mark, engaged him in courteous conversation (it was crucial to do everything courteously; any hint of vulgarity would probably scare him away), learned his name ("Steven Matthews, but you can call me Captain Matthews!"), graciously accepted his invitation to come aboard for snacks, plied him with vodka, champagne and biscuits, then asked him to take them to Britain. They half expected a polite refusal, but only half, because they were young and attractive and nicely dressed, and, if life had taught them anything, it was that such a combination usually opened locked doors. In the event, he cast off with a song and a smile. It would be a *privilege* to take them!

As they crossed the Channel, they all smoked cigars and sang songs. Valentina put her head on Captain Matthews's shoulder, and he put his arm round her waist, and she tried to imagine what it might be like being in love with him, even though he was nearly twice her age. In an excess of abandonment, but also 'for luck', Kseniya gave him a single gold rouble. He promised to rename his boat Potemkin in their honour. He'd originally thought they were gangsters, he said, but their excellent manners had persuaded him otherwise. He was scared of all gangsters – who wasn't? - but of Russian gangsters in particular, 'because, no offence, they aren't subject to any known authority.' Valentina and Kseniya laughed breezily when Pasha translated, but inwardly shivered: they seemed to catch an oblique glimpse of their own futures.

As the Hampshire coast came in view, they fell to thinking about John Mordred. Not a bad idea to seek him out, although it wasn't originally theirs. The difficulty would lie in persuading him they had anything to offer anyone at all. An idea commissioned by the FSB's Director of Overseas Strategic Affairs, which probably hadn't even been put into effect. The Director had dismissed it out of hand, and, although Pasha left his office with the strong impression he was going to pass the idea off as his own, he had no evidence that was what had happened. For all he and his nine friends knew, everyone might have forgotten about it; Elizaveta might be alive and well somewhere; the FSB might not even be pursuing them.

Not that they could afford to take a chance on any of those things. The question remained: what had they to offer John Mordred, or anyone in the west? 'A plot to take over the BBC', that's all. It sounded crazy.

But the great thing about John Mordred, so Elizaveta had told them (and she would probably know), was that he recognised when you were telling the truth.

Yet that had to be bullshit. How could he?

When they reached London, they bought a smartphone and obtained 'the use of' a tiny bedsit in Peckham from a landlord who bitterly resented the government trying to use him to police the immigration system (or so he said). Then the full absurdity of what they were doing hit them simultaneously, hard as a sledgehammer. So far, they hadn't had chance to stop and think about it. Now it was like awaking from a dream. One in which everything seemed, fantastic, ludicrous, stupid.

More than that: they suddenly saw they'd had a growing awareness of such a thing even before crossing the border into Ukraine. It had lain dormant for a long time, but it had grown inexorably, and now it was undeniable.

They were idiots. They should go home.

But how could they?

It was time for a conference.

Valentina and Kseniya sat next to each other on the only piece of furniture in the room, a green sofa, too small to sleep on, with greyish pink cushions. There was no kitchen in here, nor a toilet or bathroom: if you wanted to cook or excrete or wash, you had to go along the corridor. The walls of their room were bare and marked lower down with what looked like shoe scuffs. The carpet was grey and heavy-duty and nailed in strips into the floorboards, as if someone was worried about it getting stolen. It smelt of tar. At night, you slept wrapped in duvets on the floor. A single window looked onto an alleyway with wheelie bins, where drug-users and prostitutes appeared intermittently throughout the night.

There wasn't space for Pasha to pace up and down the room, so he stood against the wall. They needed to make a decision, but they'd lost the willpower and also the sense that any one alternative – whatever it was – could conceivably be better than another.

Kseniya spoke first. "We need to go back to Moscow," she said. "After all, we haven't done anything wrong. As far as anyone there knows, we've just gone on a long trip at short notice."

"We were being watched 'for our own good'," Pasha told her. "That's what Kuznetsov told me. And we worked on a state secret - "

She gave a derisory sigh. "'State secret', my foot. A stupid idea which you were explicitly told was a non-starter, nothing more."

"They'll trace our movements," Valentina said. "They'll find out about the gold coins. They'll wonder where we got them. Then they'll notice that gold coins aren't exactly common. Each one's fairly unique, and those we dispensed just happen to match the missing batch in FSB HQ. Which probably adds up to a hell of a lot of time in prison."

"They couldn't work that out," Kseniya said. "They'd have to retrieve the ones we gave away. Anyway, we don't even know they're after us. We might just be victims of our own paranoia."

"What about finding this 'John Mordred' character?" Valentina asked.

"What do we expect him to do?" Kseniya asked derisorily. "Take us into protection? Give us a big house? a car? money for food? We left Russia on a whim, driven by a mad idea. Not even our own mad idea."

Pasha frowned. "What do you mean?"

"Look, Pasha," Kseniya went on, "you and Valentina obviously don't know this, and I must admit, I've only recently twigged, but John Mordred's a complete fantasy."

Valentina laughed. "I'm pretty sure he's not."

"I'm not saying he doesn't exist. I'm saying we've built him up into something he's not and can't ever be. By 'we', I don't even mean us three. We just bought into it. Maybe because we were having such a ball, and we all bonded so frenziedly, and we caught each other's delusions, like getting the flu or a dose of measles."

"I still don't get what you're saying," Pasha told her. "I didn't have any delusions."

"No, you weren't the one who transmitted them," she replied.

"Get to the point," Valentina said. "You're starting to scare me."

Kseniya folded her arms. "This is what happened. Elizaveta joined Kuznetsov's group in November, right? She was one of the first. And she was highly impressionable. It gave her a huge buzz that she was joining the Moscow branch of the FSB, and she started taking all the spy bullshit really seriously. Somehow or other, she came across John Mordred. By that, I mean someone in the FSB may have drawn her attention to him. At that point, there may have been some plot to compromise him in the pipeline. He's married, and Elizaveta's very attractive - "

"If there was such a plot, she *can't* have come up with it herself," Valentina said. "We weren't even told what we were supposed to be doing till the last minute."

"There were probably lots of plots," Kseniya told her. "It's not impossible that the people who selected us had certain ideas of their own, at least early on. One of them may have been getting John Mordred into bed with someone. Sounds lame, I know, but let's face it, if the FSB was capable of coming up with credible proposals, they wouldn't have needed us. What I do know is that Elizaveta was never the brightest intellect in the room, and that she became obsessed with John Mordred almost as soon as she started."

"I didn't buy into the idea because of her," Valentina said.

"Maybe not, but you did buy into it," Kseniya said. "Think about how you just introduced him into the discussion. *This 'John Mordred' character*, you called him, like you're not so enamoured now."

Valentina grimaced. "I was never 'enamoured'!"

"Come off it," Kseniya replied. "We all were. It's just a question of how badly you were bitten. Elizaveta had it worst, then

Olga. Do you really think Olga would have had the chutzpah to blackmail a senior policeman if she hadn't been besotted?"

Valentina turned to Pasha. "Did *you* buy into the John Mordred idea because of Elizaveta and Olga?"

"I may have done," he replied sheepishly.

"Good God."

"You see?" Kseniya said triumphantly.

"They presented it to the group in a rational way," Pasha continued. "Not as an infatuation. *Here's a man who will help us*, that's what they told me. And I took that away, and nothing more."

"You might not have believed them if you'd known where they were coming from," Kseniya said. "Their back story, I mean, since November."

"It's pretty irrelevant now," he replied.

"Is it?" Valentina asked. "Let's say we *do* decide to seek him out, just for the sake of seeing this mad episode in our lives to its bitter conclusion, where would we even find him?" She directed the question at Pasha.

"It should be simple enough," he said. "Just turn up outside London's Thames House, where he supposedly works. We know what he looks like."

"It's that easy?" Valentina said incredulously.

"His bosses must know he's out there, in the public domain," he replied in a similar tone. "How could they not? Yet they don't fire him. They don't even suspend him."

Kseniya laughed hysterically. "He's a fantasy figure! We've made a mistake, big time. God help me, I can't live the rest of my life like this! A crappy box to live in with a cold shower, a dirty kitchen, druggies and whores outside the window every night? How long till one of us gets stabbed or raped? Prison would be preferable! It'd take a bit of getting used to, but at least we'd be amongst other Russians!"

Pasha sat down next to Valentina. Perhaps Kseniya had expected an argument, but the fact is, she was right. Your enemy's enemies aren't necessarily your friends. Russia had rejected them, and, in the spirit of returning blow for blow, they'd rejected Russia. But it was a forlorn gesture, and it had failed. They didn't belong in Britain.

Pasha picked up their shared mobile phone and unlocked it. "Did you hear what the president said the other day?"

Kseniya shrugged. "Putin?"

Valentina remained immobile.

"*Our Western partners have admitted,*" he read, "*that some elements of the liberal idea, such as multiculturalism, are no longer tenable… The liberal idea has come into conflict with the interests of the overwhelming majority of the population… It cannot be destroyed; it has the right to exist and it should even be supported in some things. But it is not unconditionally entitled to be the dominating factor.* Perfectly reasonable, yet all the western media has done is abuse him. You'd think he was Hitler, going by what most of them have said!"

"We've spent two pointless mornings in Trafalgar Square now" Kseniya said. "I'd be very surprised if the others haven't gone home, at least some of them. We're just the stupid ones, carried away by our ludicrous sense of adventure."

"You're right," Valentina said. "Some of them must have gone back. Just statistically, when you think about it. Pasha, are you okay?"

Domogarov had stopped swiping the phone. He stared fixedly at the screen. He grinned idiotically. "Not really," he replied.

He turned the screen to face them. Words.

They laughed nervously. "Er, neither of us knows English, Pasha!" Valentina said.

He scrolled down to show them the picture.

"Oh my God," Kseniya said softly.

They were looking at Fydor Nikolayevich Golovin. Their friend.

Pasha translated. "GU comes under intense scrutiny after Russian citizen is stabbed to death in Köln Hauptbahnhof."

Chapter 6: Kelly's 'Brainwave'

Ruby Parker left the room with Suki and told Mordred to stay where he was. He walked to the window and watched the sparrows and starlings playing in the plane trees. Then he searched for information about Mobeen Dhanial on his phone. She called him after ten minutes.

"No more news, I'm afraid," she said. "We don't even have the CCTV yet, although it should be available. But given how driven you say he appeared, and that he depicted himself as a conspiracy-investigator, we can't rule out something more than a random murder. I'll keep you updated. In the meantime, forget about *Panorama*. You're going to spend the rest of the day focussing on the Russians. Brian Penford's on his way up to see you, and you've an appointment with Sir Harold Kelly at two pm. He'll also be coming to you in E17. Obviously, none of this affects your lunch break."

"Who's Sir Harold Kelly?"

"The supposed Head of Grey department."

He chuckled. "Given Grey's paranoid obsession with secrecy, I'm assuming he's neither a 'sir' nor its head."

"We probably need to overlook both those things. He'll certainly have the requisite authority, and if you don't behave as if you've bought into the deception, we'll probably both end up regretting it. Don't forget: they gave us this case. They'll probably tell you they didn't have to."

"Given that the Russians are apparently on their way to see me, they'd have had difficulty keeping it under wraps."

"So be accommodating, but not overly." She hung up.

Mordred sighed and immediately forgot about 'Sir Harold Kelly'. Instead, his thoughts returned to the White Horse & Bower. Poor Mobeen Dhanial.

He couldn't blame himself, but had their paths never crossed, the journalist might still be alive. It wasn't the first time he'd been in this sort of position, and it probably wouldn't be the last, and he definitely *wasn't* responsible, and yet... Well, the universe had a habit of making him a precursor to people's deaths. He wondered if Dhanial had a partner. He almost certainly had living parents, maybe siblings –

A knock at the door. Brian Penford put his head round in exactly the same way Suki had, earlier. A bearded, bespectacled fifty-five-year-old, wearing a Shetland tweed jacket and brown corduroy trousers, he gave Mordred a diffident look and said, "Hey up."

"Hi," Mordred replied.

"Everything okay? You look down." He proffered a thick A4 folder with 'Confidential' stamped on the front. "Here."

"Thanks. No, I'm not okay, although it's obviously not your fault. I just met a man in a pub and now he's dead."

"Bummer. Bad luck. How? I mean, how did it happen?"

"He was stabbed. I assume you're here to show me some sort of PowerPoint?"

"Yup. We're not scheduled to do it for an hour. I'm just here to set up and give you the file. Take five, as they say. Go to the canteen, get a strong cup of tea with lots of sugar. Good for shock obviously, although I'm not saying you *are* shocked."

"What's in the file?"

"Open it and have a look."

"Yes, of course. Sorry."

Brian scrunched his eyes. "No, *I'm* sorry, John. I didn't mean that to sound critical. I wasn't thinking. It's all about the nine missing Russians. It's got their pictures in, and information about them. Learn to recognise their faces, that's your mission should you choose to accept it, as they say. Later on, I'm going to show you some visuals; you have to point out the Russkis as fast as you can. In real life, it may be about you being able to spot them faster than any foreign agent, of which I gather there are a huge number. It should be fun, in a way. A kind of 'Where's Wally' but with, er… On the…"

"On the understanding that if I don't spot Wally quickly enough, he or she will probably be stabbed to death."

"You're right. We shouldn't make light of it."

Ten minutes later, Mordred sat in the canteen with a cup of tea and a Twix. The different departments were starting to arrive in twos and threes for lunch now, but he wasn't particularly hungry. He didn't have an office, so he finished his drink, scooped the Twix and the file up together and went downstairs to his desk where he could be in peace. When people saw you reading at your own workstation in Thames House, they generally knew to leave you alone.

The file was a wad of about fifty A4 punched documents bound with something like superglue so that no one could add to or subtract from it. Like all MI7 documents, it had a catchy title: RUS19/786641B. He opened it at page 4, after the preface, the contents and ten-paragraph warnings about what would happen to any reader who mislaid it or mentioned its contents to personnel without the necessary clearance.

Pavel ("Pasha") Sergeyevich Domogarov, born 1987, Moscow, to a family involved in military engineering. Graduated from Moscow State Social University (now The Russian State Social University) in 2008. Member of the organisation 'Youth for Charity' 2008-present. Marital status: single. Employment: junior executive, 'Green Pages' 2009-13; section manager 'Video Tube International' 2013-present. Believed to be in a relationship with Valentina Leontievna Morozova (see below) and possibly travelling with her at the time of writing.

Valentina Leontievna Morozova, born 1977 in Chelyabinsk. Daughter of the prominent media executive Mikhail Sukov and the actress Ekaterina Listyev. Graduated from Moscow State Institute of International Relations in 2000. Married to Alexander Mikhailovich Dodolev 2001-2009. Won a divorce settlement after allegations of marital abuse. Currently employed as middle manager in 'Media Magnum' in Krasnoyarsk Krai. Believed to be in a relationship with Pavel ("Pasha") Sergeyevich Domogarov (see above) and possibly in company with him at the time of writing.

Fydor Nikolayevich Golovin. *Born 1990 in Saint Petersburg. Graduated in Social Sciences, Amur State University 2012. Unmarried. Retrained as an actor in 2013, but appears not to have capitalised on this. 2014-2019 employed in the Accounts department of RIA Novosti, Zubovsky Boulevard 4, Moscow. Killed 6 June 2019 in Cologne Central Station, Germany. Suspected GU involvement in his murder.*

Kseniya Igorevna Yumasheva. *Born in 1996 in Moscow to Igor and Natalia (née Safina). Studied in the faculty of Law in Transbaikal State University for three years from 2016, but was transferred to Moscow in December 2018 after a recommendation from a lecturer (Sophia P Grigorieva, see separate document RUS17/6746CV) believed to 'headhunt' for sensitive intelligence posts. Keen amateur boxer.*

Olga Borisovna Pamfilova. *Born 1990 in the city of Buy, Kostroma Oblast. Graduated alongside Pavel ("Pasha") Sergeyevich Domogarov (see above) from Moscow State Social University (now The Russian State Social University) in 2008, although the two do not appear to have known each other at that time. Former member of The Russian United Democratic Party 'Yabloko' (2012-14). Until recently, employed as a marketing and public relations representative at Yellow TV Media Group, Krasnodar city.*

Yuliyr Edgardovna Chipovskaya *(deceased: suicide March 2019 – see Appendix to this document).*

Elizaveta Aleksandrova Khamatova *born 1988 in the city of Sochi. Daughter of the 1970s Soviet actress, People's Artist of the RSFSR (1981) recipient, Olesya Vasilyevna Shcherbak. Studied Applied Information Technology at Sochi State University 2007-10. Moved to Volgograd in 2010. Employed as a fashion model by My vlyubleny v samu lyubov'! magazine (rough translation: 'We Are in Love with Love Itself!') 2010-14, and also part-time as a cipher* *clerk for her local branch of the FSB, 2010-18. Promoted to the rank of corporal in 2017. Transferred to Moscow in November 2018 at the personal request of Stanislav Kuznetsov, the FSB's Director of Overseas Strategic Affairs.*

Roman Anatolyevich Shirokov *born 1986 in the city of -*

He wasn't taking in a single word. Time to speed up, glean the essentials: retaining the detail was virtually impossible and, as far as he could imagine, completely unnecessary. Who the hell even put these sorts of files together? Possibly, they'd be useful in an interrogation – *if you really* are *Valentina Leontievna Morozova, perhaps you'd care to tell us where and when you were born, and where you went to university? –* but even then, any halfway decent spy would have mugged that sort of thing up in training.

Two minutes later, he was finished. They'd all been born in Russia, they'd all gone through the Russian higher education system, some of them were men, some women, one or two had partners whom they'd left behind. He had no sense of knowing any of them even slightly better than when he'd started (apart from that 'keen amateur boxer' bit, but that might be a mistake: credulous errors happened a lot in intelligence).

The point was to remember the name-photo connection. Luckily, there were at least four or five pictures of each individual in there. It was mainly what RUS19/786641B was, actually: a glorified photo album. In an ideal world, he'd write the names on the rear of the pictures, then shuffle them, and see how many he could recall on complete run-through. But MI7 being what it was, someone had pasted them all into the file – probably with superglue again - on individual pages with the person's name in size sixteen bold at the top.

Why the hell were they coming to England to look for him? It didn't make sense.

No point obsessing over it. He ate his Twix and took the lift back to E17. Brian sat where Ruby Parker had been earlier. He dunked a teabag in an 'I Love Cornwall' cup. He squeezed all the tea out and tossed it expertly across the room and into the bin. "Goal," he said quietly.

John sat down where he'd been an hour ago. "Ready when you are."

"What's going to happen," Brian said, sliding the laser pointer across the table at him, "is that I'm going to show you sixty slides. They're all a bit like the cover of *Sgt. Pepper's Lonely Hearts Club Band*. That is to say, they're mock-ups, each with between forty and a hundred people in. Each slide contains just one of the Russians. You've got to identify the Russian, point to him or her, and ideally, say the full name. I'm going to come over there, because if you hit me in the eye with that pointer, it could be dangerous."

"How long do I get for each one? And by the way, I'm not sure I'm much of a shot with a laser pointer."

"No one is. That's why I'm coming to sit over there. There isn't a time limit, but I have got a stopwatch."

"Did you bring that on your own initiative, or did someone tell you to?"

"The former. No one's checking up on you, John."

"Apologies."

"Accepted. Ready?"

The first few slides were a mess of faces – he could see Madonna in there, and Denzel Washington – but it took him nearly five seconds to spot Olga Pamfilova and Evgeni Ponomarenko, and he mixed up Kseniya Yumasheva and Elizaveta Khamatova, calling out 'Kseniya Khamatova' then not knowing which one he'd identified.

"That's Shania Twain," Brian told him. "There aren't actually any Russians in that slide."

"Who's that then?" Mordred asked, using the laser pointer.

"That's Vladimir Putin, but he doesn't count. I meant, Russians you're looking for."

"Fair enough."

"Boris Yeltsin's in some of them. He doesn't count either. Ditto Lenin and Joseph Stalin."

"Okay, I've got the idea."

They continued. After a while, Brian paused the slideshow. "Your time's improving. But we're going to have to stop now. You've got an appointment with Sir Harold the Grey at one pm."

"It's at two, not one."

Brian picked up his cup, switched off the projector and stood up. "It's been changed. Sorry, John, they changed it and asked me not to tell you till five minutes before it was due. They want to keep you 'fresh', apparently, whatever that means. I guess it means slightly blindsided. It's how Grey rolls, so I've heard. Mind games. And I didn't say that, obviously."

"Well, I guess they must have an agenda, otherwise they wouldn't be trying to 'disorient' me, as they probably think of it. And at least they've annoyed me enough to make me bloody minded about falling in with it. Or not."

Brian smiled. "Attaboy. And I didn't say that either."

He got up, said bye and let himself out.

John had no idea what would happen now. Sir Harold Kelly was meant to be coming here. But given that Grey was Grey, he might turn up in two minutes, two hours or not at all. On the other hand, they couldn't afford to alienate him too much, and they probably knew they'd gone far enough already. He knew all about the Russians now. They couldn't have many more cards to play.

The door swung open almost to its fullest extent, and a man in a grey suit entered. A power entrance. The coming-into-the-room equivalent of facing a camera while standing with your legs unusually far apart. Mordred stood up.

'Sir Harold Kelly' looked to be in his late sixties. He had white hair, wire-rimmed glasses and his physique and demeanour suggested a possible previous career in the armed forces. He gripped the door handle as if it was his only means of controlling the ferocious beast he'd just overcome.

"Good afternoon, John," he said loudly, without making eye contact. "I trust you're well. As you've probably guessed, I'm your 2pm: Sir Harold Kelly, Head of Grey. I've heard a lot about you, not least that you used to work for Grey. I hope you didn't mind me rescheduling at the last minute. Please accept my apologies. Something urgent popped up. I don't need to tell you how intelligence can be sometimes. Good to finally meet you."

They shook hands and sat down.

"How do you feel about Pride, John?" Sir Harold asked. "Don't answer that. You don't have to. The point is, are you going on the march?"

"In London? I might do."

"You know you've got quite a few Russian agents shadowing you?"

"That's what I've been told. I'm not sure I see the connection."

"I won't beat about the bush then. We recently learned from one of our Moscow contacts that, about nine months ago – sometime in November or December, actually – the FSB toyed with the idea of sending an attractive female agent out here to seduce you. Crass, I know, and, as far as we're aware, it came to absolutely nothing. But it obviously occurred to them. Now, it just so happens that your wife's in Berlin for a while. We'd like you to go to the march, meet a man – a fellow agent, and, er, give him a kiss. I mean, in the romantic way."

Mordred laughed. "Right, okay."

"Wait a minute. I mean, before you consent – or not – let me explain the reasoning."

"Fire away."

"Like I say, your wife's out of town for a while, so it could look like you're ripe for blackmail. And, of course, a lot of Russians still see homosexuality as something shameful. In a way most of us don't, any more. Your shadows will probably have their cameras out, filming you – it's a celebration, so everyone's filming everything, it looks, and usually is, completely innocuous – and when you perform a homosexual kiss, they'll think their boat's come in. Once they start trying to blackmail you, say a few days later, we've got them. Only, it's us reeling them in, not the other way round. Obviously, your wife will be fully in the know from the start."

"Well, it's a lovely idea, but totally counterproductive, so I'm going to decline."

Sir Harold frowned. "I need you to explain why."

"From what I've been told, our primary mission is to get the nine or ten fugitives - "

"The Novelists, the Russians call them."

"Okay, because we think they've something to tell us. If you're right in saying that the average Russian is more homophobic than the average Brit, then how do we know that doesn't apply to The Novelists too? They might find a photo of me kissing a guy off-putting. It might persuade them not to make contact, after all. So we'd be reeling a few GU guys in – against whom, incidentally, we've nothing damning, so we can't control them – but we've lost sight of our main objective and quite possibly sabotaged it."

"I see, yes. Well, I think you're wrong about that. If they're coming to the West, it's probably because they accept western values. They must do, mustn't they? If they want us to help them, they must be at least open-minded?"

"My guess is, Russia's done something to them. They're running away from it, not towards us. We just happen to be here."

"Putin will have their cards marked now. We all know how much he loathes traitors. My guess is they'll be able to overlook a little kiss or two, just to stay alive. Look, John, I'll be honest: we don't actually need you. All we have to do is ensure you're watched by people who've also read file

RUS19/786641B, and can recognise the Russians' faces. Four or five of our agents can bundle any Tatiana Romanova into a waiting car faster than any GU bozo can say Jack Robinson."

"What makes you so sure?"

"Because we're on home soil and we've got communications available to us that no foreign agent or agents can realistically hope to match. We can get hold of your daily itinerary – with or without your knowledge, or even that of Red Department – and we can put agents in place to reconnoitre your destination well in advance. And, of course, we're the best."

"If you're that good, you can probably work out who the foreign spooks are without my help."

"Yes, we can, but we need them to think they've got the upper hand."

"Okay, as I understand it, if I go along with your plan, I'll get a pile of GU agents trying to blackmail me. You'll be in control of the situation, not me. You'll be responsible for what happens behind the scenes, and I have to trust you to get it right. The alternative is that I don't go along with your plan, and I'm on my own. No more contact with file RUS19B3F - "

"It's RUS19/786641B, actually."

"Sorry."

"Apology accepted."

"I mean, I'm not really sorry. What's it matter?"

"I was warned about your slightly oblique sense of humour, John. Very well, you're off the case as far as we're concerned. I'll let Ruby Parker know, obviously. And *I'm* sorry too. Really sorry."

"Thanks."

"Maybe think about it?"

"I have."

"In that case, I'll need the file back. And let's not have any attempted witticisms this time, please."

Mordred slid the file across the table. They both stood up to go. Mordred was first to the door. He held it open for Sir Harold to precede him. Partly so he wouldn't have to witness another power-open.

"No hard feelings," he said.

"We'll see about that, John," Sir Harold replied.

Chapter 7: Alec's Tuppenny Bits' Worth

As soon as he'd finished talking to Sir Harold Kelly, John went to his desk, took out a notepad and committed the ten Russian agents' names to writing. He added everything he could remember about their careers – which was hardly anything – then went to his email to see if he'd received a *What the hell did you do to upset Sir Harold Kelly?* from Ruby Parker yet.

He hadn't, but he wasn't worried. He had right on his side, and Sir Harold Kelly didn't even exist. Not really. Probably not.

What he *did* have was an email from Brian entitled, 'Sgt. Pepper's Lonely Hearts Club Band', along with an attachment.

Okay, God loved him, after all. He downloaded the Power-Point, then cut and pasted it onto the memory stick on his key fob.

If anyone was monitoring his email, they'd know he'd opened this one, so he wrote a brief reply – 'I'm off the case now, Brian, but cheers anyway' - and hit send. Now it would look as if that's why he'd opened it: tie up loose ends.

True, they might be able to tell that he'd downloaded the file, but he couldn't do anything about that. In any case, they probably wouldn't look at something from Brian Penfold with a Beatles album heading. Like nearly all the macho men and women in this place, they almost certainly considered Brian a harmless loser.

Anyway, he could spend at least some time at home tonight isolating the Russians' faces from the slide show and resuming the process of committing them to memory.

Probably unnecessary, really. When Ruby Parker learned he'd been 'taken off the case', she'd probably go AWOL; not with him necessarily (although maybe), but with Grey. She might not be able to get him back aboard, but she'd almost certainly make sure he had renewed access to file RUS19whateveritwas, because his life was potentially in danger.

What he should do in that case – yes! - was show no interest in file RUS19, not even bother picking it up, much less take it away again to read. That way, Grey would think he'd lost interest, or taken their warnings to heart. It'd give them a false sense of security.

Mind games. Two could play at those.

Time to get back to Dhanial. Thames House probably had a copy of his book in the library on the third floor. They kept all sorts of establishment-bashing, conspiracy theory tomes up there, and if you ever suggested they might have missed one, they tended to get shirty.

Half an hour later, he sat at his desk with a copy of *The BBC's True Agenda: Identity Politics, Doublethink and the End of Britain* and a cup of strong Earl Grey. He'd have preferred the canteen – much more comfortable - but you could never rule out the possibility of someone sidling up to you for a conversation there.

It was a new copy, as far as he could tell. A respectable three hundred and forty-nine pages in a decent sized font, not much in the way of blank padding between chapters: probably worth twelve ninety-nine if you were into that sort of thing. He took out his phone and looked at the ebook: £2.99 and a little orange bar against the cover announcing it was a number one bestseller.

Either news of Dhanial's death had spread quickly and there was a spate of sympathy-buying, or there was an appetite amongst the reading public for anti-Beeb material. He checked the local news: still nothing about the murder, so it was probably the latter. He checked the sales figures of the 'customers who viewed this item also viewed' titles. *The BBC's Liberal Assault on the British Mind* seemed to be doing quite well. *How and Why the BBC is Trying to Change the Way You Think* was doing even better. In fact, they were all doing well.

He turned to the acknowledgements section at the back – always a good place to start when you were researching the author as much as the book. He'd likely be going to Dhanial's funeral sometime within the next week, and he might get a heads-up on some of the other mourners.

Many people have helped me directly and indirectly in writing this book. In particular, I would like to record my thanks to Tom Ford, former BBC Group Managing Director and Chair of the think tank, Policy Renewal, and Orville Peterson MP, former Parliamentary Under-Secretary of State for Arts, Heritage and Tourism. In addition...

Sounded interesting. And what was this, a little lower down? 'Jean-Paul Crevier and his delightful family'?

... with whom I spent a delightful summer discussing the probable benefits of Brexit, and keenly anticipating the 'New Europe' that will likely emerge. I would like to wish Mlle Brigitte Crevier the very best of luck in her political career. I am convinced we will be hearing much more about her in the future.

Blast from the past. Three years ago, Mordred had been held against his will in the Creviers' chateau in southern France. Interesting to see the old man was now out of prison (assuming he'd ever been there - Mordred hadn't followed subsequent events - but he'd deserved to be), and that Brigitte had apparently inherited the Creviers' misguided sense of Destiny's siren call.

Mobeen Dhanial must have been much more than he looked. Links to a former BBC Director and a one-time Parliamentary Under-Secretary? Intimate political conversations with the Creviers, *and* at their home in France? Quite a player, by any standards. Mordred had completely underestimated him. No wonder they had his book in the library upstairs. The only mystery was why it looked so untouched.

It didn't mean they weren't all paranoid, of course: Dhanial, Ford, Peterson, the lot of them. The Creviers definitely had delusions of grandeur, but you could afford those when you were super-rich and well-connected, and sometimes history had a nasty way of making them not so delusional after all. And Peterson might be an MP, but what did that mean any more? Being ambitious and pushy was enough to get you up the ladder nowadays. Quite possibly Tom Ford was of a similar mould. He'd look them up later, see if they'd been to public school. Just out of interest.

Time for the main feature. He took a sip of tea and turned to page one.

The BBC is no longer the impartial, trusted organisation it once was, and which its founders nobly envisaged. It is a shell occupied by the forces of liberal progressivism and doing everything in its power to bend the British people to a worldview shared by a minority of metropolitan elites with no real stake in any specific geographical locality…

Two hours later, he put the book in the buckle-down briefcase Phyllis had given him on his birthday and went downstairs to sign out. Alec sat on one of the chairs on the far side of the lobby, apparently reading a magazine. He discarded it when he saw Mordred and stood up. Balding, mid-forties, tall, well-dressed, his body language suggested he'd been waiting some time but didn't want to show it.

"How did it go in the one-to-one with Ruby Parker?" he asked.

"Fine. Then I had an interview with Sir Harold Kelly, Head of Grey, and he wanted me to kiss a man, and I said no – purely for reasons of efficacy, and because I don't like my lips touching another person's without some sort of prior affection in the mix - "

"Germy, I admit, but we are spies. More importantly, should you really be telling me this? I don't think I've been given clearance, unless you know something I don't."

"That'll be the day. Anyway, I'm off the case. What case, you may ask."

"The Russian case or the *Panorama* one? Because you were only ever semi-on the former."

"The Russians."

They signed out of the building and descended the stone steps to Millbank. The sun peeped from behind a thick grey cloud. A breeze blew from the Thames. Mordred tried to spot the supposedly countless men and women that were watching him, and succeeded, he thought, in clocking four.

"Are you doing anything tonight, by the way?" Alec said. "I thought we might get a few drinks. I don't mean in a pub. You could come to mine, or vice-versa. And before you say no thanks you're married, I happen to know Phyllis is working late tonight."

"We could have a few drinks now."

"Maybe, but what about *Star Trek?*"

"I think that's on Netflix for ever."

"Don't bank on it. Look at *Spooks*. That just vanished into thin air."

"I've got to read the rest of Mobeen Dhanial's book."

"He's written a book?" Alec said. "What kind?"

"A long put-down of the BBC."

"Well argued?"

"Tolerably. So far."

"I thought he was a freelance journalist. No disrespect to the profession, but most journalists I know haven't the patience to sit down and write a textbook."

Mordred began to speak, then paused. "That's actually a good point."

"You sound like you've just had a thought."

"He didn't strike me as the academic kind. Maybe someone wrote it for him."

"Does it matter?"

"I don't know."

Alec hmm-ed. "The thing is, he's probably right. I mean about the BBC."

"Do you actually know what he says?"

"I can guess. The BBC's a mouthpiece for liberal elitism: same thing everyone's saying. Well, not everyone. Lots of people."

Mordred scoffed. "What? You actually think that's true?"

"Put it this way, I don't like Nigel Farage, but do you ever hear anyone on the BBC say anything positive about him? Given that he's pretty popular, and not a total moron, that's got to be significant. Comedy's chiefly where it happens, incidentally. Not the news. Comedians these days don't just lean on the microphone-stand, like they used to, and tell a joke or two; no, nowadays they all have 'views', which they mostly present as common sense. And they're all pretty much cut from the same cloth."

"Rubbish. I'm pretty sure that, if you tot them up, gag for gag, you'll find as many jokes about Jeremy Corbyn as you do about Nigel Farage. Tony Blair never got an easy ride. It's just whoever happens to be in the public eye. There's no agenda."

"Corbyn jokes are all about his shabbiness and his age, his supposed dottiness-stroke-unworldliness, and sometimes his bike and his allotment. Farage jokes are all about Farage's opinions. That's the difference. And they're much more vicious."

They'd reached the traffic lights on Horseferry Road. On the other side lay the White Horse & Bower, but Mordred didn't want to go in, not after this morning: it seemed disrespectful. The Barley Mow would be better. "But the BBC's a national broadcaster," he continued. "It has a duty to represent the population, and the population's diverse. You can't have it turning a blind eye to anything that looks remotely like xeno-phobia. Entertain, inform, educate, that's its remit. We all pay the licence fee. I'm sure it *does* get it wrong sometimes, but it's vastly preferable to any alternative I can imagine."

"It's London-centric, even with its efforts to set up else-where. And London's another country, everyone knows that. The thing about you, John, is you actually buy into the liberal project. Most of us don't."

"By 'liberal project', I assume you mean a respect for human rights and a celebration of what used to be called 'multicultur-alism'; before that became a dirty word. Yes, I do."

"By 'liberal project', I mean a culture divided into imagin-ary victims and imaginary oppressors, where you get kudos for belonging to the former, and where everyone's therefore encouraged to be a whinger. 'Diversity', BBC-style, is about skin colour, sexual orientation and disability – the purely su-perficial things, in other words - not about outlook. They definitely don't want you to *think* differently."

"Bloody hell, Alec, did *you* write this book?"

Alec laughed. "I'm not even sure I believe half of what I'm saying, to be honest. Devil's advocate, that's me. But that's the beauty of a conversation with you, John."

They walked into The Barley Mow. Dark wood, expensive wallpaper, a narrow tiled area round the bar, rustic chairs, plain circular tables.

"Maybe we should talk about something else," Alec said. "My round. What are you having?"

John examined the little insignia on the pumps. "A pint of Barnaby Rudge, please."

"Two Barnaby Rudges," Alec told the barman.

"I don't mind continuing to talk about the BBC. Although I think I've got your take now."

"That's one of the things I like most about talking to you, John. We can have a grown-up conversation. I mean, we can deeply disagree, and neither of us takes it personally. By now, most people I know would be like, *I can't talk to you any more, I can't even look at you at the moment, off you go to* your *corner of Facebook to be with your ugly friends and I'll go off to* my *corner of Facebook and be with my beautiful ones.* They'd never be able to grasp the notion that I'm not necessarily saying what I think."

"What *do* you think?"

"Nothing. I read lots of different people: Owen Jones, Rod Liddle, Polly Toynbee, Peter Hitchens, Yasmin Alibhai-Brown, Piers Morgan. I think they're all pretty intelligent. Any of them could be right. I don't have any real power in the present system, and I'm pretty sure I'm not on their pay grade, so I don't feel obliged to lay my life down for them in a mere pub discussion. They can do that for themselves, if that's what they want."

"Sensible attitude."

"Meanwhile, none of them rules the domain that is Alec Cunningham's head. They live there, that's all, perpetually arguing. Downside: they have a tendency to raise their voices, so sometimes I find it difficult to get to sleep at night."

"Okay, you're starting to freak me out now."

Alec leaned over as if about to divulge a secret. "Keep your eyes on the table for a moment, but when you get a chance, check out that guy in the far corner. Fifty-ish, Philip Larkin specs, brown trainers? He's been following us since we left Tracy Island five minutes ago."

Mordred smiled. "You see those two women sitting at the bar? Ditto."

"So can I take it you know what's going on?"

"I'm not sure I'm allowed to tell you too much: it was mainly what my one-to-one with Ruby Parker was about this morning. But I can tell you one thing: I'm being watched by about eight different foreign agents, plus some from Grey department."

"And you're not allowed to say why?"

"No."

"And you think I'm too stupid to work it out? Presumably, it's because the Novelists are looking to make contact with you for some reason."

"You might very well think that. I couldn't possibly comment."

Alec took a sip of his drink. "Are we in any danger? I mean here, now?"

"Not unless one of the Novelists breaks cover. Assuming they're anywhere within a thousand miles of here, of course."

"Quite a lot of people must be making the assumption that they are, John. Why the hell are the rest of us being sent to Berlin and Paris?"

"Because it's essentially Grey's case, and, of course, the original plan was for *me* to go to Berlin."

"And the Home Secretary's heebie-jeebies about *Panorama* trumps this? God help us. Ruby Parker must be losing her touch."

"If Grey have got me completely covered here, they'd probably have done the same in Berlin. We'd be redundant in both cases. At least now you've a chance of achieving something."

"Going back to the subject of danger again, you do realise you could be in an awful lot of it? I assume some of the 'foreign agents' watching you are actually Russians? People who haven't necessarily got your best interests at heart?"

"I have had that explained to me, yes."

"Does Phyllis know?"

"No, and don't tell her. She's got enough on her plate lately. The point is, the Russians are significantly outnumbered. And given how leaky the FSB is, I should think Grey knows all about them."

"Courtesy of Bellingcat, probably. You'd think we ought to be able to do that sort of thing ourselves. Er, what do you mean, 'she's got enough on her plate'? Is she okay? Ignore that question if it's none of my business."

Mordred drank some of his beer. "She's considering resigning from the Conservative Party."

"Bloody hell."

"Exactly."

"That's quite a big thing in her world, isn't it?"

John nodded. "It's massive."

"Any specific reason?"

"Let's just say she was bitterly disappointed by the choice of leader. And then the Cabinet."

Alec sighed. "Politics is upsetting everyone at the moment. We're all washing our hands of it, one way or another. Sorry if that's stating the obvious, but I'm a bit speechless."

"That's okay. Worrying, but okay."

"Democracy's rubbish, but at least you get to kick your leader out every five years. Yes, you get an equivalent dud in return. But he or she's only going to last five years too. Under every other system, they're immortal. Let's talk about something else."

"If only we had Netflix to hand."

"We'd have been well into our second episode of *Star Trek* by now."

"Instead of which, we're bitterly depressed."

"Do you think there's any connection between the Russian Novelists and *our* novelists in MI7? I mean, we've got quite a substantial group of people in Red Department writing stuff like *Nowhere in Transnistria* and *The 6.17 to Spy Central Station*."

"I doubt it. The Russians came up with the name, and I doubt they know or care about our novelists."

"It just struck me that the FSB might be like a parallel world, that's all. Like maybe everything we have in Thames House, they have an equivalent of in the Lubyanka Building. Only with a Russian twist."

"*Father Ted*, only not so funny."

Alec sipped his Barnaby Rudge. "If only it were true."

"It probably is. The Russians and the British are pretty similar in most respects. Have you ever read *Spycatcher*?"

"Bits."

"Peter Wright. We're both pretty deferential, resentful about it, obsessed with secrecy and rank and punching above our weight. Both former empire builders. Most Russians I've met are pretty decent."

"That's the beer talking," Alec said. "You do realise, by the way, that you actually figure in most of the spy novels penned in Thames House? *I* actually feature in one or two. Annabel's in most of them, I think. But the real life Annabel's so difficult to tell apart from Jet or Beatrix Rose that I may be wrong."

"That's pretty detailed information you've got. What's your source?"

"Suki's been deputed to keep an eye on them, make sure they don't breach any protocols. She reports monthly to yours truly."

Mordred laughed. "I'd love that job. I didn't realise."

"Anyway, they're only doing it for themselves. A kind of, *I once worked with the* real *John Mordred, how cool does that make me?*"

"Not very cool at all, but it's flattering."

Alec finished his beer and put his glass on the table. "Have you noticed something, John?" he said quietly.

"You mean...."

Since the two women at the bar had come in twenty minutes ago, customers had been entering at the rate of roughly two every three minutes.

"We're perfectly safe," Alec continued. "I assume they're all in competition. If only there was some way - "

Mordred took out a pen from his inside jacket pocket and dinged his empty glass three times. The conversations didn't gradually die down. Every single speaker stopped dead, and every person in the room swivelled to face him.

The realisation apparently hit them all simultaneously: everyone here was a spy.

"Sorry," Mordred said. "Just testing."

Alec grinned nervously. "Er, I think it's probably time to leave."

Chapter 8: Food for Starving Spies

After The Barley Mow, John returned to the flat he shared with Phyllis in Camden. He poured himself a glass of orange, showered, ate half a tub of coleslaw and lay on the sofa to read more of *The BBC's True Agenda.* Page two hundred would be a good target. He could make three by tomorrow, and probably finish the whole thing before the funeral – the one to which, it was true, he hadn't yet been invited. Ruby Parker would probably want to see him tomorrow morning about: (1) that very funeral; (2) alienating Sir Harold; (3) dinging that glass. Grey would have made a point of snitching: it'd almost certainly had agents in The Barley Mow. He wondered what sort of beer they drank, or whether they were strictly dry martini types.

By half past seven, he'd finished *The BBC's True Agenda.* Its final part was devoted to Amazon TV's *Transparent*, which it claimed was something the BBC probably wished it had made, but couldn't possibly have pulled off. In the BBC's hands, its protagonists would all have been likeable and psychologically well-balanced, its storylines edifying, fanciful and trite. From the outset, its 'educate' remit would have asphyxiated its supposed duty to 'entertain' - as it virtually always did. There followed a hundred pages of the BBC's attitude to minorities ('they're always wholesome, unless they're UKIP-ers or City Bankers'), religion ('W1A, where atheism is always "cool"!') and radical feminism ('always in the right, except when it comes to Islam, where the Beeb tends to keep its head down'). A grim read and Mordred found himself inwardly disputing most of it.

At eight o'clock Phyllis sent him a text saying she'd set off from Thames House. He took a curry he'd made two days earlier from the fridge, put it in the oven to warm up, and boiled some brown rice.

She arrived home three quarters of an hour later. Long dark hair, a wide cheerful-looking mouth, 'perfect' teeth, a small nose, intelligent eyes, she pecked him on the cheek as she went through into the bedroom to change out of her work clothes. "Sorry for stealing your Berlin trip. What are you cooking?"

"Your dinner."

"I haven't been in the shower yet. I don't want to go to bed on a full stomach. Could you eat some?"

"You don't have to turn in for the night as soon as you've finished it. We could stay up a while, watch half a film. Or even a quarter."

"Airport, I'm afraid. I've got to be up early. Kevin's picking me up at five."

"*Five?*"

"I know. And I'm already bushed. Incidentally, our flat's being watched. I know that's relatively normal, but I got the impression it was being *super*-watched tonight. I actually clocked three people out there, all very shifty-looking. Is there something I should know?"

"Only that I'm being shadowed by agents from about five different countries."

"So what have you done now? Don't tell me. They think these fugitive Russians are on their way to meet you?"

"Bingo."

"And are they?"

"So I've been told. And so has everyone else, apparently. You know how it is when word gets around. *Extraordinary Popular Delusions and the Madness of Crowds*, Charles Mackay, 1841."

"Pretentious, *moi?* What did you have for dinner?"

"The coleslaw."

"What? That *pathetic tiddly bit of coleslaw?* Bloody hell, John: do you want to stay six foot plus, or do you want to be five foot three? Because that's what you'll end up."

He laughed. "It's probably not good for you to have the curry, I admit. You need something non-spicy. How about the cauliflower cheese?"

"I'll have a can of tomato soup, and one of those bread rolls you bought if we've still got any."

"I might put the curry in some Tupperware and take it down to one of the spies."

She came into the room and put her head on one side. "You're joking, right?"

"They're not going to stab me. It's not that kind of a surveillance. And they know I know about them. I called at least a third of them out in The Barley Mow late this afternoon."

"You trying to be funny again, I take it?"

"No, I really did."

"Tragically, I believe you. I accept you were in The Barley Mow, presumably with Alec, since I saw him waiting for you in the lobby earlier, trying to pretend he was interested in *The Economist*. I assume you did something 'zany' like stand on a barstool and go, 'Friends, Romans, Secret Agents', because that's the sort of thing you might do, and one day, it's going to get you killed. For God's sake, John. If you can't think about yourself, think about me. Think about your mum and dad and your sisters. We don't want to lose you."

"To be fair, we *are* spies. Danger's part of the job description. Which this isn't."

"*Necessary* danger, if I recall. Which that wasn't."

"Well, look, there are some Americans down there. And some French guys, and one or two Germans. I've been periodically watching them since I got in. Some of them have been there for hours. They must be hungry. You can come with me. We don't have to give it to the Russians, not if you don't want to."

72

"Come on then."

"What?"

"Let's go and give them the curry," she said. "I'll just put a brush through my hair, and I'll go in the shower when we get back. It'll be an adventure. Not necessarily a good one, but at least it won't be food wasted. And excuse me if I pack a weapon."

"What sort of weapon?"

"It's a secret. Part of the 'jolly caper', such as it is."

"Okay."

"And another thing. Next time I see Alec, which will be to-morrow, since we're going to Berlin together, I'm going to give him an ear-bashing he'll never forget. He encourages you."

"That's not true."

"Either that, or you feel the need to impress him."

"Okay, maybe that's true, I don't know. He used to be my boss. I mean, he recruited me. Perhaps - "

"You probably need to see a psychiatrist. Okay, look, sorry, I've said enough now. I don't want a row, and I love you. I'm just very tired. I've worked hard all day, and I've done God knows how much overtime. Let's just go and give this curry to whoever, and if we're both killed in the act of giving, I expect God'll have mercy on our wretched souls, and at least we'll go to Heaven together, where we'll probably get to sing hymns all day, okay?"

He got the Tupperware out. She put the tomato soup in a plastic bowl. He transferred the rice, then the curry. She set the microwave for three minutes. He took a fork from the drawer.

"Ready?" she said.

"When you are," he replied.

She pressed 'Start' on the microwave. "We give it to the first one we see, okay? No hanging about."

He picked up the tub and the fork and preceded her out of the flat, down the external stairway and through the security gate. The street was lined on both sides with parked cars, and most of the nearby flats had their blinds or curtains drawn. On the opposite side of the road, a man and a woman walked by, hand in hand. Mordred strode across and stood in front of them.

"Hi, it's me," he said. "From The Barley Mow. I thought you might be a bit hungry, so I've brought you some curry."

Both looked panicked. The man backed off, inserting himself subtly into the space in front of the woman, as if to defend her. He held his hands up.

"Hey, Mister," he said in an American accent. "I don't know who you think I am - "

"You're Agent Aidan Taylor of the CIA," Phyllis said irritably. "Now just take the curry."

His mouth popped open. He seemed to shrink slightly. He threw a furious look at the woman. She shrugged. He accepted the curry.

Phyllis grabbed John's arm and dragged him back the way they came. She didn't speak. When they got indoors, she went straight to the microwave and retrieved her soup. He buttered her a bread roll and put it on a plate. She sat down and started eating.

He sat opposite her. "How the hell did you know who he was?"

"He was American, right? So I guessed he was CIA. Aidan Taylor's just a name I made up. For all he knows, there may well be an Aidan Taylor in the CIA. The point is, he was fazed by the fifty per cent I got right, he took the curry, I didn't have to resort to my weapon, so mission accomplished. I'm going to miss this sort of thing in Berlin. Not."

Chapter 9: Kseniya Breaks Out

It was almost impossible to roll over without disturbing the others, but necessary if the discomfort wasn't to become unbearable; they all did it, all night. But it was worse for Valentina because she'd chosen to lie between the others. She didn't want Pasha next to Kseniya - she couldn't afford to lose him, even though they were no longer in love: she had no one else to fall back on - and they *said* they didn't want to be next to each other.

Was she fighting a losing battle, though? Was it inevitable that, at some point, he and Kseniya would get together? Three was a crowd.

What would happen then? How would they break it to her? Or would they both sneak out in the middle of the night and leave her to fend for herself?

Not a chance. Any 'sneaking out at night' was a non-starter. They all slept too lightly. Apart from the discomfort, they didn't feel entirely safe. The two locks on the door might work for most practical purposes, but they'd present no obstacle to a determined assassin. And they were always on the alert for a more routine break-in. Anything was possible round here.

This couldn't possibly be the beginning of the rest of their lives, could it?

Of course it could. They'd made their beds both literally and figuratively.

Valentina was wide awake now. She eased their shared phone out from beneath her pillow. Four o'clock in the morning. Next to her, Pasha rolled onto his back and snored. She heard Kseniya swear under her breath, then slip out from under her duvet.

They'd sat in Trafalgar Square again this morning, all three of them at different ends. A complete waste of time. They'd known it was a stupid plan when they'd come up with it in Moscow, but even so, they should have tried to think of a better one. It was too late now. No one was ever going to come. Even if they did, how would that make things any better? There'd be four or five of them, instead of three. They'd still be destitute and in fear of being killed at any moment.

Kseniya was moving about now. "I'm going for a shower," she announced quietly. "Lock the door behind me. I'll knock when I want to come back in."

"You went for a shower before we went to bed," Valentina told her. "Like five hours ago."

"I feel dirty again. I don't need your permission, do I?"

"I didn't mean it like that."

"Have sex with your boyfriend while I'm out. I'm serious. It might make you both feel better. With me around, you're not going to get many chances."

Should she say something? *Pasha and I are no longer together?* Hadn't she noticed? "What do you mean by that?" she asked instead.

Kseniya chuckled. "Not that I'm after him. You can rest easy on that score. Just that I'm in the way here. You'd both be better off without me."

"Oh, right," Valentina replied bitterly. "Of *course*. Because in that case, it'd just be *a normal romantic holiday*."

Pasha raised himself on his elbows. "What's going on?" he said sleepily. "Are you two arguing?"

Valentina ignored him. "We're only on the brink of total despair," she told Kseniya sardonically, "because you being here makes sex difficult. Without that tiny little inconvenience, we'd be having the time of our lives!"

"I'm going in the shower," Kseniya repeated opening the door and stepping into the dim light of the corridor where an automatic light flickered on. "Lock up after me, for safety's sake if you're not going to have sex. I'll knock five times – three long, two short - when I want to come back in. I love you both."

"We love you too!" Valentina said emotionally.

Kseniya closed herself out. Valentina got up, locked the door then slipped back into bed.

"Should we be concerned?" Pasha said after a few seconds.

"We may have to get used to giving each other some space," Valentina answered. "We're all feeling the strain. She needs to be alone, that's all."

"Where's she gone?"

"The shower."

"But she *did* that before she got in bed! So she said."

"I know. Which probably means she's gone out for a walk. Which may in turn mean she's at risk. But what can we do? She's an adult."

"That 'I love you'. It sounded... I don't know..."

"A bit melodramatic?"

"I was going to say, *a bit final*. Like she's got something in mind. Something that might require us to remember that she told us she loved us."

Valentina groaned. "You mean, kill herself?"

"Possibly."

"So what do you think we should do? Go after her? That might just make things worse. Anyway, I think it's unlikely. She imagines she's some sort of burden to us, so she decides to help out by committing suicide: reduce the liability by a third: that's your thinking, right?"

"Something along those lines."

"But if that was her plan, she'd need to devise some way of letting us know she was actually dead, and that the burden had therefore been lifted. A suicide note wouldn't work because she'd know in advance we wouldn't necessarily believe it. And no one's ever going to come and tell us, 'Hey, your friend's dead'. Suicides are probably common in London - and of illegal immigrants probably doubly - so it wouldn't make the news. Her just 'disappearing' – which is all her death would amount to from our point of view – would prompt us to go out and search, making us even more vulnerable than we already are. She'd have become more of a burden in death than she ever was in life. And I'm pretty sure she knows that. She's not stupid."

"But you don't think she's in the shower."

"Like you just said, she *went* in the shower five hours ago. So, unless she's developing some sort of obsessive-compulsive behaviour - "

"Which isn't impossible," Pasha said.

"Let's just give it twenty minutes. If she's not back then, I'll go and check."

"Maybe we should work on the assumption that she is coming back. That she's doing exactly what she says she is, and she wants to give us a bit of space. I mean… perhaps we *could* have sex. We might as well. It'll take our minds off things for ten minutes."

"We broke up, remember?" she said.

"I know, but what else is there? What the hell have we got to look forward to?"

He got up and walked to the window. "No, you're right," he said after a while. "We shouldn't think like that. It's sinful."

"Maybe we should pray."

"I still love you, Valentina."

"I love you too, Pasha. I care for you. I always will."

It was dark, so she couldn't tell where he was. Since she couldn't hear him moving, she assumed he was still looking out of the window. After a few moments, she heard him muttering The Lord's Prayer.

She joined him in a whisper and she had to make an effort to stop herself crying. Such a long time since these words had crossed her lips, now it was like the faintest little fresh breeze from home.

There were lots of open-all-day churches in London. To-morrow, they'd find one and spend the entire day on their knees. Light a candle, if they did that sort of thing in England. God would help them. They hadn't trusted in Him sufficiently before. That needed to change. She flooded with a sudden sense of happiness, as if she'd found the solution to all their problems. She noticed she'd stopped whispering the Lord's Prayer and replaced it with an inward recital of *Jesus Christ, Son of God, have mercy on me, a sinner.* Then that too faded into quiet.

When she awoke, Pasha was lying next to her on his side. It was light outside. She took the phone from under her pillow and looked at the time. Eight o'clock.

Then *where she was* hit her, as it always did, after a delay just long enough to make it feel like someone had stuck a knife in. She groaned.

Then the events of last night crowded on her. Kseniya.

She looked round the flat, as if Kseniya might be hiding somewhere, and shook Pasha awake.

"Kseniya's still not back!" she said.

"What time is it?"

"It's eight o'clock. She's been gone four hours!"

"Oh shit. We locked her out."

"I wasn't that unconscious. I never am. If she'd been hammering on the door, I'd have heard. We both would. I'll check the shower," she said, and she heard her own words like a joke. *Of course* she wouldn't be in the shower: it'd been four hours! "Sorry, I'm not thinking."

"You *are* thinking. What if the bathroom door's locked? What if there's the usual queue of tenants waiting to get in? What if she's done what we both thought she might do, and no one's yet had the sense to kick the door in?"

She pulled on her clothes, unlocked the door and sprang into the corridor. Six doors down, the bathroom.

Oh, my God: there *was* a queue.

No longer than normal, though.

Then the bathroom door opened and a middle-aged Arab-looking man came out with a towel wrapped round his waist and a pair of brogues on his bare feet. Someone else went in, and the queue diminished by one.

Thank you God. Valentina did an about-turn and re-entered the flat.

She found Pasha reaching down inside the back of the sofa. Their money, of course. He pulled out a plastic envelope. It looked as thick as the last time they'd had it out, which wasn't very thick at all. The point was it hadn't gone. She hadn't taken it. Pasha began counting it.

"Look around the flat," he told her. "If she left a note – which I'm guessing she has – it'll be in here somewhere. Like you said: she's clever. She'll have put it somewhere we wouldn't have stumbled across it earlier. But it *has* to be in here. Because where else could it be?"

Valentina thought for a moment. Where the hell could you hide something – anything – in a space this small? Pasha had already checked the sofa –

Then she knew. She went to Kseniya's side of the bed, reached under her pillow, and retrieved a folded piece of lined notepaper.

"*I've got it!*" she almost shrieked, opening it in the same moment. "It says… It just says: 'I've gone back home. I'll make sure everything's all right for us. Don't worry. I love you both. K.'"

Valentina put her hands on her head. Was this for the best? How could it be? Maybe it could! But how was Kseniya going to get home, without any money? Maybe she had a secret stash of her own?

"How's she going to get home without any money?" Pasha said.

"I don't know. Maybe she's got some of her own?"

But he'd turned pale. "She's not planning to 'go home' the way we came, that's obvious. She'd have taken some cash, because she definitely hasn't got any of her own. She didn't even take her phone. She's – Oh, my God. We've got to get out of here. She's gone to the Russian embassy!"

Chapter 10: Not Actually in Trouble

John made Phyllis two slices of toast and jam, two cups of tea, a lunch box – four cheese and tomato sandwiches, a bottle of orange juice and a granola bar – and kept out of her way while she packed her travel case and put her makeup on. Kevin pulled up outside at 4.55.

"No more feeding the spies," she told him sternly as she pulled her coat on.

"I love you. Go easy on Alec."

"I'll probably let it go. Tragically, I think it's more you than him."

"Sorry you married me?"

"I will be, if you get killed. I meant what I said a moment ago. Mind your own business while I'm out of town."

He carried her suitcase down the stairs and put it in the boot – both things she was perfectly capable of doing herself – then kissed her, told her to text him when she reached Berlin, and watched the car pull out and disappear round the corner. He returned to the flat and went back to bed for two hours.

When he awoke, he switched to autopilot. Make the bed, wash, shave, two Weetabix in front of the TV, a mug of strong tea, wash up, dry up, clothes on, shoes on, briefcase, walk to the bus stop, get on the 254, read the news on his phone, disembark at Lambeth Bridge, stroll along Millbank, enter Thames House.

"Ruby Parker wants to see you at nine o'clock sharp," Colin said, as he signed in.

"Thank you," Mordred replied. He looked at his watch. 8.55.

Weird: Colin couldn't possibly know he was in trouble, although his tone of voice suggested otherwise. Maybe he'd learned to divine Ruby Parker's moods.

He went upstairs to his desk, switched on his computer and went to his email. There it was: subject heading: *9am*, content: *Please come to my office at 9am, RP.*

Pretty unambiguous.

Autopilot again. He logged off, took the lift to the basement and strode along an empty corridor to her office. She called her usual 'enter' when he knocked: nothing in the tone to suggest he was in for a carpeting, but then it *was* only a single word: difficult to extract too much from it.

"Sit down," she told him, indicating the single chair. Her office was whitewashed, just large enough for a desk, a PC, In and Out trays, and a variety of house plants on different levels. Its only decoration was a recent addition: Pietro Annigoni's *Queen Regent* in a plain wooden frame on the wall facing the door.

He did as commanded. Probably pointless saying good morning.

"I got a phone call from Sir Harold Kelly after he spoke to you yesterday," she told him. "'Informing' me that you were off the case, or attempting to. I 'informed' him that, given your centrality in all this, he should change his mind: bluntly, if any of those Russians were to make direct contact with you, we might conceivably decide not to share their intelligence. Of course, we probably couldn't keep that up for very long – Grey has a fairly clear-cut kind of seniority here – but we could certainly try, and throughout the time an adjudication was on its way, every card would be in our hands. Naturally, he didn't like that."

"So I'm back on the case?"

"John, I don't really see how it could be otherwise, do you? I mean, it is you these Russians are supposedly coming to find. It did help that, when I spoke to him, you'd called out several of his agents, plus ten or twelve of their foreign rivals, in The Barley Mow. I don't know why you did that – although I assume you were being bumptious again – but it worked in our favour. It gave them a sense of their own limitations."

"All's well that ends well, then. I expected to be hauled over the coals."

"In any other circumstances, you probably would have been. Anyway, it's all academic, more a point of principle than anything else. You may still be 'on' the Russian case, in the purely passive sense of being open to any approach, but *Panorama*'s still your main concern, especially given what happened to Mobeen Dhanial."

"Do we have any idea who killed him yet?"

"So far, we're assuming that it is roughly what it looks on the CCTV: a mugging that went wrong, or a straightforward murder which may or may not have been racially motivated. We are no closer to identifying either of the suspects, although there is enough – just - in terms of their facial presentation to the cameras. It's at the top of our list of priorities at the moment because, fortunately or not – I mean, for us – there's been a development. It seems that Mobeen Dhanial actually maintained a blog. Up until the time he was killed, I think its total readership was in single figures."

"Even though he's the author of a bestselling book?"

"There's no mention of the blog in *The BBC's True Agenda: Identity Politics, Doublethink and the End of Britain,* so it's not advertised there. He seems to have started it after it was published."

"I assume his blog catalogues his conviction that *Panorama* was after his blood."

"Correct."

"Have you read his book?"

"Yes," she replied. "Why?"

"I was speaking to Alec yesterday, and he made a good point: most journalists don't have the patience to write something like *The BBC's True Agenda*. Whatever you think about its premises and conclusions, it is reasonably well argued. More academic than hack. I think it might be instructive to compare its style to that in which the blog's written."

"So you believe someone else may have written *The BBC's True Agenda*?"

"I think it's possible."

"But why would they allow him to take the credit?"

"With respect, that's the wrong question. It's a fringe work, advancing a hypothesis that might be true, but which doesn't command the assent of the majority of the population. In short, it reads a bit like a conspiracy theory. The correct question is, why would they allow him to take the flack? And the answer is: because it's flack."

"I see what you're saying, yes. You think the true author may belong in the sort of circles where vilifying the BBC for its supposedly pro-liberal bias is a bad career move."

"*Like* academia, although not necessarily. Conversely, in Dhanial's line of work, pillorying the BBC might well be a *good* career move. To give an example, Rupert Murdoch's not exactly Auntie's biggest fan."

"Have you anyone in mind, as the true author? And what difference does it make?"

"I haven't yet read Dhanial's blog. If it reads like the book - "

"It doesn't, but that needn't mean much. Different enterprises often require dissimilar styles of writing."

"Of course."

"On the other hand, there are scientific ways of investigating identity of literary style. We can do that here in Thames House, but I'm still not sure what you're ultimately driving at. Do you have a theory attached to all this? You're not suggesting, I take it, that the murderers may have been in the pay of the true author?"

"I think it's possible."

She shook her head and chuckled. "Okay, possibly publishing that sort of book *could* be bad career move in some places, but, my God, not to the extent of hiring a pair of *contract killers* to conceal your contribution! It's a sorry enough theory on its own, but it also assumes that Dhanial was threatening to expose the 'true author', when we don't yet have the slightest reason to think he himself didn't write it. Sorry, John, we're way out in the realms of fantasy now."

"I wasn't suggesting that. I was thinking more that someone badly wants to bring the BBC down. They write a book for which Dhanial takes credit. Dhanial gets wind of something going on at *Panorama* and blogs about his conviction that the BBC is after him. He gets killed. Might that not look as if there's some substance to his blog claims? That they're not just paranoia? There are a hell of a lot of people out there nowadays who'll believe anything. There's never been a time like the present for conspiracy theories."

"Sorry, John, I don't think anyone's going to fall for the idea that the BBC's actually killing journalists. I know you're only thinking aloud, and I'm not discouraging you from doing that – on the contrary, I think it's good practice – but I'm convinced you're barking up the wrong tree entirely."

He sighed. "So am I, if I'm honest. The truth is, I can't shake the idea that his death had something to do with his meeting me, and that, when a person says they're on to something big, and then, within five minutes, they're killed, it's because they really *were* on to something big. And probably I've been watching too many spy films. I didn't notice anything about Dhanial's blog in the papers this morning."

"I'd imagine because the editors don't know what to make of it. I think we can both appreciate their predicament. They either take the angle that he was a crank, which seems disrespectful and a stab in the back for one of their own, or that he may have had a point, in which case, they've got their work cut out justifying that and not getting sucked into a row from which they could easily emerge looking very silly indeed. My guess is that they'll continue to ignore it, which is almost certainly their wisest policy."

"When is the funeral?" he asked.

"As usual, you're a step ahead. Three days' time. Monday. You're not invited, obviously: I doubt any of his friends or family knows he ever met you. But there's nothing to stop you, or anyone else, attending a funeral. Someone there may know you met, and you're an expert at interpreting involuntary facial expressions. And you're allowed to tell whoever asked why you're there. That too may yield something. Pick up a black suit and tie from Amber on Saturday morning. There are three people I'd particularly like you to look out for."

"Let me guess. Tom Ford, former BBC Group Managing Director and Chair of the think tank, Policy Renewal, and Orville Peterson MP, former Parliamentary Under-Secretary of State for Arts, Heritage and Tourism. And one of the charming Creviers."

"You did tell me once that they actually *were* charming."

He smiled. "That's true. I mean, yes, they kept me prisoner. But they were very civilised about it."

"They could have thrown you in a cellar or even killed you. I don't think you should be too hard on them."

"I wonder how they'll react to seeing me at the funeral."

"If they're there at all, I expect in a courteous manner. I doubt there will be any hard feelings."

"I get the impression you quite like them."

"I wouldn't go that far. In any case, we need to talk about Tom Ford and Orville Peterson. What do you know about them?"

"I haven't had chance to do any research yet, but it is on my to-do list."

"It's true Orville Peterson was a former Parliamentary Under-Secretary, but he didn't last long in the post. The consensus is that he's talented but too inflexible for a successful career at the higher levels. There are times, especially if you're aiming for a cabinet position, when you've got to blow with the wind. Peterson was all for facing down the unions all the time, and eventually it lost him the support of his colleagues. However, that's background. All you need to know is that he's been an MP for twenty years, and he's tried three times – in three different sessions – to introduce the same private member's bill. He's very persistent, in other words. He's been selected by ballot twice and he's also gone via the ten minute rule. Most PMB's only have a very small chance of success, but his are mainly introduced on an if-you-keep-on-pestering-eventually-you'll-get-somewhere conviction. Thus, it just so happens that, right now, he's making a fourth attempt."

"So what's its substance? Do we know?"

"If it's anything like the other three – and it almost certainly is - he'll be trying to get legislation through Parliament that would scrap the BBC licence fee. Under the Royal Charter, the BBC has to obtain authorisation from the Home Secretary. All that was done and dusted in 2017. The current Royal Charter isn't due to expire until 2026, and no one wants to drag the Queen into politics so that date's effectively written in stone, but the Home Secretary could in principle revoke his permit before that. That would be horribly controversial and it would take the country into uncharted territory so, even with a high level of anti-BBC feeling in the government, it's unlikely ever to happen. Renewal of the Royal Charter would be the first battleground."

"So Peterson's trying to prepare the ground for an all-out assault in seven years' time?"

"He's not upfront about it obviously, but yes, I think that's his plan."

"He must oppose the BBC pretty vehemently to keep on pressurising."

"If you're looking for some sort of personal motive, you'll probably be disappointed. He's an idealist. He thinks the BBC's the proponent of a socialist-type ideology, and it's subtly trying to indoctrinate the population with false assumptions and values."

"Very much the position of whoever wrote *True Agenda*. Which I'm not saying wasn't Dhanial."

"John, you would *expect* their positions to coincide, since Peterson's thanked in the acknowledgements, but I take your point: we shouldn't rule anything out."

"What about Ford?"

"In terms of his views, he too could have written *True Agenda*. He began life as a local radio journalist in the 1980s, and came to the BBC in 1991. He helped launch BBC Choice and jumped ship to Radio 4 when it was replaced by BBC Three. He was a senior executive at Sky Atlantic for two years, and became BBC Group Managing Director in 2017. He resigned after just three months, citing what he called 'creative differences' with other members of the Executive Committee. Nowadays, he writes a weekly column for *The Daily Mail*. One of his recurrent themes is that the BBC is brainwashing Britain with leftist propaganda, but more importantly, that he – as someone with a deep insider's knowledge of the Corporation - is uniquely placed to remedy the problem. He likes to depict himself as a kind of Director-General in waiting, but unless the tide of public opinion turns radically against the BBC for reasons he would wholeheartedly approve, his chances are negligible."

"Both dyed-in-the-wool BBC Hunters, then. I assume we've also been in touch with *Panorama*. They may hold the key to what's going on."

"Not directly. MI7 approaching the BBC about one of its current affairs programmes tends to send the wrong signals. The police have spoken to them. From what I understand, *Panorama* denied any connection to Dhanial. To all intents and purposes, they effectively told the investigating officers to mind their own business."

"Understandable. But if they knew nothing about Mobeen Dhanial, what sort of 'entry' could he have had? Because that's what he claimed."

"Your guess is as good as mine. Could he have been lying?"

"I didn't get that impression. And since he was inviting me to join him, he'd have been silly to make false promises."

"It looks like the funeral's your best lead. I think, if that gets us nowhere, we may just have to wait, like everyone else, till *Panorama* actually airs. The embarrassment of not knowing what was happening – assuming they really are onto something big – is probably preferable to the likely fallout if we're perceived to be spying on them."

"Dhanial approached me. I didn't approach him."

"Go to the funeral, see what you can dig up, write me a report. If we get no new leads and no information, we'll draw a line under the whole thing, and I'll send you to Paris. Thank you for your time this morning, John."

Chapter 11: Not Such a Great Homecoming

Kseniya Yumasheva stood outside a substantial building in Kensington Palace Gardens. The Russian embassy. In some ways it looked like a lot of old buildings in London: big bays, wide windows, something monstrous about it and at the same time, tame. Very English, but given the portico and the colonnaded porch, it probably wouldn't have been out of place on the outskirts of Moscow either. Especially the high railings and the even taller gate with thick pillars either side.

The first time she'd been here, early this morning, she'd expected to find guards outside. Instead, it had been deserted and eerily quiet. Probably – almost certainly, actually – external 'guards' were something closed-circuit TV had long since rendered obsolete. Later that day, she wondered if anyone inside had seen her. She didn't think so. She'd worn a headscarf and even she could tell her appearance had changed significantly over the last few weeks. She looked thin and defeated now, nothing like the attractive law student she'd so recently been, click-clacking along marble-tiled corridors in heels and a black skirt-suit to attend yet another mock-court case.

This was her second visit to 5-7 Kensington Palace Gardens, and she was determined to go through with her plan this time. The dream – or nightmare – had to be laid to rest. Time to go home, by whatever means the occupants here saw fit, in their mercy, to grant her. Even a coffin would be better than Peckham, though she didn't think it would come to that. A spell in prison, probably, that's all. And since she knew the statutes, and could fight a lawsuit, and her faith in the Russian justice system was far from dead (though she'd seen one or two bad things), she was reasonably confident she could be out in a couple of years. Less, if she could persuade the others to give themselves up. She could defend them all together.

It was nine o'clock at night now and dusk was creeping in. All she had to do was remove her headscarf and stand at the front gate for as long as it took, like a one-person protest. They'd wonder who she was at first, but hopefully, it wouldn't take them long to realise.

Inside the embassy, the security team – two middle-aged ex-soldiers eating pot noodles and drinking orange juice – registered the suspicious looking woman as soon as she appeared. This time of night, there wasn't that much to look at. They sat up but didn't stop eating. She gave off the air of someone on a mission of some kind. Wearing a headscarf and completely alone. The term 'suicide bomber' appeared spectrally in both their minds, but in each case, it had too many question marks attached. She didn't look like she had an explosive belt, for a start, and then there was the time and place. If you were going to set off a bomb, you'd want maximum casualties, maximum damage. You wouldn't stand outside a set of heavy railings in a quiet part of London at dusk. Besides, the British security services were supposed to be more or less on top of that sort of thing: nowadays, the terrorists had to use knives or vehicles, like the pathetic, mentally retarded losers they all were.

The likelier probability was that she was a Crazy of some kind, in which case, it might be best to just leave her alone for a while. If she stayed too long, call the British police, make a complaint about 'loitering'.

She suddenly removed her headscarf and walked right up to the gate and looked directly into camera six. Blonde hair, sharp eyes, plump nose and lips, slightly haggard. Maybe a Romanian beggar. Definitely a Crazy.

Ultimately, they'd probably ring the British police. First, however, there was standard procedure to go through. Purely a formality in this case, just so they could say they'd ticked all the boxes.

They had to take a screenshot and email it to the Defence Attaché's Office in Highgate.

"I'll do it," the older one said in a bored voice.

Half an hour later, Kseniya Igorevna Yumasheva sat on one side of a table in a basement office. Opposite her, two GU officers, both men, one quite slim with a short beard and very little hair, the other stockier with a double chin and a gold wristwatch, both about forty. Neither looked pleased to see her, but then, she hadn't expected to be welcomed back into the claustrophobic fold that was modern-day Russia with open arms. Short of putting handcuffs on her they'd done everything they could to show their contempt. Nevertheless, just hearing her own language from strangers' voices gave her the feeling of being halfway home. Part of her wanted to cry with gratitude. Above her, the room was illuminated by a single light bulb with a plain shade. Apart from the shade, it was the most stereotypical interrogation room she'd ever seen – and she'd encountered all but this one in films.

The stocky man produced a digital recorder. He turned it on and placed it gently on the desk. He went through the formality of stating her name and theirs, then the time and place.

"Why did you leave Moscow, Kseniya?" he asked.

"I wanted to see a bit of the world," she replied.

They exchanged weary looks. The stocky man sighed. "We're not going to get anywhere if you waste our time trying to be witty. This is supposed to be the pleasant version, Kseniya. This is where we *ask* you for information. We expect you to be equally pleasant in return, and give it, preferably with a smile on your face."

"You could even be back in Russia tomorrow or the day after," the slim one said. "If you cooperate."

"No one else knows you're here," the stocky one said. "You're currently a non-person. You can stay that way – get my drift? - or we can rehabilitate you. Now, I'll ask you again: why did you leave Moscow?"

She swallowed. "Because I thought I was being watched," she replied meekly. She understood what they were doing – nice cop, nasty cop, and that they already knew most of what they were going to ask: the stuff they didn't know wouldn't come up till near the end. "I'd been working on a top secret project for the FSB, and it was discontinued, and I was made to feel I'd done something wrong, and I was told I'd be watched, and I - "

"Where's the 'we' in all this, Kseniya?" the slim man interrupted.

"What do you mean?" she asked. She saw she was trembling. She hadn't noticed till now.

Then the realisation hit her hard: coming here had been yet another big mistake. My God, how stupid *was* she?

Silence from the interrogators.

"What do you mean?" she asked again.

"I mean, you were part of a *team*," the slim man said gently. "You were *all* working on that project. You were pretty chummy. We know all about Kuznetsov's little venture, how it began as a hypothetical plan to get Elizaveta Aleksandrova Khamatova into bed with the British agent, John Mordred, and how, in reality, that was just a ruse to get her into bed with Stanislav Viktorovich Kuznetsov."

"Which never happened in the end," the stocky man said. "Because she wisely took flight."

"And then one day, you all came up with something useful," the slim man said. "And what we want to know is, how much do you know about that?"

Before she could answer, the stocky man leaned over the recorder, as if confiding a secret. "Let the records show, we're about to call the technicians to apply the lie detector," he said.

For a split second, Kseniya was terrified: she thought the words 'lie detector' might be some kind of sick joke, like they were going to hit her or something. But then the door buzzed open. Two more men entered, wearing casual clothes, and began unpacking instruments from a case. The faces of her two interrogators glazed over. "Did you catch the tennis the other day?" the slim one asked.

For a moment, she thought he was talking to her.

"I'm more of an ice-hockey man myself," the stocky one replied.

"You missed a good match," the slim one said.

"Stand up and take off your blouse," one of the new entrants told her.

She did as commanded. To their credit, none of the men looked at her in anything like a lurid way: as far as they were concerned, she was just an inmate.

One of the technicians wrapped a band round her chest. "This is a pneumograph," he said matter-of-factly, as if it was really important she knew the name of whatever it was, in case anything went wrong. "It'll measure your respiration,"

The stocky man laughed. "Ivan, don't tell her what it *does*! She might use the information to cheat!"

"You can't cheat," the slim man said.

"I was *joking*, dummy," he replied.

"Give me your fingers," the other technician said. "You can sit down now. These are electrodes. They'll measure skin con-ductivity."

The other man wrapped a band round her arm and muttered 'blood pressure'.

Everything was hooked to a machine at the far end of the table, then the two technicians left.

"Okay, I'm going to ask you a number of questions," the stocky man said, "to establish what you telling the truth looks like."

He asked her what her name was, where and in what year she was born, what her marital status was, where she'd been to school, how many fingers he was holding up. He put an earpiece in and nodded to his partner, then removed it again. "Okay, we're ready to begin," he said. He switched the digital recorder back on and recited names, dates and times. "Resuming interview with the aid of a lie detection kit," he said.

"What was the task you and your team were working on?" the slim man asked. "I mean, in Moscow, under Director Kuznetsov?"

"We were assigned to devise the next phase in the disruption of Russia's enemies abroad," she replied.

"And what did you eventually came up with?"

"A plan to bring the BBC – the British Broadcasting Corporation - under the control of people more attuned to Russian values."

"And who came up with this idea?"

"We all did. Probably one or two more than others, but I can't remember any one of us specifically claiming the credit, or being given it by the others."

"Explain the detail of that plan," the stocky man said.

"It didn't *have* any detail," she replied. "There wasn't time."

"You know no more about it than what you've just told us?" the slim man said.

"No," she replied. She could see something had happened. In some unknown way, her answer had taken them by surprise. They exchanged sceptical looks.

"I'll check," the slim one said. He stood up and left the room.

The stocky man switched the recorder off. "Shame, a nice girl like you getting mixed up in something like this," he said. He grinned. "You're quite attractive, you know that? I mean, for a *traitor*."

The word hit her like a slap. In a flash, she saw a million bad futures, but most prominently, how awful it'd be for her in prison if that tag followed her there. Terror gripped her a second time, but she grabbed it by the throat and thrust it down. She had to show she despised traitors. In one lightning movement, she thrust her chair back, and threw a right hook which hit him square in the face.

She'd done a bit of boxing at university, so knew her own strength. Roughly 300 psi, this occasion. She saw him fly back on his chair as if in slow motion, the best bit of which was the total surprise on his face.

He hit the concrete floor at speed. The whiplash meant his skull struck the ground a second later than the rest of him, and the blow from in front was supplemented by an equal and opposite clout from behind.

He lay still. His nose pumped blood but not in any kind of enthusiastic way. Thankfully, the whole thing had been more or less silent, so no one rushed in from outside.

Ten seconds later, the slim man re-entered. "She's telling the truth," he announced indifferently as he closed the door.

He turned round and registered the empty space where his partner had been.

Then his partner on the floor, in what was now a small pool of blood.

He reopened the door and bolted, yelling *help*. A second later, an alarm sounded. Ten seconds later, six men entered in a hurry. A man in his fifties knelt down and examined the stout man, feeling his wrist, his neck, then pummelling his chest, while the other five forced Kseniya to the floor and pinned her there. More pummelling. Someone called her a bitch, then more silence.

"My God, he's – he's *dead*," someone whispered.

"He called me a traitor," Kseniya said.

Murder at the Russian embassy was a first, and this was a freak occurrence – had he hit the ground just slightly slower or from any other angle, he'd merely be concussed - and for about half an hour, no one knew what to do. Incredulity and horror followed shock as high-ranking members of staff frantically bombarded Moscow with encrypted messages.

The victim had been killed on British soil, but within what was technically known as the chancery, the diplomatic building. What that meant juridically had never been fully tested. The chancery didn't have anything like full extraterritorial status - contrary to popular belief, such buildings hardly ever did – but it did have certain privileges under the Vienna Convention on Diplomatic Relations, one being immunity to certain local laws. Murder – or manslaughter, to give Kseniya the benefit of the doubt - probably wasn't exempted *as a rule*, but things were likely different when both killer *and* victim were Russian citizens, and where the former had entered the embassy of her own free will.

The corpse was a major part of the problem. One solution was to transfer it to a Russian plane at Heathrow under the cloak of diplomatic privilege, but no one knew how this might work, and after the stink caused by the murder of Fydor Nikolayevich Golovin in Cologne, it was risky. If MI7 caught wind, and decided to jeopardise the operation, or something unforeseen went wrong, all hell might be let loose.

The final decision went to the ambassador who decided, as ambassadors nearly always did, to play it by the book. According to Article 37 of The Vienna Convention on Consular relations – *information in cases of deaths, guardianship or trustee-ship, wrecks and air accidents* – the Russians had a duty, 'in the case of the death of a national of the sending State, to inform without delay the consular post in whose district the death occurred.'

In other words, the British had to be told. And there wasn't much time. Any delay might look conspiratorial.

Not everyone liked this. Moscow hired a team of British lawyers at short notice to smooth the most foreseeable creases. The lawyers advised that, although the Foreign and Commonwealth Office would demand to know the identity of both victim and perpetrator, under at least one interpretation of international law, it possessed no entitlement to such information. A court case might in theory ensue, but it was highly unlikely things would go that far: over the last few years, the UK had alienated many of its former friends, while the Russians arguably had natural justice on their side. In any case, formal legal proceedings would drag on too long.

A bigger problem was the British Security Services. They would undoubtedly want to know why the Russians were being so secretive. Kseniya Igorevna couldn't stay in 5-7 Kensington Palace Gardens forever: sooner or later, she'd have to be extradited, and the British would be waiting with cameras and possibly even (because you couldn't rule out mavericks in some sections MI7) and exfiltration plan. Either way, they'd quickly discover who she was.

But then someone had a brainwave. Why not tell the British everything? If they learned that Kseniya Igorevna Yumasheva was sitting pretty in the Russian embassy, and had entered of her accord, and that the Russians were treating her deed as a tragic mishap, not a murder at all, they'd assume 'The Novelists' were beginning to give themselves up to the mother country. At the very least, they'd find that demoralising. At best, it might even persuade them to throw in the towel and focus their resources elsewhere. Britain, at least, had lots of problems right now, and getting hold of The Novelists probably wasn't sustainable in an environment of diminishing returns.

The killing occurred at 22.35. At 23.55, the Russian ambassador informed the British Foreign Secretary in person. The latter expressed his condolences, but said he would need to consult with the Permanent Under Secretary, the Head of the Diplomatic Service, and the Prime Minister before deciding how to proceed. Three-quarters of an hour later, he called back, conveyed the Prime Minister's deepest sympathy and said that, provisionally at least, providing the proper protocols were observed – largely a matter of filling in the right forms in the right order and supplying documentary verification of the key points – he saw no reason why it should not remain a purely Russian concern.

The next problem was a practical one. How to proceed with Kseniya Igorevna's interrogation. By this time, she'd been handcuffed and beaten and was barely conscious. The GU's chief First Directorate (Europe) representative in London, Commander Yuri Bryzgalov, noted that she was in no condition for a lie detector, and for purely pragmatic reasons he'd never favoured torture: victims tended to simply to tell you what they thought you wanted to hear.

Meanwhile, the ambassador still believed in the rule of law. At his insistence, the six men who had beaten her were placed under arrest and four were sent back to Moscow to face what he hoped would be some sort of trial. Bryzgalov made no attempt to interfere. Quite the contrary: he was supportive. Not on moral grounds, much less out of any misguided compassion for the victim, but solely because these six might have wrecked the GRU's best chance of netting the other Novelists. At the very least, they'd set the investigation back – which, in his view, ought to be an indictable offence in itself.

The big question was, set back for how long? The medical team who examined her recommended at least three days till she was re-interviewed. Its report played down the fact that she'd almost died under the severity of the beating she'd received.

But three days was too long for Commander Bryzgalov. He gave her twenty-four hours.

Chapter 12: Funeral in West Ham

No matter how the mourners arranged themselves – and they shuffled several times in the progress from the hearse to the graveside - Mordred seemed to find himself slightly adrift, an object of suspicion and perhaps hostility. The body had arrived ten minutes earlier at West Ham Cemetery wrapped in a shroud. Family and friends – some twenty-two people in all – watched six men lower the corpse into the earth on slings and an Imam lead a recital of the *Salat ul-Janazah*. The sun shone weakly from behind a thin layer of cloud, birds watched impassively from high branches, and tombstones of all shapes and sizes seemed to stretch everlastingly to all points of the compass.

Mordred quickly recognised the two mourners he was most interested in from his previous day's research. Tom Ford, small, pugnacious-looking with a beaky nose and dyed blond hair, and Orville Peterson: stout - verging on obese - double chinned, a permanently disapproving expression on his face and a habit of putting his hands in his pockets whenever he came to rest. Both in their mid-fifties.

Almost equally central to his research had been the Creviers, though he wasn't sure any of them would turn up. They might have enjoyed hosting Mobeen in France, but that didn't mean they'd come all the way here for his funeral. In any case, there was no way of knowing whether they even knew he was dead.

Nevertheless, just after he'd spotted the two men, he saw Brigitte Crevier at the back of the crowd, and thereafter Ford and Peterson flanked her like a couple of bodyguards. She was tall and thin, with a small nose, narrow eyes, dark skin, and a bob, and, although she was only twenty-one, she'd already

comfortably assumed the stereotypical French woman's min-
imalism, poise and chic.

He wasn't sure how she'd receive him once she registered
his presence here – last time they'd seen each other, she'd been
in the process of being arrested – or whether she'd even recognise him – it had been over three years, and, for her, probably
one of the most eventful periods of her life, the change from
teenager to adult. Yet when their eyes finally met, she nodded
a curt acknowledgement.

Mordred didn't have much power in this situation. Ultimately, some people here might well know who he was, and,
if they didn't, Brigitte would probably tell them. *He's a member
of the British Security Services.* That could go either way, because funerals were full of more or less intense emotion, and
sometimes, when an unwanted intrusion made itself felt, the
herd instinct kicked in. It might only take one person to start
yelling, *What the hell are YOU doing here, don't you think we've
suffered enough, etc.* for the entire gathering to turn on him like
a pack of wolves.

On the other hand, their curiosity might trump any pre-
dilection to violence. And Ford and Peterson certainly
wouldn't want to be associated with a mobbing.

But if that happened, it would at least open a line of enquiry. The worst outcome would be everyone leaving him
alone, and him departing no wiser than he'd been on arrival.
For that reason, he was relying on Brigitte. When she nodded
at him, he smiled sadly – it was a funeral, after all - and gave
a wistful little wave. She looked quickly away.

Which probably meant: the end.

Once the ceremony finished, his plan was to make the pretence of rushing off as if he had to be somewhere else soon. A
feat that, in practice, was indistinguishable from the real thing,
and just as likely to land him in Nowherewithnoleadsville. Its
chief advantage would be that he wouldn't look needy. If they
thought he wanted something, they'd probably smother their

curiosity. If they believed he was just here to pay his respects, it might just get the better of them.

So as soon as the last mourners had filed past the grave, he turned round, put his hands in his pockets, lowered his head and made towards the cemetery gates.

He was about five hundred yards away from the afterglow of the ceremony – three hundred yards farther than the point at which he'd advised himself to start abandoning hope – when he heard footsteps approaching fast from behind. Then, a voice:

"*Mr Mordred!*"

He swung round.

Orville Peterson, seriously out of breath.

Peterson stopped and put his hands on his knees, looked at the footpath and wheezed. He stayed that way for two seconds, then raised his head.

"Mr Mordred," he gasped.

"Mr Peterson," Mordred replied. It was important that, in whatever exchange now occurred, he didn't hold anything back. For this afternoon only: the truth, the whole truth and nothing but the truth.

"You know who I am?" Peterson replied, still recovering. A genuine question, not the sort of thing cabinet ministers and film stars sometimes said to perceived nonentities.

"You're Orville Peterson, MP," Mordred replied. "You're mentioned in the acknowledgements section of Mobeen Dhanial's, *The BBC's True Agenda: Identity Politics, Doublethink and the End of Britain*. As you're probably aware, I'm with the British Security Services."

"I *was* aware. I didn't expect you to admit it so readily."

"I'm not here in my capacity as a spy, and certainly not to spy on you. I'm here in a detective's role, because I feel involved. Mobeen Dhanial asked for my help investigating something – I still don't know why he chose me - and I brushed him off, and he was killed about thirty minutes afterwards. I want to get to the bottom of what happened, which I don't think was anything remotely like a simple mugging, whatever some of the papers might have us believe."

"We're – my two friends and I - going for a drink. Would you like to join us?"

"I assume you mean you and Tom Ford and Mademoiselle Crevier? Of course I'd like it, Mr Peterson. I was on my way somewhere relatively important, but it can wait. I'd very much like to speak to all three of you."

Peterson straightened up. He looked elated. "I'm buying the first round, Mr Mordred."

"Call me John, please."

"And if you could call me Orville, that would be equally good."

Chapter 13: Triumvirate of Maybe Righties

They walked back. Peterson introduced Mordred to his two companions. Ford looked less than enthused. Brigitte offered her hand in such a manner that he wasn't sure whether she wanted him to hold it, shake it or kiss it. She regarded him as distantly as if they'd never met. Maybe she *didn't* actually remember him, though that seemed unlikely.

Tom Ford's red 1972 Mercedes-Benz was only a few paths away from the graveside. Ford and Peterson sat in the front, as if they'd previously arranged it. Brigitte sat next to Mordred, put her hands in her lap and looked straight ahead without speaking.

"You ever been to The Hudson Bay, John?" Peterson asked as they left the cemetery and accelerated.

"A pub?" Mordred asked.

"A Wetherspoons," Ford said. "I hope that doesn't offend your liberal sentiments, John. I take it you're a Remainer?"

Bloody hell, not that again. *I take it you're a Roundhead, John. Or are you a Cavalier?*

"I'm past caring now," Mordred replied, trying to be diplomatic and honest at the same time. "I think everyone is."

A minute later, they parked in a side street in Forest Gate. Ford cut the engine and they walked in silence to a bar-stroke-restaurant with a blue carpet, polished oak tables and low-slung ornamental lighting. It was virtually empty.

"Now listen," Peterson said, brandishing his wallet on the way to the ale pumps, "I know it might seem disrespectful to Mobeen - I mean us having alcohol when he was a Muslim - but he wasn't really a *practising* Muslim. He went to the mosque every so often, yes, and I know he always went home to see his family for Eid, but he didn't rate the religious side, and he definitely liked a pint or three."

"And of course, he was as gay as a maypole," Ford put in. "I'll have a triple scotch with soda, *s'il vous plait.*"

Brigitte muttered something about a Cinzano Bianco, Mordred asked for a pint of Stormdrain, and Peterson waved two twenties at the barman. "A Campari bitter for me," he declared, before repeating everyone else's order.

"You and Brigitte go and sit down somewhere, John," Ford said. "I'll help Oscar back with the drinks."

"It's *Orville,*" Peterson said, but with a hint of pleasure, like he loved to show off their double act.

Mordred let Brigitte lead the way. She chose a seat by the window. He sat opposite her so they were facing each other. She put her bag on the back of the chair, smoothed her dress under the table, and faced him.

"So, Mr Mordred, we meet again," she said.

"How's Pop?"

She frowned and put her head quizzically on one side.

"Your father," he said. "Jean-Paul."

She smiled. "He's roughly the same. No thanks to you, of course, but then we *were* holding you hostage, so I don't feel sorry for him or us. I'd have done exactly the same in your situation, and I'd have regarded anything else as contemptible. He went to prison, of course, but only for six months, and he might as well have been in a hotel for all the hardship he suffered. But then, you're almost certainly aware that, in France, the best people never really have to face justice. Have you ever seen *Engrenages?*"

"It used to be my favourite programme. Series six wasn't so good."

She ignored his attempt to steer the conversation onto a lighter note. "The point is, the past is water under the bridge."

She suddenly lowered her voice. "Can I ask you a question before the others get back? Why does Tom keep calling Orville 'Oscar', and why does Orville keep calling Tom 'Glenn'?"

He had to think for a second. "I think it's a kind of joke," he announced eventually. "Oscar Peterson was a Canadian jazz pianist. Glenn Ford was a Hollywood actor in the 1940s and 50s. They've both been dead for about ten years."

"I didn't realise. I should probably have laughed."

"Too late now."

She frowned. "I've been a fool. They probably hate me."

"Look out, here they come."

Tom Ford sat next to Mordred. He set his own whisky down and Brigitte's Cinzano. Orville arrived with the real ale and his own drink.

"John has just been explaining the reason why you call each other Glenn and Oscar," she said. She made an attempt to grin. "I didn't realise it was so funny."

"We're a couple of idiots," Peterson said sourly. "Ignore us."

"The last vestiges of childhood, my dear," Ford added. "Anyway, let's leave that to one side, because it's incredibly puerile and we promise never to do it again, even after we've finished here. Let's get down to business, and, by that, I mean let's pay our proper respects to our good friend Mobeen by asking you, John, why you were at his funeral. I assume you told Orville, and you might even have told Brigitte by now, but you certainly haven't told me."

"The day of the murder," John said, "I was on my way to work when I sensed I was being followed. I went into a pub called The White Horse and Bower on Horseferry Road - "

"I know it well," Ford interrupted.

"And Mobeen followed me in and introduced himself. He said he knew who I was and that he wanted us to work together on an investigation he was conducting into the BBC programme, *Panorama*. I told him in no uncertain terms that I wasn't available. He tried to give me his card, and asked me to call him at *The Daily Mail* 'when I'd changed my mind'. I went straight in to work and reported the incident – a routine requirement, that's all – and half an hour later, I was told he was dead."

"Have you read his blog?" Ford asked.

"He thought the BBC were after him," Mordred replied. "But I don't think that's very likely."

Ford scoffed. "I beg to differ, John, and I've worked there, so I know a thing or two about it. Don't get me wrong, I'm not saying the BBC *itself* contracts killers, obviously not. But I'm pretty sure there are people out there – and again: not BBC employees, I accept that - whose interests are nicely served by whatever *Panorama*'s digging up, and who weren't averse to topping an interfering journalist from a newspaper that, as a matter of fact – and this too may or may not be coincidence – just happens to represent the flat opposite of the BBC's increasingly strident leftism. And I'd be surprised if someone in the BBC doesn't know who those people are. They could probably tell the police if they wanted to. But they won't: it's too complicated, and it's not in their interests, and they can square it with their paper-thin consciences by hiding behind some or another version of 'journalistic privilege'. They're morally bankrupt, in other words. And they'll never run any version of *Panorama* investigating themselves."

"Put it this way," Peterson chimed in: "he claimed *Panorama* was after him. His blog proves he anticipated some kind of aggro, though he probably didn't expect to be killed. He came to you, John, and asked for help. Half an hour later, he was lying face down in the gutter with a six-inch hole in his chest. Does that sound like a coincidence?"

"We can't rule it out," Mordred said. "London's a violent place nowadays."

"But does it *sound* like a coincidence, John?" Brigitte persisted.

"No," he replied.

"Look," Ford went on, "I know it's difficult for people like you, John. I don't mean that disrespectfully. You're a liberal, everyone who knows anything about you knows that, and you're in tune with the BBC's worldview, so I'm pretty sure – and don't take this the wrong way either - it goes completely over your head just how partisan it is. Take every drama they've ever made, you'll always find the protagonist's a leftie of some description: likeable or not, self-aware or not, flawed or not, they're all either knowing liberals or potential liberals. Everything the BBC does points in the same socio-political direction."

"You're talking in abstractions," Mordred said. He needed to shake them up a bit, get them talking about the subject in hand. "Look, I'm not here to discuss the BBC. As it happens, you're right, I *do* disagree with you, but let's put that aside and concentrate on Mobeen, shall we? Back a bit. You talked about 'people out there' with an interest in what *Panorama*'s supposedly investigating. What 'people' do you have in mind?" He decided to take the plunge: Ruby Parker had been right, it was a stupid theory, but in getting an airing, it might just pull something unexpected to the surface. "Because I can only think of one such group."

Ford exchanged puzzled looks with Peterson. "You mean the Russians, John?" Ford said.

"The Russians?" Mordred replied. "No, that hadn't occurred to me. Why the Russians?"

"Wait a minute," Brigitte said, "if you're not thinking of them, John, then who *are* you thinking of?"

"Someone who holds exactly the same views about the BBC as you do," Mordred replied.

"You think *we* did it?" Ford said incredulously.

"As a matter of fact, no," Mordred replied, "but it is a credible hypothesis, and it could work. Someone very *like* you, perhaps even within your ideological circle."

"How exactly do you work that out?" Peterson said irritably.

"Because John's living in a BBC drama, Orville," Ford told him, "and as such, it's inconceivable that a pair of right-wingers – and possibly a trio, if you include Mademoiselle Crevier - aren't the bad guys. We always are." He made to stand up. "Come on, you two. We're wasting our time here. Some bloody wake this has turned out to be."

"Absolutely not!" Brigitte exclaimed. "I want to hear John's reasoning. I'm not prepared to leave it like this. Mobeen was my friend. I'm not going to be accused of killing him and just leave it at that! Shame on you if you are!"

"I'm not accusing any of you," John said. "But it's important I let you know how some people in MI5 are actually thinking. You might well be able to help."

Ford and Peterson sat down again. "Okay, let's hear it then, Johnny," Peterson said.

"It's not my theory. Okay, maybe it is. Someone wants to bring the BBC down. They know Mobeen's investigating a very sensitive upcoming episode of *Panorama* and also that he's blogging that the BBC is after him. He gets killed. The blog goes public as a result. Might it not look as if there's some substance to his claims? That they're not just paranoia?"

Ford scoffed. "Well, if that was the plan, it hasn't worked out very well, has it?"

"Someone wants to hurt the BBC, yes?" Brigitte said contemptuously, "so this person kills one of its biggest critics? On the hunch that someone in the media will say, 'Oh, this man, he was blogging about the BBC wanting to hurt him, now he's dead, he must have been right?' That's *crazy*."

"But not impossible," Mordred said. "In the real world, some plans really *are* stupid. It doesn't mean they don't get put into effect. Presumably, their authors eventually realise how ludicrous they are, but too late to make a difference."

"You're saying we're *stupid* now too?" Ford said.

Mordred sighed. "Not you. Someone who shares your views. And that's not to say your views are stupid either, before you start. The idea's not impossible, that's all I'm saying. It's a theory. If you think your Russian theory's better, I'm all ears."

"I think you'll find it's *vastly* better, John," Brigitte said.

"I apologise if I offended you," Mordred said. "But if we're going to get to the bottom of this, it's probably important that we put all our cards on the table."

Silence. Ford and Peterson looked at each other, then at Brigitte.

"Apology accepted," Peterson said.

"You tell him," Ford said.

"Isn't it obvious?" Brigitte put in.

"Vladimir Putin's the great disruptor," Peterson said. "Look, this episode of *Panorama*: whatever it's actually about – and amazingly, not even MI5 seems to know – there's a pretty big consensus that it's set to cause a major upset. Veritable gunpowder treason and plot stuff. It's got the potential – so they say – to bring the government down. Now why wouldn't Mr Putin want that?"

Mordred finished his beer. "So Mobeen Dhanial was killed simply because he stood in its way?"

"It's one theory," Ford said, "and it's better than yours."

"It doesn't square with what you told me earlier," Mordred said. "You said you thought the BBC might be in on his murder in some way. 'I'd be surprised if someone in the BBC doesn't know who those people are': those were your words."

"They don't know they're *Russians*," Peterson said. "The Russians aren't stupid: they'll have kept *that* under wraps. But the BBC guys I'm talking about will know, on some level, that 'these people', whoever they are, eliminated Mobeen."

"But they wouldn't leave it there," Mordred said. "They must think 'these people' had a motive. And it couldn't possibly be the defence of free speech as represented by Auntie. That wouldn't cover murder. So who do your hypothetical BBC-morally-bankrupt-people *think* the murderers are?"

More silence. Once again, Ford and Peterson looked at each other, then at Brigitte.

"You're right," Ford said. "If we're correct, and it was Russians, probably no one in the BBC *would* know."

"And yet, it seems odd that they don't seem to care," Peterson said.

"Does it?" Brigitte said. "Why should they? Here was an enemy of theirs, poking his nose in where it didn't belong, and now he's been taken out of the picture. They didn't know him, except perhaps as an irritant. They certainly didn't owe him anything. Why should they care? I wouldn't."

"If it was the Russians," Mordred said, "they'd have to know what *Panorama's* investigating, something even the British security services haven't been able to discover. So how would they have found out about it? Who'd have told them? And why would they then become convinced enough to kill someone who probably wasn't actually much of a threat?"

"The Russians wouldn't necessarily know he wasn't a genuine hazard," Ford said. "But I take your more general point. What we're suggesting doesn't quite hold up."

Brigitte caught the waiter's eye and ordered another round of drinks, same again. "I disagree," she said. "All it means is that what *Panorama* is investigating isn't real. It's a Russian plant, the whole thing. Their baby, so they've got to protect it. And before you ask, they haven't put it on YouTube because the BBC's a zillion times more respectable. Their aim is to bring down your government, Orville, and sow discord."

"It's a good theory," Ford told her, "but seriously out on a limb. We've no evidence for it or anything of the sort. And it would take an awful lot of setting up. Financially as much as anything: you'd have to pay a huge number of strategically well-placed people to lie on your behalf. It'd be con trick of the century. But it wouldn't work. In practice, not all of the people you offered to pay would be biddable, and word would get out that the Russians were trying to pull a fast one. Which would be a quadrillion roubles down the drain. Money the Kremlin can scarcely afford nowadays."

Peterson chuckled. "Although you *are* right in another sense, Brigitte."

"What do you mean?" Ford asked him indignantly.

"In that the next general election could well spell the end for the UK," he replied. "Corbyn's a disaster all ways up, Johnson's a cack-handed egomaniac, the Lib Dems – well, no one even knows who they are any more, except that they're *really nice people* – and the SNP will probably triumph in Scotland and then demolish the Union. We'll get a bog standard, probably hung Parliament, and permanent devolution. Both of which would suit the Russians down to the ground."

"And *now* can you tell me why the potential reward wouldn't outweigh the risks?" Brigitte said.

"*Panorama's* not staffed by a bunch of dilettantes," Ford told her. "They have trained staff for that sort of thing, bods whose job it is to fact-check to the nth degree. One or two things might get past them, I admit, but enough for an entire programme?"

Peterson took a sip of his drink. "Maybe tell that to Lord McAlpine and Cliff Richard."

"There wouldn't necessarily need to be many factoids in the programme," Mordred said. "Just enough to give all the actual facts a new context, requiring a new interpretation."

Brigitte laughed. "You see, John agrees with me!"

"I'm not even sure what John means," Ford said. "And I'm not sure John does either."

Mordred took a sip of his beer to allow himself a moment's thought. "Okay," he said. "Let's say we've got a marksman who won a gold medal for the 'rifle three positions' event in the Rio Olympics. All his biographers agree that he did a lot of shooting, supervised by his parents, when he was a child, and that he's never been formally trained. However, *I* then discover that, in the last six years, he's shot at least three people dead in three separate countries. I present a theory - on *Panorama*, just for the sake of preserving the parallel - that he's an international assassin. Now, not only am I *not disputing* that he's an Olympic champion who trained with his mum and dad all those years ago, but those indisputable facts actually *support* my theory, because they establish that he has a long-standing interest in shooting, and that he's good at it."

"But then his biographers would focus all their scrutiny on your three murders," Ford said. "They wouldn't fact-check the things on which everyone agrees."

"Only, I'm not the person who's trying to frame him," Mordred replied. "Whoever fabricated the factoids had unlimited time and money to make them look convincing. By contrast, I'm working for *Panorama*, so I'm up against a deadline, on a tight budget, and in competition with other media outlets who are trying to get 'my' story out there first. The question becomes: could a fabricator create something convincing enough to defeat me in the limited amount of time I actually have? Remember, he or she doesn't have to defeat me for ever. If I keep on probing for all time, it may be that I'll eventually reach the truth. But this is journalism. I don't have that luxury."

"I really hope it *isn't* the Russians," Peterson said. "I think we should be trying to build bridges with them."

Tom Ford and Brigitte nodded as if this was a mere truism.

Mordred couldn't let it pass. "In what way?"

"Values," Brigitte said. "The primacy of the family, nationalism, an appropriate respect for Christianity, less about the rights of so-called victims, less of indulging parasites, harsher treatment for criminals up to and including the death-penalty, a more thoroughgoing anti-racism, less glorification of weakness, more scepticism about immigrants – by 'scepticism' I don't mean hostility, just critical thinking – more respect for authority - the church, teachers, your elders, the state, the police, the armed forces – and more deference to tradition all round."

Mordred laughed. "'More anti-racism'? Where does that fit in?"

"What's wrong with it?" she said.

"Nothing, obviously," he replied, "only - "

"Come on, John," Peterson said. "The left's replete with anti-Semitism nowadays, that's common knowledge. It's only a matter of time before people wake up to the fact that it's got a racism problem more generally. Racism's when you use someone's skin colour to denigrate them, yes? So you explain to me, then, why it's not racist when lefties talk about 'white saviour complex' and put out books with titles like *Why I Don't Talk to White People about Race*, or whatever it is. Because it's an 'acceptable' kind of racism, that's why. Just like some kinds of anti-Jewish feeling used to be 'acceptable', until - "

"Until the BBC, among others, woke up to it," Mordred said. "*Panorama* was a big part of that, as I remember."

"It came fairly late to the discussion, as I remember," Ford said. "Then presented itself as a ground breaker." He sighed. "Look, John, everyone says there is no right and left any more. They may be correct, but I doubt it. Us three here are what are called *Old Liberals*. 'Old' as in traditional. We've just been bundled in with the fascists, that's all."

"I take it it's 'New Liberals' you object to," John said.

"Too bloody right we do," Peterson said.

"I'm surprised you don't recognise the distinction, John," Brigitte said drily. "I always considered you a thinker."

"I haven't actually come across the distinction," John replied. "But I'm always open to new ideas and penetrating insights."

"We believe in toleration," Ford told him. "That might sound dour but it's based on the sensible notion that most people are self-interested, so they'll probably shaft you if there's enough at stake. You tolerate them till they do that, but purely on a case by case basis: individuals, not groups. New Liberalism, on the other hand, wants to replace tolerating each other with celebrating each other. Life's now supposed to be one big shindig. So, for example, you can't ask awkward questions about what's going on in the room: you might spoil the mood. You can't have a serious discussion: you might spoil the mood. You can't call someone out, even if you spot them pocketing the cutlery, because some ignorant do-gooder might turn on you and call you a party pooper. God help us, even bloody funerals have to be celebrations nowadays. Which is seriously creepy, when you think about it. At least we spared poor Mobeen that indignity. *Wear fancy dress and bring a balloon.*"

Peterson half-scoffed, and turned to Brigitte. "To get back to the original point, my dear," he said, before Mordred could get a word in, "you can't build bridges with the Russians."

"Why not, if we admire them?" Brigitte said.

"Because they've got two contradictory approaches," Peterson said. "On the one hand, they want us to resemble them more – in that regard, you're quite right: they are fairly admirable, although far from perfect. On the other hand, Mr Putin's got to stay in power, and he thinks his best means is to convince the electorate that everyone else in the world's anti-Russia, and only he can save them. In other words, he wants every other country to both emulate Russia and to hate it. There's no making friends with someone like that; only endless self-recrimination, confusion and misery."

"I'm getting bored now," Peterson said. "Let's get back to Mobeen." He held up his empty glass. "John, I do believe it's thine round."

Mordred caught the waiter's eye. "Same again."

"Look, John," Ford said. "I think we can probably help each other here. You want to find out who killed Mobeen, so do we. How about us working together? Before you say no, have a proper think. We're not three little nobodies asking James

Bond to take us along on his latest jaunt. We're powerful people and we can look under rocks that most others – including you, probably - couldn't even budge."

"When you say, 'work together'," Mordred said, "what precisely do you mean?"

"We help each other lift rocks in deep pools," Peterson said, "and we share the facts about what we've found underneath them."

"My first loyalty's to Thames House," Mordred said.

"It's only a question of us lifting the rocks," Peterson said, "and you going in underneath them and reporting your findings to us."

"Not exclusively, obviously," Brigitte said. "We know we can't expect that. But a rock we lift, you go under, you have to tell us what you've found. And I know if you agree," she said, looking hard at Ford and Peterson, "you'll honour your word, because you're an honourable man."

"If you lift a rock," Mordred said, "as a result of what we've agreed here, and I find something under it – anything – I'll share it with you. But I don't really know what the metaphor refers to, and I've had three pints of beer and I'm beginning to wonder what any of us is talking about."

Peterson burst into laughter. "We're talking about *lifting bloody rocks*, John! Have you never been to *The Sea Life Centre?*"

Ford started laughing too. "Have you never seen *Finding* bloody *Nemo*, John?"

Suddenly, they were all roaring. Peterson slapped the table several times in an unsuccessful attempt to stop himself. Brigitte's Cinzano went up her nose and she sneezed several times, and she had to cover her face with a napkin. 'I love *Finding Nemo!'* she exclaimed defensively as if that was all that was at stake. Ford pushed himself back on his chair, and twice almost lost his balance. After a few seconds, they stopped laughing at their witticisms – which hadn't been funny anyway, only they were drunk – and started laughing at each other: Brigitte wheezing like she was going to die and her mad makeup after the application of the napkin, Tom nearly falling backwards, Orville's teary face on the table, Mordred almost choking on his last sip of Stormdrain.

Because they were sitting at a window table, several people outside slowed down to take a closer look like they were peering into a freak show. They moved on with faintly disgusted expressions. Which was also hilarious. The waiter brought their new drinks and retired, obviously torn between asking them to leave and minding his own business in the hope they'd calm down.

After five minutes, they did.

"So, John, what do you think?" Peterson said solemnly and started laughing again.

"I need to know the nature of the rock you're intending to lift," Mordred replied.

They nearly lost control again, but somehow, this time, they all caught sight of how they must look from the pavement, and screeched to a halt.

"You may or may not know," Ford said, "that I write a weekly column for *The Daily Mail*. I'm going to use it to publicise Mobeen Dhanial's blog. I'm going to send a torpedo into *Panorama*'s hull. My guess is that they'll come swimming to the authorities, John, try and deflect the bad publicity. There's still a week to go yet till that programme airs, and they definitely won't want the Director General getting jumpy. This will be one way they can pre-empt him: open themselves up to scrutiny, prove everything's kosher: they call for you to give them a full service, get your official seal of approval. All you've got to do, John, is be in the right time and place when the call comes."

"I think I can manage that," Mordred said.

Brigitte raised her glass. Mordred expected her to propose a polite toast to success, but instead she said, "To Peter Jonathan Hitchens."

"To Peter Hitchens," Ford and Peterson said solemnly, clinking glasses.

"Er…" Mordred said.

"Barman!" Peterson called. "Four more drinks!"

Chapter 14: Bryzgalov and the Ambassador

They threw Kseniya into the corner of the interrogation room and hit and kicked her until she coughed blood. After they'd finished, they handcuffed her, bound her feet and gagged her, and she lay on the ground and whimpered for a long time. The blood on the floor grew drier and stickier and she fluctuated between semi-consciousness and a kind of horrible sleep in which people with clubs chased her along everlasting tunnels and knocked her down and cut her and bashed her.

At some point, the lights went on. She felt herself being hauled to her feet and injected. She lost consciousness again.

When she awoke, she was in a bed in a windowless room. She wore a nightdress. Her arms were bandaged and her legs were bruised. A middle-aged woman in a trouser suit stood over and gave her an injection. Things returned gradually to something close to normality. The pain went away, she felt incredibly light-headed, and, though there was nothing like a mirror to hand, she knew roughly what she must look like: a bloody mess of welts, swellings and bruises. She probably looked barely human. She didn't know where she was, but it didn't matter because she could tell she was being hauled somewhere else. Someone said, 'Be careful with her', someone else asked if it might be better to fetch a stretcher, a third person called her a bitch.

Later, when she remembered what had happened, her first feeling was guilt. All he'd done was call her a traitor, and she'd killed him. He might not have been even been serious. He probably had a family.

Time passed, she had no idea how much, but on each occasion she opened her eyes, things were slightly different. A change of bedding, or new people in the room, lower or more intense lighting, a subtle shift in the shadows.

Commander Yuri Bryzgalov – a well-built, splenetic-looking man with close-cropped silver hair, who looked like he might have been a wrestler in his day - sat on an antique sofa in a furnished room. Opposite him, on a Queen Anne wingback, sat the ambassador, His Excellency Feodor Pisemsky, a thin fifty-nine-year-old with half a head of grey hair and circular steel-framed spectacles. Around them, two GU men, four FSB officers and the Defence Attaché stood or sat like acolytes. These men were all Bryzgalov supporters: he'd brought them in to cow the ambassador. The only other occupant of the room was the minute-taker, a young woman in a beige dress who sat poised on a stool with a notepad. On opposite walls, two framed portraits: Vladimir Putin and Peter the Great, facing each other as if they had something in common. The carpet was deep pile and the room was warm, though there was no fire in here. A man in a suit entered with a tray and poured two cups of tea, one for each of the principal interlocutors. The ambassador waved him away irritably before he could make his usual enquiries about milk and sugar.

"Kseniya Igorevna Yumasheva's a criminal and probably a traitor," Bryzgalov said. "With respect, Your Excellency, doing it your way is likely to end in lies. She'll have us running round in circles, chasing our own tails."

"Have you actually been to see her, Commander?" the ambassador asked. He took a sip of his tea. "No, you haven't," he went on, cutting the GU man off before he could open his mouth. "I have. And I can tell you, she's in no fit state to have a lie detector strapped to her. Those sorts of devices measure reactions under conditions of normal stress. In her condition, she might give all sorts of truthful answers, and they might all come up as lies. I know that too for a fact, before you interrupt. I've spoken to experts."

Bryzgalov grimaced. "I sincerely hope you don't feel sorry for her, Your Excellency. She killed an innocent man."

"She says he called her a traitor, and I'm pretty sure she didn't mean to kill him. Don't you think it *good* that a Russian should react angrily to being called a defector? I mean, did she really deserve to be beaten insensible?"

"She'll recover."

"And yet she was telling the truth," the ambassador said drily.

"What about? I don't follow."

"Let me remind you, then. According to the written report, Kantemir asked her if she knew any of the detail of the plan Domogarov provided back in Moscow. She said, and I quote, 'It didn't *have* any detail. There wasn't time.' That prompted Simolyn to leave the room. He wanted to check the lie detector was working, because, of course, it was categorically *not* the answer either of them were expecting."

"And while he was out of the room, she killed one of my best men."

The ambassador gave a contemptuous laugh. "The device wasn't malfunctioning, so, to the best of our knowledge, she must have been telling the truth. So what are you saying, Yuri? Let me see. Your claim, it would appear, is that she told the truth solely so Simolyn would leave the room, thus giving her the opportunity she'd been waiting for all along to kill Kantemir." He laughed again. "Talk about a cunning plan!"

Faint smirks crossed the faces of some of the men standing around. They exchanged involuntary glances. The ambassador knew Bryzgalov had brought them in to witness a textbook display of *who's the boss here* and he'd allowed them to stay for precisely the same reason.

"I'm pretty sure she's putting a lot of it on," Bryzgalov said grouchily. "She wasn't that badly beaten."

"Unless you were there at the time, Yuri, I don't see how you can possibly judge. You have read the medical report, I take it?"

"Yes, but - "

"Well, then you'll know the phrase 'badly beaten' appears on page one."

"Okay, look, you win, Your Excellency. What exactly are you proposing? That we just wait? For how long?"

"Well, the medical report says three days. You say you can't wait any longer than twenty-four hours - "

"Which expired *three hours ago!*"

The ambassador nodded, took another sip of his tea. "So now we interview her."

"Thank you!"

"Or rather, I do. You just sit and watch."

"But - "

"And I want your entourage outside. With respect, I think a massive police presence is only likely to intimidate her further."

Bryzgalov ground his teeth, but said nothing. He knew only too well: a foot wrong now and he might also be excluded. "Maybe *we* should go to *her*," he said. "If you think she's that frail."

The ambassador smiled thinly. "Let's not get too carried away."

She knew something important was about to happen when five people entered the room with a wheelchair. The woman in the trouser suit leant over her, smiled, and asked her if she was feeling any better.

"I didn't mean to kill him," Kseniya said.

"You're starting to sound lucid," the woman replied and inserted another needle into her arm. "This should help. We're going to see the ambassador now *in person*, and if you behave yourself and answer his questions, things might not be so bad for you in the long run. What happened was an accident, we all know that. It doesn't excuse what you did, but it does make a difference. The ambassador can help you."

"But you've got to bloody cooperate this time," someone out of view said; a man.

The pain subsided and she felt light-headed again, but relatively lucid. A tall man picked her up from the bed and transferred her gently to the wheelchair. Four people got behind her, and suddenly they were moving.

For the first time in what seemed like aeons, she thought about Pasha and Valentina. She'd almost certainly have to give them up now, but, well, that was okay - wasn't it? They couldn't make it in England alone, not living like they were. Sooner or later, the FSB or the GU would catch up with them. For their sake, it might as well be sooner. At least they wouldn't make the same mistake she had. Nobody could be as unlucky as she'd been: she'd taken a wrong turn at every available opportunity.

A moment later, they were ascending in a lift. When the doors opened, she found herself looking out at a hallway with expensive furnishings, antique wallpaper, two chandeliers, four gilt framed portraits, and a thick patterned carpet, everything complementing the exquisite good taste of everything else. Another world.

More than anything else, her attention was drawn to a large window just in front of her and to the left, where a shaft of sunlight entered.

She was back in the land of the living. For how long?

The ambassador and Commander Bryzgalov sat on two chairs angled equidistantly around a circular coffee table in such a way that the wheelchair would appear to fill the natural third position. They stood up when Kseniya entered, introduced themselves and asked her kindly how she was. Tea and biscuits had been set out on the table, and the ambassador asked her if she would like to join them. She declined. The woman who had wheeled her in applied what must be the brake on her wheelchair – it juddered slightly – and then retired, closing the doors on herself. The two men sat down and turned to look at Kseniya.

"I didn't mean to kill him," she said.

"It was unfortunate," the ambassador said, "but from what I understand, not a deliberate killing. How could it have been? More a culpable accident. Manslaughter." He sighed, as if yes, it was very regrettable, but there were more important matters to talk about now. "We need your assistance, Kseniya. If you can help us, I might be able to help you. Put in a good word for you, back in Moscow."

"What do you want to know?"

"The last time we were talking to you, we asked if you knew any detail of the plan that Pasha Domogarov hatched to make the BBC more Russia-friendly."

"The plan didn't *have* any detail," she said. "As I told the interviewers."

"And you were telling the truth," the ambassador said. "We've confirmed that."

"How *well* did you know Pasha Domogarov?" Bryzgalov asked.

"Pretty well," she replied. "We came to England together."

Bryzgalov was taking a sip of tea. He almost choked. He tried to conceal his agitation with a laugh, but the panicked look he flung at the ambassador completely betrayed him.

"You actually know him *intimately* then," the ambassador said. He looked rather less disconcerted, probably because – as became obvious in his next question - he didn't believe her. "We were given to understand that Pasha Domogarov had a girlfriend and that he left Moscow with her. Are you trying to tell us *you're* his girlfriend, because that would contradict... I mean - "

"No, three of us left together. Valentina's his girlfriend."

Both men looked as if they'd hit the jackpot.

"Do you know where they are now?" Bryzgalov said.

"We're not going to hurt them," the ambassador said.

"You hurt Fydor Nikolayevich," she said. "In Cologne. You killed him."

"That was an idiotic mistake," the ambassador told her. He probably didn't sound convincing even to himself. "Look, excuse us for a moment, would you, please, Kseniya? I need to have a word with Commander Bryzgalov."

They left the room in a hurry. When they'd closed the door, she realised she'd made yet another mistake. She'd forgotten all about Fydor Nikolayevich until just now. These people were killers.

Unfortunately, she'd told them enough now to make them reasonably confident she knew where they could find Pasha and Valentina.

But that wouldn't matter. She'd been gone a long time now. They'd have moved on, wouldn't they? She'd told them she'd gone 'home', but she hadn't taken any of their money. They weren't stupid. They'd probably twigged she was here. They'd have bolted like rats from a trap. She could safely tell the ambassador where they 'were' – which would only amount to where they'd been.

But where did that leave her?

There had to be a third way. But what did she have to offer?

Then she knew.

But she'd have to extract promises. She couldn't live with herself if either of them was killed.

The door opened. Bryzgalov and the ambassador marched back in and resumed their seats. There was nothing of the cosy-chat-over-tea-and-biscuits about them now. They looked manic.

"Look, Kseniya," the ambassador said, "it's true: Fydor Nikolayevich was killed, but that's because we thought you all knew about the details of our plan, and the evidence suggests that at least some of you were – are - intent on finding a British agent called John Mordred."

"That's nonsense," Kseniya said. "It was Elizaveta and Olga who wanted to find him. They became besotted for some reason, and they got us on board because we were going through a period of collective insanity. I'm pretty sure we've all got over it now."

"In any case, we're having him closely watched," Bryzgalov said – she got the impression more for the ambassador's benefit than her own – "if any of them had tried to make contact with him, we'd know."

"Okay, that's good," the ambassador said. "Now look, Kseniya, there *is* a detailed version of this taking-over-the-BBC plan of yours. When you told us you didn't know about it, that surprised us, because we naturally assumed Pasha Domogarov would have shared it with the other members of the group."

"He definitely didn't share it with *me*," she said.

"And the lie detector confirms it," he said. "Now, all we want to do is stop the detailed version getting out. If we can get hold of Pasha – well, actually, if we can get hold of Valentina - "

"As I understand it, Pasha and Valentina are 'in love'," Bryzgalov said.

"See if you can follow my logic, Kseniya," the ambassador went on. "We know Pasha didn't tell you about the detailed version. That raises the possibility – which we didn't recognise when we killed Fydor Nikolayevich: how could we have? – that he didn't tell *any* of the other members of your group. Now, we can confirm that possibility if we can get hold of him and Valentina and subject them to a lie detector test, just as we did you. If we ask Pasha, 'Did you tell any others members of the group?' and he truthfully says no; and if we ask Valentina, 'Do you know of any detailed version of the plan?' and she truthfully says no, then we can all relax. If he didn't tell the person he loves most in the world, then obviously he won't have told anyone else."

"On the other hand," Bryzgalov said, "if we can't confirm that he hasn't told any of the others, then, if any of them appear, we may have to kill them, just to protect our interests."

"Just to be on the safe side," the ambassador said.

"To stop that happening," Bryzgalov added, "we need to get hold of Pasha and Valentina. As soon as possible, to stop others getting killed. Do you see? We can't be intending to kill them, either, if you think about it. In order to subject them to those tests, we need them *alive*. We can't test dead people. So it's against our *interests* to kill them. Do you follow?"

She nodded. Like he hadn't underlined it twice, as if he thought she was stupid.

The ambassador patted her hand. "And once we've cleared everything up and confirmed that Pasha's actually kept the secret, you can all go home. A slap on the wrists, that's all. Even you, if you help us."

"What if he hasn't?" she asked. "I mean, kept the secret?"

"Then it becomes more complicated," the ambassador replied. "I'm not saying we'll kill anyone else – I mean, just for practical reasons: every time we kill someone on foreign soil, even one of our own, all hell breaks loose." He laughed. "There's a limit to how much hell even *we* can take! But we'll have to have a re-think, for sure."

"We're asking you to take a gamble," Bryzgalov said. "On the likelihood that Pasha hasn't told any of the others. We know he hasn't told *you*, and I'm assuming he travelled with you for a fairly long time. And I take it Valentina hasn't told you anything about a detailed version, otherwise that would have shown up on the lie detector. I'd say the odds in favour of him having kept quiet are pretty good. *I'd* take them, and I'm not even a gambling man. The question is, *can* you help us? Do you actually know where we can find them?"

"I do," she replied. "I can give you their address in Peckham, but I don't think they'll be there. Failing that, we've all got a plan to meet in Trafalgar Square. They'll be in disguise, but if they see me there, they'll probably come over."

Bryzgalov smiled. "We'll set it up then. Well done, Kseniya."

"You're doing the right thing," the ambassador told her.

For the first time since her arrival in Britain, she felt good about herself.

"I know," she said.

Chapter 15: Tom Gets to Work

Mordred's alarm went off at 6.15am, but something about it was different. It took him a moment to realise that someone was also ringing the doorbell.

It paid to be careful when your flat was being watched by a truckload of spies, but likely someone out there would have told him if there was any danger – Ruby Parker probably had agents in the mix too. He peered through the front outside viewer and saw a middle-aged man with a large parcel. He opened the door.

"I'm from Deliveryquick," the man said. "Package for John Mordred?"

"That's me."

The courier passed him a digital signature pad and handed over the parcel. Mordred brought it inside and locked the door.

If someone was trying to kill him, this likely wasn't the way they'd do it. And if they were trying to send him a message, they presumably thought he'd received it now. In their minds, they'd be picturing him tearing the wrapping paper off and his reaction as he found – what? It wasn't heavy enough for a mafia-style severed limb, but it might contain a thumb.

Or anthrax.

He needed to stay calm and get ready to bolt. He carefully peeled away a strip of the outer layer.

Something hard and plastic and translucent.

He suddenly knew.

He tore the paper off. His Tupperware, cleaned, a packet of Weetabix, and a printed note: 'Compliments of the CIA.'

He chuckled, but not entirely comfortably. How did they know he had Weetabix for breakfast?

130

Still, who cared? He'd given them supper, they'd bought him breakfast. The future of US-UK relations was bright.

He deviated from his morning routine only to buy a copy of *The Daily Mail* on his way into work. Tom Ford had initially promised to write something that would 'flush *Panorama* out of its hiding place', but in the event, he'd been even more successful. He'd called John the previous evening: his editor was considering an article on the subject for the front page. With Parliament in recess and half the country on holiday, news was slow, and readers had short memories: if it didn't move mountains, well, it'd be yesterday's news tomorrow. The important thing was that, barring some sort of international crisis, Mobeen Dhanial's blog was guaranteed its deserved fifteen minutes of fame. Stones were being lifted!

And when Mordred went to look at the newspaper front pages on his phone that morning, there it was: 'Death of an Investigative Journalist.'

He had to wait to buy a hard copy to get the detail. He bought one as soon as he left the flat and read it on the bus into work.

Or tried to. He couldn't stop noticing that the attitudes of his fellow commuters were undergoing a subtle transformation. Most were regulars: they'd done this journey every day with him for years. All that time, he'd caught up on the day's news on his phone, so they couldn't really see what he was reading or, by implication, *what he thought and therefore who he was*. Now they realised, or thought they did: he was *a* Daily Mail *reader*. Some people were approving, some the opposite. Either way, henceforth he was a fully known quantity. No going back.

Unless he bought a *Guardian* tomorrow. That would bamboozle them. Their heads would probably explode.

He had to wait till he got to Thames House to properly digest what he'd looked through. He checked in with Colin, went to the canteen, sat next to the window with a cup of tea, then re-read the front page.

It didn't accuse the BBC of anything, but he hadn't expected it to. It simply juxtaposed facts: Mobeen Dhanial's blog, the secrecy over *Panorama*, the BBC's refusal to address Tom Ford's written questions, a quote from Orville Peterson about the Corporation's 'arrogance', extracts from *The BBC's True Agenda*, an anonymous BBC 'insider source' who spoke of anger 'at executive level' regarding the claims in Dhanial's book and perhaps even a wish for vengeance, the 'woeful failure' of the police to catch his killers, his prophetic sense that someone was after him, his appeal to MI5 for help just before his murder, a report from another 'insider source' about the left-wing culture at the BBC and its supposed sense of being 'untouchable'.

He finished reading at 8.55, went to his desk and switched on his PC. As expected, Ruby Parker had scheduled a meeting for him, in her office, at nine.

"Two things," she said, as he sat down. "Firstly, the Russians have got hold of one of the Novelists, Kseniya Igorevna Yumasheva, who we believed was in company with two other members of that group, but apparently isn't. From the CCTV we've been able to piece together – and there's quite a lot of it: that part of London is watched relatively intensely – we believe she handed herself in voluntarily, which is what the embassy claims. However, it gets stranger, because it turns out that, shortly after her arrival, she committed an act of manslaughter. The Russian ambassador informed the Foreign Secretary last night, and the decision's been taken not to pursue it from our end."

"Bloody hell."

"She's not in the country legally, she's a Russian citizen who killed a Russian citizen on what's legally quasi-Russian soil. The Russians could probably have got away with not informing us, but they chose to eschew that route. As a reward for good behaviour, they want to deal with it themselves and since, as I've just said, she almost certainly entered the building of her own free will, we've got scant moral grounds for an objection. Needless to say, we're having the building very carefully watched from about ten different places, just in case they decide to use her for anything … unexpected."

"You mean to lure the other Novelists out from their hiding places?"

"Something like that. If she really was in company with Pasha Domogarov and Valentina Morozova, she might know where they are. As always in these sorts of cases, the Russians will know we're watching them, so they'll be very careful. But watch this space. Now, the second thing - "

"Hang on, I don't fully understand. You say she entered the building of her own free will, but then she committed an act of manslaughter. How long between her going in there, and the Russians reporting the crime?"

"She entered the building at 9.15pm. The FCO was informed of the killing at five minutes to midnight."

"It does sound as if they might have done something pretty nasty to her to have provoked something like that. Are you absolutely sure we've no moral grounds for an objection?"

"I didn't say 'no grounds', I said 'scant'. Firstly, from their perspective, she's officially a killer. I take your point that they probably provoked her, but I'm not sure anything's sufficient to justify killing a man. Secondly, from our standpoint, she's officially an illegal immigrant and, as I'm sure you've noticed, The FCO isn't exactly keen to uphold the rights of illegal immigrants. The third point is, it's not finished. We've got them in our sights. Now, let's move on. I take it you've read this," she said, holding up a copy of *The Daily Mail*.

"Just now," he replied.

"Whoever wrote it certainly lacks Dhanial's talent for argument. But then, I suppose it's probably not meant to persuade the already unpersuaded."

"It's simply designed to pique the BBC. I have that on the author's own authority."

"Tom Ford. Yes, I've read your report. Well, you might be interested to know it's paid off. Terry McNamara, the BBC's Director General, contacted me this morning. Dhanial's eleventh hour appeal to MI5 was a bit of a bombshell, apparently. He wanted to know if it was true and, if so, why he hadn't been informed. I explained that we go to great lengths to avoid getting involved with the BBC on any level, because whatever we may do is always open to misinterpretation. The police are invariably better placed."

"But you did tell him it was true?"

"Obviously, yes. We want a way in, Tom Ford's supposedly helping us get it. This is a chance that won't come around again. He guessed it was you, by the way."

"Great."

"I say 'by the way', but as a matter of fact, it's central, and it really is 'great'. He's decided you're someone he can trust. So he's arranged to give you very limited access to *Panorama*, in the hope of allaying some people's suspicions and taking some of the pressure off his staff. It won't be going on air till next Monday, but I get the impression he wishes it was out of the way right now."

"So when do I meet the guys?"

"They probably won't be as obliging as the Director General. They may even be resentful. My question is, do they have any reason to be?"

"I'm not sure I follow."

"According to your report, you agreed to work with Tom Ford, Orville Peterson and Brigitte Crevier. Tom Ford's now fulfilled his end of the bargain, if we can call it that. He now expects you to probe and report back to him. He'll want to

know what *Panorama*'s working on. They won't want him to
know, because he'll share it with Orville Peterson, who'll share
it with the government. But you're apparently morally committed to telling him."

"I'm committed to sharing any information that sheds light
on why Dhanial was killed. Not anything and everything."

"I'm pretty sure the BBC don't know who killed him or why
he was killed."

"But that's mainly what I'm going to be concentrating on.
Ideally, I'd like something to give Ford: as you say, we did
make a bargain of sorts. But that doesn't oblige me to tell him
what the programme's about, assuming I find out."

"I don't see how Ford can even know you've been invited
there."

"Firstly, he thinks he's probably piqued Terry McNamara
sufficiently to get me access. Having worked there himself, I
would imagine he knows something of the BBC's panic-levels
and willingness to make concessions. Secondly, Terry's almost
certainly not inviting me over for fun. He's doing it to show
he's got nothing to hide. If he doesn't publicise my visit on
some level, that's not going to work."

"So how do you intend to proceed?"

"Ford and Orville are convinced the Russians are involved
on some level. They don't want *Panorama* to go ahead because
they think it's got the potential to bring down the government."

She sighed wearily. "So I understand, yes. So let's go back.
You're committed to sharing any information that sheds light
on why Dhanial was killed. But there won't be any. On the
other hand, as you also point out, you can't go back to Ford
empty-handed. So as far as I can see, you're caught between a
rock and a hard place."

"As I said in our last meeting, when a person says they're on
to something big, and then, within five minutes, they're killed,

I can't resist the feeling that it's because they really *were* on to something big."

"I think you're playing a dangerous game here, John. Tom Ford's using you to get information about *Panorama*, that's all. A heads-up from him to the government will have its rewards, and you probably won't get so much as a thank you. Can I just ask you, partly out of interest, what you think about the BBC? I mean, generally? Do you, on any level, agree with Dhanial, that it's had its day?"

"I think it's about the only decent major institution left in this country."

"Okay…"

"Yes, it maybe does have a bit of a left-wing feel to it sometimes – I can see where people like Dhanial are coming from – but that's purely coincidental. Its universalism just happens to coincide with other forms of universalism. Everyone pays the licence fee, so that's who it has a duty to: everyone. In the abstract as well as the concrete. That's its ideology. Just inclusion, that's all. Nothing sinister. And let's face it: it's pretty much the envy of the world. Nothing much else Britain's got nowadays is."

"Then I don't understand how you can have got along so well with Ford, Peterson and Brigitte Crevier. Because you obviously did."

"I don't think that's a bad thing."

"I'm not saying it is."

"*I* don't entirely know how me getting along with them works either. People are just people. Maybe, in the end, it's about having a good laugh at nothing at all. And beer. And perhaps food - although we didn't actually have any that day. And the fact that we're all going to die, and the universe is mainly empty space, and God's behind a big grey cloud. I don't know. We're all alive at the same time, maybe."

She expelled another sigh. "Okay, John, you can go now. Your appointment at Broadcasting House is at 2pm. I've already sent you the details, and I'll assign someone to accompany you over there. I don't want you going out alone any more, not till all this is over. Good luck."

Chapter 16: On the Way to W1A

At noon, Mordred left his desk and went up to the canteen, where he queued behind a well-built man - one of Colin's team in Admin - called Russell Crowe. Russell looked exactly like a younger version of the eponymous Hollywood actor, only he had a high-pitched voice that usually surprised people, and even made one or two of his co-workers pity him: if it hadn't been for that, they agreed quietly, he'd have been 'perfect'. Mandy Collins, one of the MI7 novelists, had dated him for a year, and forced him - so the rumour went - to see a vocal therapist. She'd succeeded in getting his voice down a semitone, but she'd been aiming for an entire octave, and she broke up with him when the realisation finally dawned that eight full notes would take her two decades and thus into her late forties. After they split, he told everyone that she'd also been trying to get him to speak with an American accent. She vehemently denied it, and one afternoon they rowed in front of ten colleagues at the eastern end of Lambeth Bridge, where the A3203 met the roundabout. His hair began to fall out shortly afterwards, perhaps for congenital reasons: his father and grandfather had both had alopecia; but theirs hadn't manifested till their early fifties, whereas Russell was only in his late twenties, so maybe stress had something to do with it. Nowadays, he was seeing Ngozi Ogiemwonyi, a high-ranking field officer in Blue Department. They'd joined the Territorial Army together six months ago and they shared an interest in prize budgerigars and a love of Nando's. His voice had returned to its original pitch. He and Mandy Collins still weren't speaking, though he'd apparently sent her flowers on her birthday, six weeks ago to the day, via Interflora. More a please-let's-bury-the-hatchet bouquet than anything romantic. She'd put them in the bin beside her desk, possibly be-

cause she suffered from hay fever, but there were rival theories about that: why, for instance, dump them so publicly? Why
right beside her desk? On the other hand, she did sneeze a lot
in the spring sometimes.

And that was all Mordred knew about Russell Crowe. They
exchanged hellos in the queue, and Russell took his lunch on
a tray to the other side of the canteen, where the chess players
usually gathered.

Mordred ordered the tofu and bean stew. When he went to
pay, the lady at the checkout stopped him.

"It's already been taken care of," she said.

"By who?" he said.

"No idea. I only know there's nothing to pay. Next, please."

He made himself a cup of tea from the urn and went to sit
alone by one of the windows overlooking the Thames.

A mystery. Ruby Parker, maybe? Possibly the BBC. But why
didn't the checkout lady know who'd paid? If the BBC was
trying to butter him up, surely it'd have made a point of informing him.

An incoming text pinged in his pocket. He took his phone
out.

Bloody hell. The CIA.

Enjoy your meal, John.

He smiled. Muchos surrealos.

He decided to make the journey from Millbank to Broadcasting House on foot, partly in hope of meeting one of the Russian Novelists, although his expectations there were slowly diminishing – even if one of them appeared, a rival intelligence
agent would probably beat him to the point of interception –
and partly to allow himself to think about the rock + hard
place whose existence Ruby Parker had so perceptively dis-
cerned.

"You're not allowed to leave unaccompanied any more,"
Colin told him as he signed the 'out' section of the register.

"I've just had it up on my screen. And you need to fill in a form – only a short one - for your own safety, stating your destination and probable route."

Mordred completed the documentation without complaining. Kevin, one of the staff drivers, a forty-something ex-soldier with lean features and a shaven head, appeared from the lift behind Colin.

"Howdy, John," he said.

Long gone were the days when Kevin declined to speak to him as a matter of personal policy. Proof that people could change.

"Howdy, Kevin," Mordred said.

"How's things?"

"Fine, thanks. You?"

"Fine. Good. The beautiful wife?"

"In Berlin with Alec."

"Sorry to hear that. My own wife, I've got to say - "

"I mean, just on a job. They haven't run off together."

"Aye… Aye, okay," Kevin said, as if he only half-appreciated the lie, given how completely see-through it was. In his world, Alec was irresistible to women, John invisible.

"So you're going to accompany me to Broadcasting House?" Mordred said.

"Aye, but not alongside you. I'll be keeping an eagle-eyed watch from a distance, ready to leap in if you get attacked. I'm armed, so don't worry."

"That's reassuring."

"You won't know I'm there unless something goes wrong."

Mordred handed Colin the completed form. "Is that okay?"

"It's perfect," Colin replied. "Thank you."

"I'll give you a minute's head start, then I'll come after you," Kevin said.

Mordred strode out of the building and turned left. Horseferry Road then across St James's Park.

Just as he'd been unable to focus on the task in hand during the bus journey this morning, so now he was unable to concentrate on the BBC. He felt old, though he was only thirty-four. Somewhere along the line in the last five years, people like Mobeen Dhanial and Brigitte Crevier had come to the fore – it was fashionable and wise nowadays to cast doubt on the drive for greater equality and more diversity – and people like him had lost ground they might never retrieve. Bloody hell, how could an organisation that had given the world Stacey Dooley and *The Misadventures of Romesh Ranganathan* conceivably be bad? And it was bullshit to say feminism had all-but succeeded and what remained of it was needless aggression. He wished Dhanial was still alive, if only so he could give him a copy of Caroline Perez's *Invisible Women*, or something like it. Get a proper discussion going, introduce him to his own sisters, though they'd probably kill him.

Maybe these things went in cycles. Maybe right-wing and left-wing were just fashions, like hair or clothes. There hadn't been many young right-wingers for such a long time that they'd come back in vogue, just like your granddad's shoes might make a comeback because they were old enough to look strangely new. That would be equally depressing.

Some people said populism was on the wane now the moderates had regained power in Greece, like that was some kind of touchstone. Golden Dawn had sunk without a trace.

But that was just wishful thinking. The right was on the rise. Russia was right wing, so was America, so was Britain. Liberals were on the back foot. They were yesterday's people. He was one of them.

On the other hand, he got on well with most right-wingers he knew. Ruby Parker was right about that: he certainly didn't dislike Tom Ford, Orville Peterson and Brigitte Crevier as human beings, quite the contrary. And his own wife was hardly Karl Marx. How did that work? Most people weren't like him.

They saw opposing views as barriers to friendship. Was that sensible? Was it -

He was suddenly aware of a disturbance on the edge of his field of vision. He turned.

A young woman, early to mid twenties, homeless by the look of her, advancing fast towards him.

Their eyes locked. She looked euphoric, like she was on some sort of pill. She accelerated, and he had the blindingly hyperreal sense of something crucial unfolding.

My God.

Elizaveta Aleksandrova Khamatova born 1988 in the city of Sochi. Daughter of -

Something exploded in his brain. He advanced at speed to meet her, machine-like, because everything was concentrated in the action of closing the gap between them. This was The Mall, it really wasn't a dream. Someone else came from one side to grab her, a man, gnarled as a tree and about forty.

Mordred's body had disappeared. What took its place was a Mordred-shaped block of adrenalin. He stepped into the man, grasped his head at the temples, and smashed it – really smashed it - with his own forehead. He grabbed Elizaveta's hand and turned her in his direction, and they ran.

Three other men advanced on him, so close that they could probably have grabbed him had it not been for two shadowy figures who closed on the attackers from some third level of action – assailants of the assailants - and tackled them all like it was a rugby match before any rules had been invented.

Elizaveta wasn't a sprinter. He kept hold of her, but he had to slow to accommodate her. He didn't look back: right now, she might have been nothing but a disembodied hand for all he knew, but he sensed men were pursuing him and gaining. A crack rang out like a twig being snapped in two: a gun in the mix. She slumped and, in the jerk of the sudden brake, he released her hand.

He turned and met two men coming to scoop her up: ex-special forces, by the look of them, and hostile, and he prepared to fight for her and probably come out broken. She was in between them, like prey caught between two species of predator, prone, bleeding copiously, but clearly not finished.

Out of nowhere, a London taxi ploughed into the two men, simply battering them out of the way and screeched to a halt. They landed on the central reservation like scarecrows. Kevin leaned out of the window.

"Sorry about the delay," he said. He jumped out, holding a pistol, and opened the rear door. "Get in, John."

Mordred did as commanded. Kevin lifted Elizaveta, put her on top of him and scurried back into the driver's seat. She'd apparently lost consciousness. A foreign agent advanced until he was level with the steering wheel. Kevin retrieved a large aerosol from the passenger seat and fired pepper spray into his eyes. Probably Ruby Parker's orders, not his personal preference.

More men were advancing at speed, with rage, like something from *28 Days Later*. Kevin was covered with Elizaveta's blood, so was Mordred, and then they were doing forty, then sixty, and Elizaveta continued to pump red all over everything like she was a cistern and someone had removed her plug.

In the midst of all this horror and confusion, she opened her eyes and looked at Mordred, sleepily. Her lips moved. She was praying.

He took her hand. "We're going to get you to a hospital," he said.

He couldn't tell her she was going to live. She almost certainly wasn't. Even the hospital was more than he had the right to promise. He frantically undid her blouse, looking for where the blood was surging. He couldn't find anything.

Her leg. Her left thigh, that's where –

Bloody, *bloody* hell!

Her eyes suddenly filled with exultation. She startled him by almost sitting up.

"I love you, John," she said in Russian. "I love you with all my heart! I'll always love you! Always, always, *always!*"

She gasped in pain, closed her eyes and died.

Chapter 17: After the Blood

Whenever uncharted territory comes within the realms of the imaginable, it has protocols. In all other circumstances, things tend to happen faster than people can level-headedly react. When Elizaveta Aleksandrova Khamatova died on the back seat of a getaway car, was it necessary to get confirmation of her death? From who? Where should Kevin drive? The hospital? Thames House? A morgue?

Tragedy immediately became farce. Two police cars forced them to pull over. A uniformed officer walked solemnly over, knocked on Kevin's window and asked him to get out of the car. Kevin rolled the window down an inch. The officer asked him sarcastically if he knew what speed he'd been doing. Kevin applied the central locking. The officer apparently registered the fact that the driver was covered in blood and had a corpse on the back seat, and he retreated at speed, calling for backup. Mordred phoned Ruby Parker. Two panda cars became six, the police sealed off the A3214 between Palace Street and Bressenden Place, and a firearms unit arrived and took up positions. A helicopter circled.

After twenty minutes' standoff, two more policemen approached in a much more leisurely manner. They gave Kevin instructions to follow one of their cars while their colleagues removed the cordon. An ambulance arrived to receive the corpse. The police had cleared the route to Millbank of both civilians and traffic.

When Mordred arrived back at Thames House, everyone was moving at twice their normal speed in order to accomplish four times the usual tasks. Senior intelligence officers from Grey and Red had already reviewed the CCTV footage of the attack, isolating faces for identification. Ruby Parker had spoken to Sir Timothy Wallsgrove, the Permanent Secretary at the Home Office, and she was due in Marsham Street in ten minutes' time to confer with the Minister himself. The press had been issued with a DSMA-notice asking them to refrain from reporting the disturbances in The Mall, but since DSMA-notices were merely requests, no one knew how effective this one would be. John and Kevin were taken to separate rooms to be debriefed, then to sign statements, then to review the video footage. *Why do you think she said she loved you?* the interrogating officer kept asking. *It could be important.* Mordred didn't know. Drugs, maybe. Maybe she was hungry and confused. Delirium of some kind, obviously: significant blood loss could do that.

The Home Secretary contacted the Russians, who were obviously expecting him. As anticipated, they disavowed all knowledge of Elizaveta Khamatova. And the fact was, with nothing to cross-reference the corpse to – no DNA profile, dental records, passport, not even any evidence that there *was* an Elizaveta Khamatova, since she'd entered the country illegally - no foothold existed from which to challenge them. For all practical purposes, she might as well have been a ghost. Even the CCTV footage, apparently showing the faces of four known GU agents attacking her, wasn't conclusive. As His Excellency Feodor Pisemsky 'humbly' pointed out, it was grainy and erratic. The Russians, he lamented, always got the blame for everything nowadays – this being just the latest in a long line of unfair allegations.

Nevertheless, Pisemsky took a strenuously conciliatory approach – *tell us how we can help, we'll do anything in our power to assist, you need only ask.* He was in a precarious position. Not only had he just reported a killing in his embassy, but he'd admitted Kseniya Igorevna Yumasheva was under his roof. An idiotic blunder, in retrospect. He now told the Home Secretary she'd been flown home to Moscow. Which was risky – the British had almost certainly been watching the building, so they'd know for a fact she was still in there - but containable: they wouldn't dare call him a liar.

Yet this little side-show in the eternal Great Game had turned slightly against him. Both sides knew his slightest error on the next move could well be fatal, the precipitation of a rapid flight across the chessboard towards an inglorious checkmate.

Meanwhile, down in the basement rooms of MI7's IT department, Tariq al-Banna was laboriously examining hours of CCTV footage from scores of different locations across the capital trying to piece together the victim's last movements. Five questions needed urgently answering: where had she been today, immediately prior to approaching Mordred? How long had she been in London? How long had she been in Britain? Had she been alone? Why had she broken cover when she had?

By 6pm, he had a provisional set of answers to at least the first question. He requisitioned Lecture Room One to show a highly condensed version of five hours' footage to twenty officers including Mordred, fast-forwarding, rewinding and freezing to highlight salient episodes in her day.

She'd begun the morning in Hackney where she was apparently living beneath an abandoned office block. She'd breakfasted in McDonald's on Mare Street at 9am, then walked into Central London and circumambulated Trafalgar Square for thirty minutes. At 10.30, she left for Victoria Park. She sat on the grass for two hours and then got up and tramped the streets, apparently aimlessly. She sat in The Mall, opposite the King George VI and Queen Elizabeth Memorial. When Mordred arrived she'd been there for well over an hour.

Towards the end of the presentation, Mordred's phone vibrated in his pocket. *Tom Ford.* He showed the screen to Ruby Parker, sitting on his left. She rolled her eyes.

Ten minutes later, when Tariq had wrapped up and everyone was leaving, she made a point of leaning over. "You'd better call him," she said irritably. "It's probably not wise for us to make ourselves too inaccessible when there's a D-notice in the pipeline. I'll ask Tariq to make the footage available for a more detailed analysis. Did anything occur to you?"

"I've an odd feeling it will. As if I've had an idea but it's bubbling somewhere below the surface. I definitely need a second viewing. As soon as possible."

"Call me the second you think of anything. You can ring Ford from seminar room H11. It should be empty this time of day. If not, and you can't locate anywhere private, come down to my office. And John: I don't want you going home tonight. Phyllis is away in Berlin and you've just had a nasty shock. No one's mentioned it - we've had other priorities - but it won't go away until we deal with it professionally, and that probably means some sort of counselling. Spend the night in one of the pods. I'll assign someone to keep you company this evening, and you can both eat and drink on the house. That's an order, by the way."

He took the lift to H11. Empty, as promised. He settled in a chair by the whiteboard and called Tom Ford.

"Hi, you tried to catch me earlier," he said when Ford picked up, trying to sound upbeat, although he was shattered. He could just slip onto the floor and go to sleep.

"You've had quite an exciting day by the sounds of things," Ford said. "You were attacked by Russians."

Mordred sat up. "Who told you that?"

"Common knowledge, John. Don't worry, your D-notice is perfectly secure. We'll respect it. This time. Here, let me put my editor on."

There was a slight click. "Mike Grimes here, John. Nice to speak to you again. We met once, in the Shard. You probably won't remember. I was slightly pickled that day anyway. Now, as Tom rightly says, we're going to respect that little D-notice of yours... this time. But if I was you, I'd tell Ruby Parker she might just be storing up problems for herself, not coming clean. It sounds like this might be something that'll happen again. Then it'll be twice the price to pay, exposure-wise. At that point, we'll have to give our readers at least a bit of background, and they'll wonder why you – *you*, not us - weren't more upfront first time round. Then they might start thinking there's even more to the story. That's where conspiracy theories come from, John. Plebs not getting trusted with info. The authorities withhold ten per cent, and when they're rumbled, ordinary people leap to the natural conclusion that it was a hell of a lot more than ten. More like seventy. If the authorities had been a bit more transparent at the outset, they could have saved themselves a lot of unnecessary aggro and retained Joe Public's trust."

"You're probably right," Mordred said. Ruby Parker's *keep them sweet* - or words to that effect – recurred. "It's not my call. But I'd be very interested to know how you found out it was the Russians who attacked me."

"I like your attitude. Not snotty."

"Thank you. I realise you don't have to tell me."

"Careful, John. Not too ingratiating. It doesn't go with the image. Okay, I'll tell you. It turns out the Russians aren't the only people with an interest in you. The Americans have been watching you too." He laughed. "You didn't know that, did you, John? Well, the Americans told Wikipedia. Who then told us. Obviously, the Yanks couldn't tell us directly: they don't want to be seen to be 'interfering'. But they have your best interests at heart and it turns out they don't like the Russkis very much, despite – or maybe because of - all that smooching between Botox-headed Vlad Putin and America's very own latter-day Einstein, Donald J Trump. Who'd have guessed it? They actually *want* Moscow to have bad publicity. Here, I'm putting Tom back on. He wants a final word with you. Ciao."

"Hello, again," Ford said. "The point about what's happened is this: I said the Russians were behind the killing of Mobeen Dhanial, and you poo-poo-ed it. But think: we get an article on the front page of *The Daily Mail* and the Russians come after you on *the selfsame day*. We've got *Panorama* by the short and curlies now, John. If you don't nail them, we will. Just not this time, thanks to the D-notice. Have they made any overtures to you?"

"I was actually on my way to Broadcasting House when I was... waylaid." It was the truth. He couldn't calculate the ramifications, not with all he'd been through and all he still had to do - re-watch Tariq's footage at least once, possibly at five hours' worth of normal speed. *Panorama* seemed a million miles away.

"Shee-it, as the Americans say. Why were you on your way over there?"

"They asked to see me."

"So the Russians are definitely involved," Ford said. "Bloody hell, it must *really* be explosive! Now, look, John, I don't want to sound like I'm trying to teach my grandma to suck eggs, but you need to reschedule that meeting pronto. Tell them there's another story here in addition to the one they've got: the story of how the BBC allowed itself to be played by the Kremlin and bring Britain down. Which would make a pretty good title for *Dispatches*, don't you think? Channel 4, in case you missed the implication: the BBC's biggest rival, albeit they're two peas in the same outdated liberal pod. In any case, with Orville's little Private Member's Bill coming up, they might want to think twice before sticking to their gung-ho approach. Reschedule that meeting, John, tell them all that, and get back to me."

He hung up.

Mordred put his phone back in his pocket. He went downstairs, switched on his PC and watched Tariq's footage. His phone rang.

Ruby Parker.

Bloody hell, couldn't she just email him, like normal?

"John here," he said.

"I've just had the BBC on the phone. The Director General, to be more precise. To say he was put out by your 'failure to show today' is an understatement. I explained something of what had happened to you on your way over, and pointed out that he could probably confirm the bare bones of my account from his news department. But the bottom line is, he still wants to see you. And *Panorama* wasn't keen on the idea to begin with. They're less so now. You've got an appointment tomorrow. Right now, I want you to get something to eat and get some sleep. Try and put Elizaveta Khamatova out of your mind for the moment. Sleeping on the problem might actually help, but either way, you're probably exhausted, whatever you might think. Go to the canteen then the pods."

Chapter 18: Kseniya Gets Rescheduled

Kseniya lay in bed in a small upstairs room with a sofa, her wheelchair and a coffee table. She'd taken tablets she'd been given and succumbed to the injection. She still felt very ill, but the nurse had been kind and stayed with her. She had no idea whether they'd posted a guard outside, but she didn't imagine they'd have considered it necessary. She wasn't going anywhere, not in this state. Later on, they were going to give her 'walking practice' so she could look like nothing had happened to her when she presented herself in Trafalgar Square. Of course, they'd also have to put makeup on her eyes and pump her full of painkillers, but they'd know that, they weren't idiots. Nothing would be left to chance.

She became aware of an unusual amount of activity a few hours after her interview with Commander Bryzgalov and the ambassador. Running up and downstairs, urgent shouts, phones ringing.

"What's happening?" she asked the nurse.

The nurse chortled. "I've no idea. I don't know what sort of things cause commotion in embassies, dear. Maybe a terrorist attack, or something's happened in Moscow. I really don't know, and I'm not in a position to ask. It wouldn't concern the likes of me, anyway. You concentrate on getting better."

"When am I going to practise walking?"

"Later. This evening, probably. Not now."

"What time is it?"

The nurse looked at her watch. "Five minutes to two. There's a clock just over there. Try to sleep, there's a good girl."

Kseniya put her hands flat on the sheets and closed her eyes. She dreamed about the past: being beaten up all over again, and the stocky man she'd killed – she still didn't know his name – and then the future: confessing to a priest and going to prison. She woke up six or seven times, but at what must have been tiny intervals, because the light hadn't changed, and the nurse hardly moved.

And then someone was shaking her and, for once – wasn't it just like her? - she couldn't wake up. Whoever it was, kept saying her name. A man.

Commander Bryzgalov. She blinked her eyes open and tried to sit up.

There were four people in the room, all standing. The nurse and the doctor were on one side of her bed. The commander and the ambassador stood on the other.

"Do you want me to practise walking now?" she said drowsily.

"She's probably okay to be transferred," the doctor said.

"You've got a little more time," the ambassador said. "We won't be doing Trafalgar Square till the day after tomorrow now. Which will give you more time to prepare, of course. Good news," he added, as if he wasn't quite sure it was.

"Your friend Elizaveta was killed today," Bryzgalov said. "We don't know who killed her. The British or the Americans. We were trying to save her."

"I didn't know she was still alive!" Kseniya said. "Oh my God."

Bryzgalov nodded solemnly. "We're telling you in order to impress on you the need for your complete cooperation now. You've got to put however ill you might feel to the back of your mind. We need you like never before."

"Nod if you understand," the ambassador said.

"She's not an idiot," Bryzgalov said. "As I keep telling you, she's perfectly capable of carrying this out. Aren't you, Kseniya?"

She nodded.

"Okay," Bryzgalov went on. "What we've got to do now is get you out of this building and put you somewhere else. The

British and the Americans are watching us all very closely. They know you're in here. We had to tell them something about, er, your little accident the other night. And we thought we might as well tell them you're here while we're on. Make it look like you're back on our side again. They know all about you, you see. But they're not your friends. We are."

The ambassador sighed. "You're rambling, Yuri. You've just told her they were chasing Elizaveta Aleksandrova. She doesn't need the implications of that spelling out."

"Okay," Bryzgalov said. "We've got to get you out of here undetected if we're to stand any chance of putting you in Trafalgar Square the day after tomorrow - "

"Why not tomorrow?" she said.

"Because there's been a lot of fallout over Elizaveta's death," Bryzgalov said. "Everyone in London will be on high alert tomorrow."

"Plus, we've got a lot of loose ends need tying up here in the embassy," the ambassador said.

"We want to see how it plays out in the British press," Bryzgalov said. "The British are notoriously timid. If they think they're winning, it'll be all over the front pages of every newspaper. But they might decide to keep it low-key, avoid 'complications with international relations', so to speak. The Brits need all the friends they can get these days."

"Give it a day, it'll be yesterday's news," the ambassador said. "We also need to be sure the British haven't followed you to your new destination. You see, they might give the appearance of not knowing where we've taken you, while actually having certain knowledge. They've probably got spy satellites trained on us now. I'm not exaggerating. The minute we put you in Trafalgar Square, they spring."

"Thankfully, we've got 'people' who can tell if they know where we are," Bryzgalov said. "Experts."

"You'll be going to your new destination via a long series of normal roads," the ambassador said, "on a route that includes four different covered locations. Car parks; invisible from the air, you see. And we won't be coming out of any one of them the way we went in. And they'll try to follow us, but we've got six or seven different vehicles in place to appear in just the right places to confuse them."

"They haven't a chance, really," Bryzgalov said. "The British have always been amateurs. Very good amateurs, don't get me wrong. It doesn't pay to underestimate them because mostly, they're in it for love, not money. But love only gets you so far."

"We're telling you all this because we want you to know we're all in this together," the ambassador said. "And we need you to trust us. We're going to put you to sleep now, and when you wake up, you're going to be some place else. Trust us, we're only putting you to sleep so we can keep you safe. We might have to drive at speed, erratically, and we might have to get you from A to B by unorthodox means – carry you, say, from one vehicle to another. If you're awake, you'll be in pain. You might be afraid. This way, you'll wake up in your new bed, and it'll be as if nothing happened."

"And tomorrow, we'll do a *lot* of walking practice," the nurse said. "Get you ready for your big moment!"

She nodded. "Okay."

The doctor came forward with a sedative in a syringe. As she fell unconscious, she thought about how stupid her world had become, a game of stay-ahead played by utter morons. Everything they'd just told her was insane.

Chapter 19: Discreet Disclosures at BBC HQ

Mordred ate a bean burger in the Thames House canteen then descended by lift to First Underground, where he took the shuttle to the gents' cloakrooms. He changed into a pair of pyjamas and went through into a bare metallic room with ten or twelve large drawers. He pressed the button on the nearest. Out came his bed. He climbed on, lay down and felt it return to its original position. The lights went off. He slept.

He dreamed about Elizaveta Khamatova, who was intermittently also Phyllis, but a Russian Phyllis, because he was Russian. They went ice-skating and threw snowballs at each other, and they were Lara and Yuri in *Doctor Zhivago*. Sometimes she was the Julie Christie version, sometimes the Keira Knightley, sometimes she was Phyllis. He kept revisiting the scene in Varykino where he sent Lara away for ever and he ran upstairs like his life depended on it and he put the window through and the theme tune blasted out and everyone in the cinema who had any humanity at all burst into tears. He woke up twice, gasping for breath.

At eight o'clock, the alarm went off: a gentle, slowly repeated ding. His new clothes – socks, underwear, white shirt and a dark suit - were in the cloakroom. He showered, feeling as if he hadn't slept at all. He ate two slices of toast and jam morosely in the canteen. When he left the building, his ride to Broadcasting House – a company Range Rover driven by Sheila Magnus – awaited him, with that morning's *Times* on the back seat. Next to Sheila, in the front passenger seat, an armed bodyguard. He bade them both good morning and settled down to pretend to read the newspaper. He thought about Tariq's footage.

It should have been a twenty-five minute journey, but due to roadworks and unexpected, inexplicable delays, it took twice that. He arrived at Broadcasting House just before ten.

He switched his phone off, walked across the U-shaped forecourt, entered via the revolving doors and checked in at the front desk. He signed a non-disclosure form. A fluffy-haired, middle-aged man in a waistcoat appeared from behind double doors to accompany him to his destination on the top floor. The man - 'Bernard' - smiled deferentially and said how brilliant it was to finally meet "sorry, it's on the tip of my tongue, God, would you believe it... *John*, of course! Apologies. Late night last night, my bad." They took the lift. Bernard didn't speak again. Select members of the *Panorama* team were apparently waiting to meet Mordred in an office along a long, twisty corridor lined with Renaissance-style oil paintings of BBC immortals: Annie Nightingale, Michael Bentine, Meera Syal, Robert Robinson, Lord Reith, Pinky and Perky.

Bernard opened the door, then closed himself out. Three people – two men and a woman – sat looking gloomy around a long table with a state-of-the-art urn, a variety of tea and coffee sachets, four cups and a pile of expensive-looking biscuits on a large plate. A small window high up at the far end of the room gave a view of a blue sky and made the occupants look shadowy. Terry McNamara, the BBC's Director General - thin with faded film star looks - stood up when Mordred entered. He advanced with a smile and a handshake. "Pleased you could finally make it, John," he said, without the sarcastic tone his words alone might have suggested.

"Sorry about yesterday," Mordred said. "I got held up."

The man and the woman had also risen, but less enthusiastically. They were about forty and wore suits.

"Philip Toussaint-Molloy and Juliet Randhawa," the DG said. "John Mordred, with Her Majesty's Secret Service, if that's not giving anything away. Don't worry, John, we've signed non-disclosure forms as well. We can't show you any of our *Panorama* programme, I'm afraid, nor go into specific details – all our rivals are trying to beat us to the scoop, as it were - but we can talk generally, give you a broad idea of the sort of thing to expect when you sit down in front of the TV at eight-thirty next Monday. Let's all take a pew, shall we? Who's for tea and who's for coffee? I'll play mother."

Someone had obviously gone to a lot of effort to bring in beverage making equipment, and Philip and Juliet looked miserable enough to say they didn't want anything, so Mordred thought he'd better show willing.

"I'll have a cup of tea, please. Milk, no sugar."

Juliet and Philip followed suit, so maybe the meeting wasn't set to be a total disaster, after all. Juliet even reached over for a bespoke bourbon cream.

"Now, who wants to go first?" the DG said, when everyone was seated.

Juliet put her hand up. "What's your opinion of Mobeen Dhanial's book, John? I'm assuming you've read it. Do *you* think the BBC's spearheading some sort of liberal plot to change the face of British society?"

"Yes," Mordred said. "But I don't care. I think it's a good thing."

Silence.

"I'm not sure I follow, John," the DG said tetchily.

"Plot's an emotive word," Mordred said. "So is 'liberal' up to a point, so is 'change'. Replace 'plot' with 'project', 'liberal' with 'enlightenment' and get rid of 'change' entirely: everything's 'changing' all the time. Now, suddenly what the BBC's doing doesn't look so sinister any more. Educating and informing people is good. It's part of an enlightenment project that's been around since at least the eighteenth century. It's based on the assumption that everyone's capable of under-standing facts and arguments, which is also good. And it's a heck of a lot better than trying to inculcate patriotism and re-spect for law and order and obedience to the ruling classes, and all the other things its opponents think it should be doing instead."

More silence.

"People blame us for *not* educating them, though," Philip said, obviously fishing for some reason to dislike Mordred, or maybe to justify his existing dislike. "They say we buried the truth about immigration, and that's partly why we got Brexit."

"No one knows the truth about immigration," Mordred replied. "They know statistics, but not what they mean. But in any case, it's not the job of the BBC to set the political agenda, or to re-set it in any major way once it's been decided. That's Parliament's job. We've had quite a few pro-immigration governments this century and the people voted them in, no one else. They're not now entitled to blame you."

"Right, okay," Philip said.

"I didn't really come here to make speeches," Mordred told him. "But thanks for the opportunity."

"Glad you're on our side," the DG said. "Although obviously, that's a crass turn of phrase. It's not about that."

Philip and Juliet also seemed to have relaxed significantly, although they were still on their guard. Mordred could tell what they were thinking. *He's a member of the security services. He'll tell us whatever he thinks we want to hear in the hope that we'll drop our guard and divulge everything.*

"I'm not just telling you what I think you want to hear," he said. "I'm not entirely a spook in the traditional sense. I used to be, but then things happened, and I became a little bit too well-known for certain jobs. You can look me up on the internet."

"We have," Juliet said, as if anything else would have been stupid - which, to be fair, it probably would. "You're the Ultimate Londoner, or used to be." She laughed. "You're not going to believe this, but I was one of the few real people who actually voted for you. I mean, I don't know what happened, but you couldn't possibly have got however many votes you actually ended up with. I mean, what *was* that?"

"Look it up on Wikipedia," Philip told her. "A scam, is one theory."

"A topic for a future *Panorama*, maybe," the DG put in, as if to put the matter to bed.

"So am I now allowed to ask what next week's *Panorama*'s going to be about?" Mordred said.

Juliet and Philip looked portentously at each other. Time for them to take the plunge.

"Have you ever heard of the hostile immigration policy?" Juliet asked.

"A little," Mordred said.

Philip looked at his phone. "Wikipedia calls it 'a set of administrative and legislative measures designed to make staying in the United Kingdom as difficult as possible for people without leave to remain, in the hope that they may "voluntarily leave".'"

Juliet nodded. "The Conservative Party wanted to get immigration figures down to the level they'd promised in their manifesto. In the words of Theresa May, who was Home Secretary when the policy was introduced, its aim was to create, 'here in Britain, a really hostile environment for illegal immigrants.'"

"Since the policy was introduced," Philip said, "there have been a number of deaths in custody in immigration removal centres. Several victims of human trafficking and modern slavery have been deported."

"All that's a matter of public record," the DG said. "However, we've discovered it goes much deeper than virtually everyone thinks."

Juliet nodded. "We've discovered an underground detention centre in Aylesbury. Astonishing enough in itself, but we've got evidence that over a hundred refugees were kept there in 2014, and that they were all shipped secretly back to their two countries of origin – Belarus and Russia – where they were murdered on arrival. The British government kept the mass deportation secret, which is just as well because it probably wasn't expecting the killings. But we've got a tranche of documents from the Kremlin that proves there was collusion between the Russians, the Belarusians and the British. The British government wanted to avoid its obligations under the 1951 UN Convention on Refugees as well as Article 3 of the European Convention on Human Rights, which also forms part of British law. The Russians and the Belarusians wanted to avoid the embarrassment of a large number of their own citizens seeking 'leave to remain' in one of its least favourite countries abroad. The forced return of the refugees coincided with – 'inspired' is probably a better word, I suppose - a vigorous prosecution of human traffickers and prostitution racketeers in Moscow and Minsk. At least seven hundred people are supposed to have been killed in total."

"Which might not matter if they were all pimps and gangsters," Philip said. "But of course, a lot of them were 'white slaves', as some human rights lawyers might call them. And of course, there were no trials. It was all done extra-judicially: the authorities thought they knew who the culprits were, and they weren't in the business of pussyfooting around."

"Seven hundred deaths is a conservative estimate," Juliet said. "Some of our sources suggest the true figure may run to three thousand plus."

The DG smiled. "The title of our programme is going to be, 'the government's secret genocide'," he said, as if he was worried this might be a little strong, and he wanted Mordred's opinion. "Question mark after 'genocide' at the lawyers' insistence."

"Strong stuff," Mordred said. "I'm not sure it'll bring the government down. It breaks my heart to say this – and that's not just a turn of phrase – but a lot of people in this country don't care about refugees any more. We're a long way into the process of pulling up the drawbridge."

"They care about being lied to," the DG said. "It's the word 'genocide' that might provoke a reaction. Which, paradoxically, is why I'm in two minds about it. And we're not aiming to bring the government down, whatever some more hysterical commentators may have said. We're in the business of reporting facts, not provoking regime change."

"Regime change comes under the 'entertain' remit," Philip said. "Sorry, I've a very dark sense of humour."

"Dark times," Juliet said.

"And it goes without saying you can verify all this," Mordred said.

"We've several ex-members of the Russian and Belarusian governments, on camera, admitting to it and supplying lurid details," Philip said. "And we've got leaked records pertaining to Aylesbury. It's pretty watertight."

"I was in contact with Mike Grimes of *The Daily Mail* this morning," the DG said. "Contrary to what you may have been led to believe, he and I get on well; professionally, bitter rivals, but it doesn't mean we can't enjoy a drink together. Anyway, he tells me there's a theory afoot about the Russians. We've told you a lot, John. Perhaps you'd like to share something with us now?"

"I've been speaking to one or two friends of Mobeen Dhanial's," Mordred said. "They're of the opinion that he was killed by Russians because he threatened to derail *Panorama*'s investigation. I use the term 'derail' loosely. And the reason I was stopped from coming over here yesterday was because the Russians don't want anyone to interfere with the BBC's *Panorama* broadcast next Monday."

"Yes, that's broadly what Mike said," the DG put in.

"It's highly plausible too," Juliet said. "The Russians and the Belarusians have nothing to fear from the facts coming to light. I don't want to appear overly critical, but in their countries, killing a bunch of perceived lowlifes is broadly – not universally, but broadly – considered justifiable. Most people have bought into the cult of the strong leader, big time. Even Alexei Navalny, Putin's biggest political critic in Russia, is not exactly averse to a bit of xenophobia. The British government doesn't have that luxury. Not yet, thank God, anyway. When this comes to light, the Russians and the Belarusians will just shrug. There's likely to be a very different reaction in this country. At least, we hope so. That's what I *personally* hope, of course, not professionally."

"Amen to that," the DG said. "Also personally, I mean."

Out of the blue, Mordred suddenly had an idea about Elizaveta. He knew how to proceed, or thought he did. Luckily, he'd learned everything he possibly could here today.

He stood up. He felt strangely moved. He wanted to say something corny: 'It's nice to see the spirit of Voltaire isn't dead', or 'long live free speech and the spirit of free enquiry.'

"Thank you for your time," he said.

"It was a pleasure meeting you," the DG said. Juliet and Philip made concurring noises. Juliet took another bourbon cream.

Outside, Sheila was waiting to take him back to Thames House in the car. His minder opened the rear door for him. Passers-by looked on from a distance with quizzical expressions. Here, someone opening a car door for you usually meant you were famous. Which Mordred was, just not in a very big way. One or two rungs below a mid-afternoon weather forecaster, or some farmer who'd been on *Countryfile* two weeks ago. He switched his phone back on. No missed calls.

As the car pulled out into the traffic on Portland Place, Mordred remembered Ruby Parker on why the FCO wasn't keen to probe the supposed killing in the Russian embassy. *As I'm sure you've noticed, The FCO isn't exactly keen to uphold the rights of illegal immigrants*. Could its timidity be the repercussion of some prior collaboration between the two countries, one the FCO wouldn't want dredging up? If *Panorama* was right, then yes, almost certainly.

His phone rang. *Ruby Parker*.

"I'm on my way back," he told her before she could speak.

"I know. I asked Sheila to keep me updated."

"Is anything wrong?"

"I think the Russians may have completely outflanked us. Grey was supposedly keeping an eye on the embassy, but yesterday afternoon at about 2pm – roughly three-quarters of an hour after Elizaveta Khamatova was killed - a car left the embassy compound at speed, heading north. Two of ours gave chase, and others further afield were alerted to resume the pursuit, but the whole thing was very carefully organised. The Russians must have been planning it for some time. To cut a long story short, we lost sight of them somewhere between Willesden Green and Brent Cross."

"I'm assuming we think they were taking Kseniya Yumasheva somewhere."

"As far as we know, she's the only person they'd have any reason to conceal. The ambassador claimed she'd gone home to Russia, which we know she hasn't. And we know she still hasn't: we've been watching all those airports where they could conceivably smuggle someone out of the country. Nothing."

"So they're almost certainly keeping her in the country with the intention of flushing out the other Novelists somehow."

"That would be the obvious conclusion, John, but I'm not sure how helpful it is, given that we've lost her. From here on, Red's assuming complete control of the operation to retrieve the Novelists. Which probably should have been the case from the start. Only, of course, it's a poisoned chalice now that all our best leads have been squandered. It's difficult to see how it's not a failure waiting to happen."

"We'll see. I've had an idea, but it needs researching. Is it okay to put my report about Broadcasting House on ice for an hour or two when I get back?"

"Gladly, but stay by the phone. Depending on how desperate the Home Secretary's feeling about the whole thing, I may need to be briefed at short notice."

Chapter 20: Really Great Breakthrough

Mordred didn't have five hours to spare, so he put Tariq's video footage of Elizaveta Aleksandrova on fast forward. His first question: was there any point in the day when she'd been in a hurry to get to or from a location, or were all her movements carried out at the same speed?

He quickly discovered there was only one transition that fitted the bill. From Mare Street, it was four and a half miles to Trafalgar Square. Google maps made it ninety minutes at an average walk. She'd done it in an hour. Easily the fastest she'd gone all day.

Chance seemed unlikely. So was she trying to get *to* or *away* from something, or both?

Answer: *to something*, because when he reviewed the footage again, she accelerated slightly as she closed on her destination. An increase of half a mile an hour from Tottenham Court Road tube station onwards. And apparently unconsciously: no effort of will in it, not like she had to remind herself of anything. And the way she looked absently at the ground: this was a journey she'd done before, more than once.

And then, when she reached Trafalgar Square... She just sat. And walked leisurely, throwing furtive side-glances.

My God, he'd got it.

He called Tariq. More footage, everything he could extract: Trafalgar Square, the last five days, all cameras, all angles.

An hour later, he completed the breakthrough. Tariq helped him construct a montage and he booked Seminar Room H11. He called Ruby Parker.

7pm, the three of them in the room. Mordred got the blinds, Tariq hit play, Mordred picked up the laser pointer.

"First things first," he said. "Kseniya Yumasheva can't have told the Russians where the other Novelists are, otherwise they wouldn't need to keep her in the country. Obviously, they'd just have asked her where they were, then they'd have gone there. No, it must be more complicated than that. Either she won't tell them where they are – unlikely, since she supposedly entered the embassy voluntarily – or, like you said, they must be anticipating *using* her to flush them out. Which suggests there's some *place* they can put her where they think the others will be, and where the others will recognise her and break cover.

"On each of the last five days," he went on, "which is the farthest back I went once I realised what was happening, Elizaveta Khamatova has been sitting in Trafalgar Square for thirty minutes precisely. Here she is five days ago... here, four days... three days... two... one... and finally, today. She always arrives at ten am precisely and she leaves at ten-thirty. If you examine her body language, it's clear she's doing two things at once. She's both looking for someone, and doing everything in her power not to be recognised. Now, the question is, who's she looking for? Well, it took me a while to work it out, because they've changed quite considerably, but we've got at least five people, all on the scene at exactly the same time *and* exhibiting identical behaviour to Elizaveta Aleksandrova. Here, we have Pavel Sergeyevich Domogarov five days ago... three... one. He seems to be alternating with Valentina Leontievna Morozova, which may suggest they're cooperating, which would in turn be consistent with the contents of file RUS19/786641B, which suggests they may be in a relationship. Here's Valentina four days ago... now two. We've also got Roman Anatolyevich Shirokov on all five days, here... here... here... here... and here."

"Stop," Ruby Parker said. "Switch on the lights."

Mordred obeyed.

"I only have one question," she said. "Kseniya Yumasheva disappeared yesterday afternoon. Have you examined this morning's footage… of Trafalgar Square? I mean, *obviously* Trafalgar Square."

Mordred was used to seeing her calm, impassive, sceptical. But somehow, she was none of those things. She was galvanised and possibly a little shocked, though doing her best to conceal it.

"Yes," he said. "She doesn't appear there today. But I'm pretty sure that's where the Russians are considering putting her."

"And the reason they don't recognise each other is simply because they've changed so much?" she asked. "even though there are at least five of them there?"

"They've all got two concerns," Mordred said. "Firstly, to recognise the others; secondly, to avoid being recognised by the GU. They've probably all heard what happened to Fydor Golovin in Cologne. Their concern for their own personal safety is understandably stronger than their desire to find their friends, even though that last desire is strong. So they're all *looking at* each other all the time, but none of them *see* each other. In addition, obviously, a relatively long time has passed since they last saw each other in Moscow. Then, they were well dressed and groomed. Let's just say that, except to the trained eye, they're unrecognisable as the same people now. You've got to look hard. Harder than they think they do."

A beat. Ruby Parker let out a flute of air. "You've done some pretty impressive detective work in your time, John," she said, "but you've surpassed yourself today. Can I just ask, though: why do you think the Russians didn't put Kseniya Yumasheva into Trafalgar Square this morning? Why leave it? Why not strike while the iron's hot?"

"My guess is that, after what happened yesterday, they've got their hands full, and having evacuated her from the embassy, they think they can bide their time. In any case, we don't need her now. Even if she *had* appeared today, she might have lured two or three to capture. Others would have seen what happened and held back. We've only got the advantage because we've got access to the CCTV. If the Russians had access to it, they'd probably have beaten us to the truth by now. But they're on foreign soil and they're working blind, so to speak."

"And we can actually sit in front of all cameras tomorrow," she said, "and monitor the whole area. We'll know exactly who's there. Not only the Novelists, but also any Russian agents."

"Should we inform the French, Germans and Americans?" Mordred asked. "I mean, just to avoid any repeat of today?"

"Ideally, I'd like to enlist their help. But my instinct with something like this is to restrict the number of people in the know to as few as possible, because any leak would prove catastrophic. I'll recall the others from Berlin, Paris and Vienna, and we'll put them in charge of ten agents apiece, not to be briefed until just before they go into action. John, I want you to take overall charge of the operation and I'd like you to spend another night in the pods. I don't want to leave anything else to chance. If all goes well tomorrow we may be able to stop watching your back for good."

"Until the next adventure, that is," Tariq put in.

"Cheers," Mordred replied.

Chapter 21: God Knows What Nelson Made of This

Trafalgar Square, 9.55am

Kseniya Igorevna Yumasheva sat on the back seat of a London taxi that had been circling Central London for two hours now. She'd begun the day by leaving the house they'd put her in last night. She didn't know where it was, only that it was small, terraced, with a long tree-lined street and hardly any traffic. Commander Bryzgalov and her two drivers had spent the night upstairs; she'd stayed in the living room on a camp bed. She still felt very uncomfortable, but not in too much pain, although that was probably the drugs.

At eight o'clock, they'd woken her, given her breakfast cereal and a glass of water, and helped her walk the short distance from the house to the front drive, where a black cab waited with its engine idling. This was as much walking as she'd done since being beaten up, and it wasn't too onerous. Bryzgalov and two other men – not her drivers from yesterday: more military-looking, a bit like the Commander himself – sat opposite her, and her nurse took up position beside her.

"We're going to drive very slowly into London," Bryzgalov said, as they pulled out into the empty street. "When we get close to Trafalgar Square, we'll let you out. You'll probably have about a hundred metres to walk, because we can't risk any of your friends seeing you get out of a car: they'll panic and take flight if they suspect anything's up. Do you think you can manage a hundred metres?"

She nodded.

"I'm *sure* she can!" the nurse said chirpily.

"We'll be watching you supportively all the way," Bryzgalov said. "If you get into trouble, lean against the nearest wall with your left hand. We'll take that as the signal to abort and we'll try again tomorrow. The important thing is to get it right, not to rush it. We've probably only got one chance. If we scare them off, they probably won't come back, and then the killing will continue."

"You do appreciate that, don't you, Kseniya?" the man on Bryzgalov's right said in an unctuous tone. "That you can bring an end to all the bloodshed? If we get hold of Pasha Domogarov today, and we can satisfy ourselves that he's behaved as a good citizen should – something we're almost sure of already – all this can still end happily, for all of you."

"Believe it or not," Bryzgalov said. "We've got forty-two men *in situ*. More than enough to keep all of you safe. The minute anything happens, we'll be on it. Benevolently. Providing Pasha turns up, we'll have him. Or Valentina, she'll be nearly as good. We could probably do it without you, but it'll be easier with. If he or she sees a friend, they're much more likely to cooperate. They'll trust you and they'll believe you when you tell them we're helping. The last thing we want is some sort of struggle. Not after what happened with Elizaveta."

"Try to keep him as calm as you can," the man said.

"I will," she said.

Nevertheless, as the car got closer and closer to its destination, she felt increasingly the way she imagined Judas must have felt on his way to the Garden of Gethsemane. She tried to say The Lord's Prayer, but got stuck halfway through: *forgive us our sins.*

Mordred sat alongside four other officers in front of a row of monitors – six in length and four high - in an underground room in Whitehall. Together, the twenty-four screens gave a complete view of Trafalgar Square: probably more than one brain could process at the required speed, so selected screens were highlighted and text supplied by individual members of the surveillance team: 'Identity confirmed from File RUS/

C56G: GU agent Nikolai Matynov; rank, corporal', 'Requesting identification male seated second bollard along from the Charles Napier Obelisk'.

Lone men had begun arriving in the Square an hour earlier, and showed no signs of dispersing. They obviously had no idea MI7 was on to them, because they made no attempt to moderate their body language. By turns cocky, aggressive, furtive, jumpy, their subliminal behaviour might have escaped notice under ordinary circumstances, but today it screamed. By 9.55, the surveillance team had tallied thirty-eight Russian feet – nineteen individuals - on the ground, all watching, watching. As far as anyone in MI7 could tell, none of them were armed, but no one underground was taking that for granted. Meanwhile, Phyllis, Annabel, Alec, Edna and Ian were scrutinising the Square from four separate windows at least twenty metres above ground level in the surrounding environs: the National Gallery, Pret a Manger, the Grand Building, Canada House. At ground level, and behind the closed doors of vans, they each had teams of between ten and fifteen agents, ready to spring simultaneously, and whom they were continually updating as regards the situation.

Mordred's earpiece had been silent for some time now, Ruby Parker was watching from Thames House, where she'd remained to keep an eye on Grey. Having been pushed out of the investigation under a cloud, there was no telling whether it knew what was unfolding now, and whether, if it did, it would attempt to muscle in unexpectedly. In that case, the best place for the Head of Red Department to be was undoubtedly back at base.

"John, there's been a newsflash," she said suddenly. "I mean, an official, national item of breaking news. Bellingcat has just published information, based on the CCTV, identifying the two men who killed Mobeen Dhanial as GU officers. Of course, this had to come at the most inconvenient moment.

Keep your phone switched off, because I have a feeling that right now, Tom Ford will want a very long discussion."

"John, I think we've got one of the Novelists," a man said, also into his earpiece. "Celine thinks it may be Roman Shirokov. We've applied FRP for analysis, but of course the result's indecisive. Camera 16. What do you think?"

Mordred looked carefully and threw his mind back to Ruby Parker's PowerPoint in E17 that day, the group photo: the guy just off from centre?

Probably.

But then that body-language: a desperate scanning of the locale, the effort to look nonchalant undermined by the obvious terror of being recognised by the wrong people.

More than probably.

Mordred looked at his watch 10.05. "I'm pretty sure that's him. Virender, I need you to bring up the Russian agents for me, please, one by one. Give me five seconds on each, no more. Monitor one."

As spy followed spy in quick succession, Mordred relaxed a notch. The Russians had over-populated the area: from now on, because they couldn't look in all directions at once, every agent would assume that every new male arrival had been there a while and was another of their own. Whoever choreographed this had miscalculated: there were just too many agents in place.

Of course, it would probably be different when a woman arrived, especially a lone woman. Unless it was Kseniya Yumasheva.

"10.07, John," Annabel said from above the National Gallery. "I'm sending my people in. Pairs, five at a time."

He looked at his watch again. Yes, she was right. As agreed: she was closest, and they couldn't all pour out at once, fifty or sixty agents. There had to be a gradual influx.

"Roger," he told her.

"John, take a look at Monitor 14," a woman's voice said. "Pasha Domogarov. And presumably, that's Valentina Morozova with him."

"I've got Olga Borisovna Pamfilova entering from St Martin-in-the-Fields," someone said.

"John, would you like more boots on the ground?" Phyllis said into his earpiece.

"Yes, please," he said. "Sorry, I meant, 'Roger'."

A male voice: "John, we've a woman approaching from the junction of Haymarket and Pall Mall. In some pain, apparently, the way she's walking. Monitor 12. FRP suggests she's Kseniya Yumasheva."

My God, it was - that was her!

They had as many as they needed. No point prolonging the agony. Act now, and they could net five or six Novelists and forestall any histrionics when the Russians realised they'd been outmanoeuvred.

"Alec," he said as calmly as he could. "You're nearest. Grab Kseniya."

"Roger," Alec said. "Moving in."

"John, we've got problems," Annabel said, apparently levelly.

But she rarely got emotional and, over the years, he'd got used to gauging the precise timbre of her voice. Right now, she was freaking out.

He scanned all twenty-four monitors almost simultaneously.

Bloody hell. Six or seven GU officers were signalling to each other, talking into lapel microphones. In their sight lines: Pasha Domogarov.

They were moving in.

"All units into Trafalgar Square," he said. "Repeat: all units into Trafalgar Square."

He looked at the monitors. Annabel ran towards Domogarov but too late. A man glanced him hard; he looked in astonishment at his arm, then crumpled.

Valentina Morozova seemed to register what had happened with shock, then with revulsion, then as if she'd expected it from time immemorial. She yelled. She fought off two GU agents, then punched Annabel, who'd arrived to defend her. Then she ran.

Five vans screeched to halts at different points of the perimeter of the Square. Agents exited in in bulletproof vests and pointed guns. People screamed.

The Russians looked at each other then began to walk away.

"Stop them!" Mordred yelled.

"We've been countermanded," Alec said through his earpiece. "We're supposed to let them go. Shit! Is Pasha Domogarov dead? I presume that's what happened to him? Annabel?"

"Confirmed," Annabel came back.

"We've got three of the Novelists," Alec said. "Enough."

"What the hell?" Mordred said. "Where's Valentina?"

"We're on her tail," Alec said.

When Valentina Morozova registered that her lover had been glanced by someone, she knew immediately what had happened. Her nightmares had finally come true, just as, if she was honest with herself, she'd always expected. She filled with the strength of Hercules and began punching: two men first, then a woman in a suit.

After that, she was leaving the Square. She might as well have been flying for all she knew or cared. She was invincible at the very point in her life when invincibility was a pointless add-on. Just as everything would be now.

She ran and ran. Ten seconds? Ten minutes? She rounded a corner and fell over and grazed her knees and palms, and sobbed.

A London taxi stood in front of her, otherwise the road was more or less empty. The back door opened and a man stepped into the street. Well-built, splenetic-looking, with close-cropped silver hair. Russian. Somehow, she knew he was Russian.

Then she saw she was surrounded. Men on all sides. All the same nationality as her.

"Get in," the silver-haired man said.

She went into battle. She'd done it in Trafalgar Square. She could do it again.

But then they closed on her. Someone struck her hard from behind – simple as that, my God, so much for her warrior spirit! - and everything went black. The last thing she remembered was laughing at herself.

Chapter 22: What Valentina Did Next

When Bryzgalov got Valentina Morozova onto the back seat of the taxi – no need to put her into the trunk: she was out cold, and it'd only set hurdles later – he waited till his two subordinates climbed in beside him then told the driver to pull away at a leisurely pace: anything else would send even more alarm bells ringing. This was the same car that had ferried Kseniya from her overnight stop in Borehamwood, and the nurse was sitting impassively in the same place she'd been throughout.

"Shall I give her an injection, Commander?" the nurse said. "We don't want her waking up halfway there."

"Leave it," Bryzgalov said. "We need to bring her round as soon as possible once we're back, and I don't want her reactions affected by drugs. We had enough of that with Kseniya Igorevna. We can't afford to lose any more time."

He'd anticipated that the British might – *might* just - turn up, and he'd made contingency plans for a swift getaway. But only on the theoretical principle of never underestimating your opponent. He hadn't expected to have to fall back those plans, not seriously.

Now he was furious, and for the first time in decades, slightly scared. God, talk about *ambushed!* How the hell had the British known they were coming? Given the number of bodies they piled in, they must have known *everything!* There'd be expulsions in Kensington Palace Gardens for sure, followed by the usual round of tit-for-tats, all very truculent, both sides pointing their chins at each other. But when it had all apparently blown over then, back in Moscow, behind closed doors, heads would quietly begin to roll. Beginning, almost certainly, with his.

Well, *what went wrong at Trafalgar Square* would have to wait. Right now, the priority was escape. He called the other members of his team and told the driver to take Route A. They made their way out of Central London, changed cars three times in covered locations, moved into and out of buildings, separated and reformed. They couldn't be certain of not being on a GCHQ radar – these days, no one at all could - but when they arrived back in Borehamwood, they could honestly say they'd exhausted the manual. If the British caught them now, they had no technical reason to reproach themselves.

The driver pulled the car onto the drive. Bryzgalov got out in a hurry and ran into the house. The two men transferred Valentina to Kseniya's wheelchair and took her inside. They laid her on the sofa in the living room and settled gloomily into armchairs. The nurse went to get a bowl of hot water and some disinfectant. She examined Valentina cursorily, lifting her head and checking her breathing.

"She's got a nasty bump, that's all," she said. "But there's no bleeding. Give her twenty minutes."

"Let's hope she wakes up before the British get here," one of the men quipped darkly.

"If that happens, then so be it," the nurse replied. "As God wills matters, we did our best. Where's Commander Bryzgalov?"

"Upstairs," the first man said.

"On the phone's my guess," the second said. "To his superiors. Not a conversation I'd like to be having right now."

"If you can even call it a conversation," the first said. He drew his index finger across his throat.

His Excellency Feodor Pisemsky sat waiting for Bryzgalov's phone call at his desk in his office overlooking the street. He had a variety of contacts at all levels, so he already knew Trafalgar Square had been a barely qualified catastrophe. They'd lost Kseniya, yet they'd managed to 'eliminate' – horrible word - Pasha Domogarov and 'capture' Valentina Morozova.

War terminology. Stupid terminology. The vocabulary of a neurotic nation with an unwarranted inferiority complex.

He was angry, but not with Bryzgalov. Russia was supposed to be a civilised country. Why the hell was it always involved in petty games of one-upmanship? Now 'answers' would be demanded at the highest level. 'Answers' to questions only idiots and children ever thought to ask.

His phone rang. "Yes?"

"Your Excellency? Commander - "

"I know who it is, Yuri. And I know what happened. I've heard none of your men were taken. Is that true?"

"The British seemed eager not to… complicate matters. Domogarov's dead. It's regrettable, of course, but preferable to him falling in to enemy hands. The - "

"We need to stop calling them that, especially since, as you've just implied, they seemed to have deliberately refrained from taking 'prisoners of war'."

"We must have a mole, Your Excellency."

Pisemsky chuckled. "Well, good luck finding him or her. After today, I'm going to be down to a skeleton staff. In the medium to long term, I'll be replaced. You'll probably be first out of the door."

"I know! And that's what I'll tell everyone! A traitor! Someone within the embassy leaked our plan! What other explanation is there?"

"Maybe you need to start looking for suspects then. Who was in the know? You had quite a few men out there today. Any one of them could be your traitor."

"I will find out."

"Of course you will," the ambassador replied sarcastically. "Your job depends on it. Although some people might say whatever you discover now, it'll be too little, too late. You should have been ahead of events, not clearing up yesterday's mess. I understand you have Valentina Morozova, is that right?"

"She's downstairs, unconscious."

"You need to find out what she knows as soon as possible. Has she been sedated?"

"No, I was very careful about that. Unfortunately, she and Domogarov were together when we killed him. She might not be cooperative."

"Wake her up, give her something to eat and drink, be nice to her. Make out it was the British who killed him. Do what we did with Kseniya Igorevna: tell her she'll be saving the others' lives if she cooperates. Keep quiet about the British having got away with … however many they got away with. How many was it? I mean, not including Kseniya."

"We don't know. We have to assume the worst, of course."

"Do you think Kseniya knows Domogarov's dead? It might make her more inclined to help the British."

"The British will have told her. They'll have told her we did it. They'll have shown her the CCTV."

The ambassador sighed. "Yes, of course."

"The game's only up if Valentina Morozova knows of a more detailed version of the plan. If Domogarov didn't tell her, he probably didn't tell anyone. We agreed that. Get her up, calm her down and get the lie detector on her. I can't believe I'm talking like this. Other ambassadors don't do this sort of thing. Not remotely."

"We like to do things differently in Russia," Bryzgalov said. in a tone that suggested he was equally fed up.

An hour later, Valentina Morozova sat at the kitchen table with a digital recorder in front of her. Two rows of empty cupboards ran the lengths of two walls, with a sink and a cooker on opposite sides. The blinds had been drawn on the single window to her left. Every surface was covered in dust. The two men who'd been present when she'd awoken sat on a low bench against a door, looking curious, as if they'd seen this sort of thing before, but they thought something unexpected might happen this time. Thirty minutes earlier, the nurse had declared her fit to be interviewed. She'd been offered bread and water, which she'd refused; she'd also declined to speak. So she expected to be assaulted at some point. She was determined not to break.

Commander Bryzgalov sat on the chair directly facing her. He introduced himself and said he needed her to answer a few questions. "Look, Valentina," he went on immediately. "I know what's probably going through your mind now, but when Director Kuznetsov hired you, you knew you were coming to work for the FSB. You knew you were working on an intelligence project. No one forced you. You were well paid. But those sorts of things require discretion. When we hear, therefore, that you've all left Russia – all of you at once – and that you're heading for the West, that's naturally going to provoke a chase. What did you expect? Did you think we'd just let you go? Three of you have died now, four if we count Yuliyr Edgardovna. I don't want to be killing civilians any more than you do, but I've got to put the interests of Russia first. Kseniya realised that, which is why she led us to you."

She forgot her resolve not to speak. *"Kseniya?"*

"Obviously, if you think about it. But she did it for *you*. We didn't compel her. She did it to save *all* of you. We interrogated her in the embassy. She told us something that, if true, suggested we might be able to stop the killings; something indicating that perhaps so far we'd been... over-zealous. Look, we didn't want to *kill* Pasha. We simply wanted to talk to him, find out how much he'd told the rest of you."

"What do you mean?" She was talking despite herself now. She noticed the expressions of her two-man audience. Admiration for Bryzgalov: he'd got her to open up.

"Look, Valentina, four of your original twelve-person team are now dead. That leaves eight. In a few months, unless *you* cooperate – and I mean *you* personally: you're the person we most wanted to speak to after we'd talked to Kseniya: even more than we wanted to talk to Pasha – all twelve of you will probably end up dead. You can help us. If you answer our questions today, you can save eight lives, including your own."

"I don't care about my life any more."

"But you care about the others, right? You must do." He slipped a group photo of the twelve Novelists across the table, all smiling.

"Where did you get this?" she asked.

"No mystery. One of you must have left it behind in Moscow. You left just about everything else, although you did steal something very valuable from the Ongoing Cases room on the Lubyanka Building's fifth floor. Which I could arrange to be overlooked, in return for your cooperation."

"Why should I believe you?"

He laughed. "What choice do you have? It's not as if you can walk out of here."

She swallowed, rubbed her eyes. "Where are we? Is this someone's kitchen? Why are we in someone's kitchen?"

"Because we're in Britain, and we don't have access to bespoke interview rooms. Concentrate on the matter in hand, Valentina. You asked why you should believe me. I said you've no choice. But put it another way. I don't *have* to promise you *anything*. Not a fig. I could easily get you to speak by removing your fingers with a bolt cutter, then your toes, one every hour. You'd talk soon enough. Everyone does. So instead of asking why I should keep my promise, ask yourself why I'm promising anything at all. How *could* I have ulterior motives, when I can get whatever I might want by other means? You're a Russian citizen, and so are your friends on the run. Whatever you might think about me, I don't like killing my fellow countrymen, and I go to great lengths to avoid it when I have to. Including making genuine promises. I'm an honest man. Come on, Valentina, I'm asking you to help save the lives of your friends. I don't want them to die either. All you have to do is answer a few simple questions. We'll hook you up to a lie detector, so we'll know whether you're telling the truth or not. From your point of view, it'll prevent us trying to extract information from you that you don't possess. But we already know you have limited knowledge. We know, for example, that you don't know where any of the other members of your Moscow group are, because Kseniya told us you don't. You've got nothing to hide, so you've got nothing to lose, think of it like that."

She blinked slowly.

"Come on," he said. "Yes?"

She swallowed bitterly and nodded.

"Good girl. That's a *good* girl!"

The two men on the bench stood up leisurely, like they'd long foreseen this, and left the room. When they returned, it was with the lie detector. They attached sensors to her chest, arms and fingers, explained roughly what they were doing, then stood by the monitor.

Bryzgalov asked her to tell him her name, date of birth, nationality, how many fingers he was holding up, and to make six true factual statements about herself, no matter how trivial. "The colour of your eyes, for example," he said.

The men nodded their approval. "It's working," one of them said.

Bryzgalov gestured for them to return to their bench. "Are you ready?" he asked Valentina.

She nodded.

"What was the task you and your team were working on?" he asked. "In Moscow, under Director Kuznetsov?"

"We were assigned to devise the next phase in the disruption of Russia's enemies abroad," she replied.

"And what did you eventually come up with?"

"A plan to bring the BBC – the British Broadcasting Corporation - under the control of people more attuned to Russian values."

"And who came up with this idea?"

"All of us. The whole team. It was Communism in the true sense of the word. Public-spirited intellectuals working together for the common good, and no thoughts about individual glory."

"Explain the detail of that plan," he said.

"There wasn't any," she replied. "There wasn't time. It was all very general."

"You know no more about it than what you've just told us?" Bryzgalov said.

"No," she replied.

"After you'd left Moscow with Pasha Domogarov, to go on the run, did the two of you ever discuss the plan?"

"No."

The two men had got to their feet again. They were staring at the monitor.

"Are you sure?" Bryzgalov said.

"Yes. Why would we? We had other things to consider. When I think about it, it wasn't even a plan. Just a vague idea. 'Take over the BBC.' I'm assuming Kuznetsov gave it the go-ahead."

"Why do you say that?"

"Because you'd hardly be going to all this trouble otherwise."

"We might be," Bryzgalov said defensively. "But it's not the BBC we're planning on taking over. It's the British government."

She laughed.

"What's so funny?" Bryzgalov said.

"Sorry, I couldn't help myself," she replied. "I'd have thought it was in Russia's interests to have a bunch of complete incompetents in Parliament. Why on earth are you thinking of changing that?"

Everyone chuckled.

"She's been telling the truth throughout," one of the men said.

"In that case, I think we can take a break for the moment," Bryzgalov said. "Thank you, Valentina. You've been very helpful."

Ten minutes later, Bryzgalov sat alone in the second floor bedroom where no one could overhear him. He took his phone out, went to *Feodor Pisemsky* and pressed Call. It rang just once.

"News?" the ambassador said.

"Good. Very good. On two fronts. Firstly, she knows nothing whatsoever about an accelerated version. Secondly, she'd obviously worked out that there *is* such a version, and she subtly challenged me to confirm it. I thought I'd better err on the side of caution – what if she's captured? – so I fed her an alternative story. I said we were thinking of taking over *the British government.*"

The ambassador chuckled. "I'm assuming the 'good news' is a little more substantial than that you had a gentle laugh at her expense."

"It got me thinking. What to do with her now? Neither of us wants to kill her. But we can use her. I propose we fill her mind with false information and arrange for the British to 'capture' her."

"Yes, yes, I see. And is there an 'accelerated' version of this plan, Commander?"

"One of us invents, writes up and prints off the story we want her to believe. Five hundred words should be sufficient. We get her to read it through, then we hook up to the lie detector and ask her to confirm she's never seen it before. All we're really doing is fixing in her mind the idea that it's real. Then we start being nasty to her. For example, I tell her we've been lying to her, and that we're going to kill the other Novelists, and that we're shipping her back to Russia where she'll probably be executed, etcetera, etcetera. Finally, we drive her back to the embassy. The British will be watching, and they'll want to get hold of her – now they've got Kseniya, probably for exactly the same reasons we did: see if she knows about a more detailed version – and they'll be smarting after they lost us last time."

"So, we make as if we're leaving for the airport with her, allow them to intercept us, abduct Valentina - "

"And she's bitter and resentful enough to want to tell them everything. Luckily, she's now in a position to do just that."

The ambassador took a deep breath then expelled it. "Okay. It's desperate, but we're in a desperate position."

Chapter 23: Harmless Fun or Dangerous Liaisons?

From the perspective of MI7, the Trafalgar Square operation was a qualified success, despite the loss of Pasha Domogarov and the disappearance of Valentina Morozova. Three of the Novelists were taken into safe custody so it seemed reasonable to anticipate an intelligence breakthrough in the imminent future.

The following morning, *The Daily Mail* devoted its cover headline, and pages three, four, five and fifteen to the murder of Mobeen Dhanial. Other news channels joined the bandwagon, and the *Times, Telegraph* and *Guardian* linked his killing to yesterday's mysterious 'disturbance' in Trafalgar Square, in which unconfirmed reports said a man had been knifed and Russian agents – again, identified by Bellingcat – were pictured fleeing the scene just as the area was invaded by what looked to be plain clothes police officers. All very 'spooky', in the worst sense.

From the diplomatic point of view, nothing much could be done about Pasha Domogarov or Valentina Morozova: both presented the same problem as Elizaveta, two days ago: they were in the country illegally and their identities couldn't be officially established. The killing had been carried out with ruthless professionalism by a man whose face never quite appeared on CCTV.

Mobeen Dhanial was a different matter: he was a British citizen. The government had to be seen to be doing something, and at noon, the Foreign Secretary summoned the Russian ambassador to Whitehall and served expulsion orders on twenty-three embassy staff and the Defence Attaché. Other European countries were rumoured to be preparing similar measures.

Orville Peterson applied to the Speaker of the House of Commons for an emergency debate under the rules of Standing Order 24. His spectacularly wide-ranging three-minute speech linked Dhanial's killing to his blog, his sense of being hounded by the BBC and the death of 'Victim X' (a term Peterson, with one eye on the headlines, invented for the occasion) in Trafalgar Square. Some honourable members tut-tutted, but Peterson's aim, as he frankly admitted, later that day on *Newsnight*, was to raise important questions about the BBC in people's minds, and pile further pressure on *Panorama*. Tom Ford wrote an article for *The Evening Standard* in which he attacked Terry McNamara, the BBC's DG, and in which he innovatively used the term 'row' of relations between the Corporation and the government.

By this time, MI7 had spoken to the three Novelists it had apprehended. And, much to its surprise, it seemed Ford and Peterson's forebodings might not be so wide of the mark, after all.

After her arrest on Pall Mall, Kseniya Yumasheva was taken to a secure hospital in Middlesex for a medical. Olga Pamfilova and Roman Shirokov went straight to Thames House. The plan was that Mordred should interview all three. His view was that, unless someone in MI7 alienated them, they'd probably divulge everything they knew. So Grey needed keeping at a distance; so, probably, did any number of self-styled expert in-house interrogators. Tea and biscuits and possibly a square meal were the order of the day, plus a shower and a change of clothes, plus a friendly face or three. Suki, Bruce and Jonathan were pressed into service, as being considerate, outgoing and, most importantly, roughly the same age. They were told to 'just be themselves'.

Olga Pamfilova was small and athletic-looking twenty-nine-year-old with short red hair and a carefree smile which being a fugitive hadn't managed to sour. Roman Shirokov was four

years her senior with the sort of handsome face romantic novelists always describe as 'chiselled', and prematurely grey hair
around his temples. Both were outraged by the killing of
Pasha Domogarov and thus predisposed to cooperate with
MI7. Kseniya Yumasheva followed their lead. God help her,
she didn't like the west, didn't hold to its values, but the
Kremlin had lied to her. It had no intention – not now, not
ever! - of showing them any mercy whatsoever; in its eyes, all
the 'Novelists' were guilty of treason, and her in particular.
Henceforth, she'd do everything possible to bring it down,
with or without British promises of leave to remain under a
new identity. It deserved to eat its own excrement.

The three all told the same story: they'd been part of a working group, assembled in Moscow over several months, by
Stanislav Viktorovich Kuznetsov, the FSB's Director of Overseas Strategic Affairs, with a brief to devise the second stage in
the obstruction of Russia's enemies abroad. They eventually
came up with a plan to bring the BBC under the control of British people more attuned to Russian values.

More than that, none of them knew, although, according to
Kseniya, Commander Bryzgalov, the GU's chief executive in
Kensington Palace Gardens, believed there was a more detailed version of the plan, and that the group's leader, Pasha
Domogarov knew what it was - presumably why he'd been
killed. Bryzgalov also believed that Valentina Morozova, as
the person Domogarov was most likely to confide in, might
have learned about it. He'd promised Kseniya the killing
would stop if he could just get hold of Domogarov. Instead,
he'd had him murdered in broad daylight.

Two hours after the debrief, Mordred left Kseniya, Olga and
Roman alone with Suki, Bruce and Jonathan and three interpreters. When he looked in on them, through the glass in the
door, after twenty minutes, they looked like they were having
a good time.

Too good? They'd paired off: Roman and Suki, Jonathan and Olga, Bruce and Kseniya. And yes, they were - my God, they were flirting. Everything about all six of them gave them away, like an evening's speed dating, and would you believe it? Here are three couples who've already found their ideals! Record time! Give then a big hand!

Not that he'd ever been speed dating. You probably didn't get applause when you found a match, but he'd seen it on TV. And he knew what happened when two people 'clicked', how they looked at each other. And he was seeing it again, right now.

The interpreters' expressions showed they weren't entirely oblivious to the situation, but also that they thought it was innocent. They were probably right. So far.

Luckily, the interpreters had to write reports for Ruby Parker's consumption. So if they had concerns, they'd record them. Which meant it wasn't his problem.

Nevertheless, even he could see it might *turn into someone's* problem. Should he go in there and put a stop to it?

No.

It sounded crass, but there was too little love in the world right now. They were young. They were having fun. Probably more than the three Russians had experienced in a long time. Let them be.

His phone rang. He moved away from the door, forgot about the three blossoming couples, and looked at his screen. *Tom Ford.*

Bloody hell. Still, he'd been expecting it. He picked up.

"Where the hell have you been?" Ford said. "I've been trying and trying. I've spent about an hour pressing redial."

Mordred laughed. "Sorry, I've only just noticed the message: two hundred and fifty missed calls."

"You're a secret agent. I'm not going to treat you like you're obliged to tell me what you've been doing, John, but we *did* have a deal. I take it you've now been to Broadcasting House.

You're at least morally obliged to tell me what you found out there."

"Not quite. I agreed to help you investigate Mobeen Dhanial's death, but we all know who killed him now. As you surmised – and I admit, I was wrong, you weren't: you were spot on, in fact – it was the Russians. You may be right that the Russians have a vested interest in seeing *Panorama* get screened, but there's not the slightest evidence that the BBC's collaborating with them. No one in their right mind could conceivably think that. So it won't be a surprise when I tell you that nothing I learned at Broadcasting House threw any light whatsoever on why Dhanial died."

"Who did you meet? Did you see Big Tez himself?"

"He poured tea for me."

"So you're not going to tell me what this episode of *Panorama*'s about?"

"I signed a non-disclosure agreement. Which I admit would involve me in a conflict of interest if I'd discovered anything to indicate the BBC had a hand in Mobeen Dhanial's death. But I didn't."

"Yet McNamara must know the Russians want *Panorama* to go out. Bit shabby of him, wouldn't you say, still going ahead with it? I mean, he must know he's doing Moscow's dirty work. Not to mention it being disrespectful to Mobeen. Think of the Dhanial family. Typical, though. Typical new liberal: put so-called universal-duty-to-abstract-truth above good neighbourliness, compassion and patriotism every time. Citizens of nowhere, the bloody lot of them. I say 'them'. You're no better, John. I'm disappointed in you."

"I'm sorry, but - "

Ford hung up.

Once Kseniya Yumasheva, Olga Pamfilova and Roman Shirokov had been exhaustively questioned, they were moved to a heavily guarded secret location in south London. Twenty-eight hours after Trafalgar Square, Ruby Parker called a meeting in H14 on the top floor of Thames House. Present: John and Phyllis Mordred, Edna Watson, Ian Leonard, Annabel al-Banna, Alec Cunningham. They sat around four tables arranged in a rectangle. Outside, clouds scudded by and a wind shook the trees. 2pm on a cold, but intermittently sunny afternoon. Primary topic for discussion: putative existence of an FSB-originated plan, with presently unknown 'further detail', to bring the BBC under the control of Russian interests.

Alec was the first to comment. "For 'more detailed version'," he said, "read, 'something else entirely.'"

"Are you suggesting they're trying to pull the wool over our eyes?" Ruby Parker asked.

"Not them, no," Alec said. "I think they're being used by the Kremlin to pull wool over our eyes. Which is academic really, because what it amounts to in either case, is us being duped. This is what I think happened. The Russians devised a plan to pull off some big act of sabotage in the West. They assembled a team to work on it, and this group of people came up with a workable plan. We'll call this lot Team A. But the Russians were scared we might find out. To safeguard against that, they put another team together – a dummy team - "

"Let's call them Team B," Phyllis put in.

"And this team also came up with a plan. And the Kremlin put the fear of God into them and chased them across Europe in the hope of diverting our attention. Sooner or later, the calculation was that we'd pick one or two of them up. They'd tell us all about Plan B, and we'd frantically investigate it. Meanwhile, Plan A would be unfolding. But because we were so focused on Plan B, we'd miss it. Classic false flag."

"Don't you think there would be more surface detail to Plan B?" Annabel said. "I mean, assuming the Russians expected us to take it seriously. They wouldn't hide that detail from Team B itself."

"There would be detail to it if it was real or if it was fake," Ian said. "The lack of that's a problem in either case."

"But there was – or is – detail," Alec said. "Pasha Domogarov supposedly knew it. For some reason, he didn't tell the others."

"Maybe he stumbled into the discovery that the whole thing's an elaborate hoax," Edna said. "I mean, back in Moscow, sometime before his working group completed its assignment. Perhaps he thought that by devising an ersatz detailed version and presenting it to his superiors, but keeping it from his colleagues, he was protecting the team. Something just clever enough to make the bosses think he'd done his job conscientiously, but not really prioritising practicality."

"Again, he might have been trying to protect his team in either case," Ian said. "Whether it was real or not."

"Isn't it much more likely," Phyllis said, "that Orville Peterson's theory is correct? In your report, John, you said that, in The Hudson Bay that day, he claimed the Russians were using *Panorama* to undermine confidence in the British government. Let's take that a step further, and add what *Panorama* itself told you, the other day. The British government collaborated with the Russians and the Belarusians to make refugees disappear. Now, suppose the Russians always knew that one day, they could reveal that, and use it to destabilise our government?"

"Except I can't see that being much more than a major embarrassment nowadays," Mordred said. "It wouldn't force an election."

"The government's currently got a single seat majority in the Commons," Edna said. "Anything's possible."

"But the Russians couldn't have foreseen that when they began working on Plan A," Alec said.

"They were lucky," Edna replied. "And good luck happens."

Alec shrugged. "What's your point?"

"Think for a moment about the Russians taking over the BBC," Phyllis said, "or filling it with sympathisers. Firstly, who fits the bill? Because Tom Ford certainly doesn't. Right-wing he might be, but he doesn't trust Vladimir Putin. Secondly, how is a hard-hitting *Panorama* documentary going to hurt the BBC? It isn't. The government might well feel mortified, enough even to want revenge. But that'll pass. These things always do, especially in democracies: the culprits resign, or they're thrown out, or they retire or, in the end, they're just replaced by someone up-and-coming and younger. Meanwhile, no one's going to tolerate government interference with the BBC as a result of it telling truth to power. That's partly what it's there for."

There was a knock at the door. A middle-aged man in a suit put his head round, looking diffident. Ruby Parker left, closing herself and the man out.

"I'm not saying any of the three 'Novelists' are lying," Alec went on, as if nothing had just happened. "Quite the contrary. They'd never get a deliberate fib past John. But from what I've heard, they came looking for John. Which means someone in Russia must have directed them that way."

"That would have been Elizaveta Khamatova," John said.

"Supposedly because someone selected her to seduce you," Alec went on. "Which is another tall story. I'm not saying she didn't become infatuated with you. Obviously, she did, but that was probably an unintended, and unwanted, side-effect of the team being focused on you at some point. Why would anyone send Team B specifically to meet you? Because they know you're a living lie-detector. If Plan B gets past you, it gets past everyone."

"It's a good theory, Alec," Annabel said, "but it's speculation."

"But don't you see?" Alec replied. "That's exactly my point. Speculation's all we have. We've got three of the so-called Novelists giving us their full cooperation, and we *still* don't know a thing. We're still hoping to pick up Valentina Morozova – God knows where she's gone – but we've no reason to believe that's going to improve our intel one jot."

Ruby Parker came back in and resumed her seat.

"Valentina Morozova's just arrived at the Russian embassy," she said. "From what aerial reconnaissance suggests, they're getting ready to move her to the airport under cover of two of their expelled diplomats. This time we'll be ready for them."

"I was just saying," Alec said, "I'm not sure that'll improve matters."

Ruby Parker nodded. "You may be right. We'll see."

Chapter 24: The Further Adventures of Valentina

Sunday morning, 7am. The gates of the Russian embassy opened with an electronic hum and a black Toyota Camry emerged at a crawl. It accelerated onto Kensington High Street, then turned right onto Addison Road. It slowed for a junction and, just as it was about to turn north, a Ford Fiesta came out of nowhere and rammed it side-on. Two youths emerged, carrying guns.

The Russians didn't waste time asking what had happened. None were armed, and they hadn't thought it necessary to bring a bodyguard. They got out with their hands up, looking scared. The thieves told them to remove their jewellery and put it in a bag, then searched the car, and instructed the driver to open the boot. He tried to argue, but caved in when - as the official report later put it - he was 'manhandled'.

The boot contained an unconscious white woman in her early forties, bound and gagged. The robbers lost some of their cool. They raised their voices, manhandled the driver a little more, and forced him to transfer her to their car. Then they drove off at speed.

Two hours later, they arrived at a flat-roofed brick building within an industrial estate in Orpington, where four British intelligence officers under Alec's supervision were anxiously awaiting their delivery. Also in place to assist were Kseniya Yumasheva, Olga Pamfilova and Roman Shirokov.

After a medical, Valentina Morozova was transferred to a bed in a room of her own, and allowed to revive in her own time. It took her four hours to fully recover, then two trained counsellors explained what had happened to her through an interpreter. Finally, the three Russians were admitted to see her, while everyone else retired. An hour followed in which she wept and accused her friends and argued with them and finally forgave them and reconciled herself to her new status and joined forces with Kseniya, Olga and Roman. The Kremlin had killed Domogarov, it had lied to gain her trust, then, once it had got what it wanted, it had shown its true colours: it was petty-minded and vindictive. Now she owed it nothing but vengeance.

She turned out to be the keystone. Her Russian interrogators had made the fatal mistake of assuming she knew more than she did, then when she denied it, testing her, in specific ways, significantly beyond the limits of her need to know. In short, they'd inadvertently taught her things she couldn't otherwise have learned.

What she'd discovered was roughly what Alec had hypothesised. The true plan was to destabilise the British government. Several years ago, Russia and Belarus had agreed to the return of a large number of indirectly-state-sponsored prostitutes (the precise nature of either government's involvement was never ascertained), all of whom had arrived in Britain as refugees. Once back in their countries of origin, these individuals had been discreetly murdered, and their governments had launched a sweeping purge of what it called 'anti-social elements'. One underlying purpose of the whole exercise had been to keep records – encrypted phone conversations, texts, emails, memos, human intelligence sources including Russian and Belarusian ministers, secret recordings of secret meetings – with a view to incriminating the British government at some indeterminate point in the not-too-distant future. The declining efficacy of the Web Brigades had triggered a consensus that now was the time.

Everything now made sense.

The obvious next step was for MI7 to fact-check *Panorama*, but there were two interrelated problems with that, both of which had already been acknowledged: firstly, the BBC had highly effective fact-checking mechanisms of its own, and secondly, even the slightest intervention might present the murky appearance of collusion with the government's party political interests.

Having no choice usually means having to settle for second best. All fact-checking would simply have to be done *post hoc*, after the programme had been broadcast. For the moment, the focus must be on what the Russians specifically hoped to achieve after the storm cloud had burst. A list was drawn up of government ministers (a) known to be sympathetic to the Kremlin, and (b) who had recently accepted Russian 'hospitality' in the shape of VIP tickets to sporting or cultural events, or gone on 'overseas fact-finding missions' at Moscow's expense. It turned out to be longer than expected.

So for the moment, it looked like a simple matter of waiting. But then, at 7am on Monday morning, Ruby Parker got three phone calls in quick succession: from the Home Secretary, The Metropolitan Police Commissioner and the BBC's Director General. There had been a burglary. One of a pair of copies of the master tape of Monday's programme had been taken from the top floor of Broadcasting House. The thief had been a professional, fully acquainted with the whereabouts of the building's CCTV internal and external, and adept at picking locks. He – or she – had entered the building with a forged identity. You didn't just come up with that sort of thing on a whim. In short, everything about the incursion screamed Intelligence Services. And in this case, Red department was the only player on the field.

It wasn't the first time Ruby Parker had been unjustly accused, and it wouldn't be the last. In general, the best way of showing you were innocent of something like this was to find the culprit. Then the burglar had to be burgled. But in this case, that was an incredibly tall order. The first task was to explore the alternatives.

For the second time in two days, John and Phyllis Mordred, Edna Watson, Ian Leonard, Annabel al-Banna, Alec Cunningham sat around a rectangular arrangement of tables in H14 with Ruby Parker at its head. This was an early morning meeting. *Panorama* was due to go out that night.

"My money's on Grey," Alec said. "I know they're officially off the case, but that doesn't necessarily mean anything. Access to a master tape would give them evidence we don't have, and possibly allow them to wrest back control of the case. Knowledge is power."

"They're off the case at Black's instruction," Ruby Parker replied. "They'd go against that at their absolute peril. It wouldn't be worth their while, and no politician could persuade them otherwise."

"It's obviously *some* kind of professional," Annabel said. "If not MI7, then the next likely candidate is some private security employee working unofficially on behalf of the government. The Home Secretary may have been among the first to cry foul, but that may be simply a smokescreen."

"If that's the case, it's lost," Phyllis said. "We can't go burgling the Home Secretary's office."

"Annabel's right, though," Edna said. "It's got to be someone in the government. Otherwise, the recipient would have put it online to speed up the government's embarrassment. It'll have been stolen so a bunch of lawyers can watch it, steal a march on Tuesday's headlines. The trouble is, we've got quite a big pool of possible suspects: twenty-three cabinet ministers, thirty-six junior ministers, and three hundred and eleven Conservative MPs. It could theoretically be with any one of them."

"Not to mention a hundred and eighty thousand party members," Alec said, "some of whom might well have the gung-ho and the means to pull something like this off."

"It would have to be deniable," John said. "A member of the Cabinet sending a thief into Broadcasting House probably *would* bring the government down, in a way *Panorama* itself probably won't. The culprit would be forever disgraced. That would be a pointless risk."

"Someone might be stupid enough to take it, though," Edna said. "There are always lots of chancers in the British government."

"Let's not over-complicate matters," Alec said. "Think Tom Ford and Orville Peterson. We know they wanted it. At one point, they thought John might get it for them. He didn't. They tried an alternative method. This time, it worked."

"Do we know what either of them have been doing since the burglary?" Ian asked.

"Sitting at home, watching *Panorama* on TV?" Alec said.

"It would be a waste of manpower to have them watched," Ruby Parker said. "Closing the stable door after the horse has bolted. None of us expect them to take receipt of something in broad daylight, and certainly not at this late stage."

"And they'll know that," Annabel said, "If either of them has it, the likelihood is they'll have hidden it somewhere ultra-safe."

"They'd have to have worked very quickly," John said. "Tom Ford rang me the other day. He said he was 'disappointed' in me, and it didn't sound like he was acting. Whoever stole this tape, they were professional, with an insider's knowledge. If Tom Ford or Orville Peterson had those sorts of contacts, they wouldn't have bothered coming to me, and, once I'd let them down, they wouldn't be upset, they'd just brush it off in the knowledge that they already have an alternative plan. And they'd have had it in the pipeline long before last night."

"Maybe they did," Alec said.

"So who's their inside person?" John said. "Peterson and Ford are effectively enemies of the BBC. How would they have made that sort of a contact?"

"An embittered employee?" Annabel said.

"There must be better, less difficult ways of getting your revenge," John said. "With that sort of access, whoever it was would have to be high-level, with an affection for the Conservative Party. Which just doesn't sound very likely."

"As a profile, it should be fairly easy to run through an identification program," Ian said.

"Do you have a positive suggestion, John?" Phyllis asked.

He thought for a moment. "No."

"How about Brigitte Crevier?" she said. "She could almost certainly afford something like that. And right-wingers often have ex-services contacts. She might well know someone who could enter and exit a building without being seen."

"Brigitte Crevier has no interest in helping the Conservative Party," John said. "She's only interested in finding out why Mobeen Dhanial was killed. Getting hold of the tape a few days early wouldn't help, and she'd be risking her political career."

"A criminal record's not always a stigma in right-wing circles," Phyllis said. "Not if it means you've been mixing with hard cases and thumbing your nose at the establishment."

"She claims she's not right-wing," Mordred said. "For what it's worth. She's an 'Old Liberal'."

"I've read John's report," Alec said. "I'm inclined to agree with her. Especially since she says she's anti-racist."

"What's your point?" Phyllis asked.

"That a criminal record may not be to her advantage in the way such a thing might be to, say, a white supremacist," Alec said.

"We shouldn't rule her out," Ruby Parker said, "but on the whole, if John's right, there's insufficient motive. She's back in Paris, and that needn't mean anything, but if she's involved in some sort of conspiracy, I'm inclined to think she'd stay closer to where it's being played out. Okay, this is what we're going to do. Annabel and Alec, I want you to get into Tom Ford's house; Phyllis and Edna, I'd like you to do Peterson's. Daylight hours, we'll just have to pray for an opportunity. John, I'd like you to visit the Director General, see if you can put his mind at rest regarding our non-involvement. I'll make you an appointment now. Ian, I'd like you to liaise with the police, see what they've dug up."

Chapter 25: Carol's Good Idea and Alec's Moral Dilemma

Outside Thames House, Sheila Magnus sat waiting in a 1976 Ford Capri. The bodyguard, a muscular man in his mid-forties, got out to let the passenger into the back.

"I didn't know we did vintage cars," John said as they pulled out into the traffic.

"It's what the bad guys never expect," Sheila replied.

"But we've just pulled out from double red lines in front of MI7 headquarters. Plus, it is fairly conspicuous."

"I don't make the decisions, John, although Vehicle Purchases would probably call it a double bluff. Thank your lucky stars they didn't send me to pick you up in the ice-cream van."

"Seriously? We've got an ice-cream van?"

"Who'd ever think to look for George Smiley or Simon Templar in an ice-cream van? No, Silly, I'm joking."

"It is a nice car, though."

"Agreed. The sort of thing James Bond drove in the old days, when he was Roger Moore."

Mordred half-expected the bodyguard to comment on this. He could see he was suddenly bursting to speak. The rest of the journey passed in tense silence, Bond's actual taste in cars hanging over it like a constipated thundercloud. After thirty minutes, they arrived outside Broadcasting House. Mordred got out, showed a card at the entrance, and presented himself at the front desk.

A long-haired receptionist in her early twenties with 'Carol' on her badge looked him up on her screen.

"I'm afraid the Director General's not available at the moment," she said. "Can I just check the time of your appointment?"

"Ten o'clock."

"Sorry, Mr Mordred, I've got it down here for eleven. Are you sure it's ten?"

"That's what I was definitely told."

She checked again. "Sorry. It must have been moved. I don't know why."

"These things happen. Where should I wait?"

More frowning at the screen. "It says to wait here."

"Is that usual? I mean, for an appointment with the top executive? Sorry, I didn't mean that to sound like, *Do you know who I am, young lady?* I don't mind waiting in the foyer. It's quite interesting. I think I saw Moira Stuart the other day. It's just - "

"It's wonderful! You see all the stars here."

"It's just, I wonder if I've done something wrong."

"Oh, no. He's probably just treating you. Look," she said quietly, "there's Rich Hall. And just behind him, that's Jack Whitehall."

"Whoa. Cool."

"I know! It so is!"

"Okay, I'll sit here. Thank you."

He sat on a bench, took out his phone and called Sheila. "Hi, I'm going to be a bit late. My appointment's been moved to eleven."

"Thank you for letting me know."

They hung up. Reggie Yates went by; then Indira Joshi from *EastEnders*; then Carol Klein, from *Gardeners' World*, sipping what looked like an orange juice, but could easily have been mango or peach. He yawned. Alexander Armstrong went by, *Pointless*.

Eleven o'clock arrived. He returned to Carol at the desk.

"I'm really sorry," she said, "but it's been moved to noon. Your appointment, I mean, obviously. This has never happened before. Something urgent must have come up."

"Or maybe Terry just doesn't want to speak to me."

"Oh, I'm sure that's not the case!"

"Could I go upstairs, see if I can catch him? I only need speak to him for a moment."

"I'm really sorry, Mr Mordred. I've strict instructions to keep you down here. I'm sure he'll be very apologetic when you finally get to see him. Please help yourself to free coffee, by the way. Or anything. Juice, even."

Mordred returned to his previous position on a bench and rang Sheila again.

"Sounds like he's taking the rise," she said. "'Strict instructions to keep you down here'? That sounds suspiciously like the brush-off to me. Sorry, not my place to say. Be angry when you see him, that's my advice. *If*."

"Anyway, sorry to keep you waiting. Again."

"It's all relaxation for me, love. I've had a very good discussion with Jason about the kind of cars James Bond drives – or doesn't - and now I'm doing the Sudoku in *The Mirror*."

"Sounds fun."

"That's right. It isn't. Not remotely. On the other hand, guess who I saw earlier? Anne Reid from *Years and Years*."

"Great."

They talked a bit longer then hung up again. John Humphrys went by. Rachel Parris and Nish Kumar passed in the opposite direction. Midday came.

Carol looked mortified. "I'm really sorry - "

"But Terry can't see me till one."

She swallowed. "Er, yes."

"And you've been given strict instructions to keep me down here in the foyer, right?"

"Er, yes. Sorry."

"What if I just made a break for the lift?"

"I'm really, *really* sorry, but I'd have to call Security."

"The stairs?"

"Same. Security. Really sorry."

He sighed. "Okay."

She leaned forward, looked nervously about her, and whispered, "Look, I've had an idea."

"Sorry?"

"Why don't you pretend to leave, and I could call up and say, 'He's gone now', and then maybe he'll come down – he usually goes out to lunch around this time - and you can pounce."

"You think he's deliberately avoiding me?"

"What do *you* think? Look, I know who you are. You're not a travelling salesman. You're The Ultimate Londoner. I think he *should* see you. Don't quote me."

"I won't."

"Anyway, he's being rude. You had an appointment for ten. Go outside and hide."

"Thank you for your help."

He left the building and stood with his head down where the shadows were deepest under Langham Street tunnel, just off the forecourt. After ten minutes, Terry McNamara emerged, carrying a briefcase and walking briskly.

Just as Mordred was about to make himself known, two men came round the corner from All Souls' Place, just in front of both of them. Something about them stopped Mordred in his tracks.

He watched them for the second's duration it took for Terry McNamara to reach the corner. My God, he and they recognised each other.

But they made no contact. McNamara's body language changed infinitesimally as he registered their presence. Scared. The men stopped and looked hard at him, and he clearly had to make an effort to avoid eye-contact. But they'd met before, that was obvious.

The tension lasted a second, no more, then Terry McNamara turned the corner towards Portland Place. The two men strode purposefully in the opposite direction, back the way they'd come.

Suddenly, Mordred knew who they were. The realisation made his head spin for a second.

They were the men who'd killed Mobeen Dhanial.

He got back in the car.

"Nice to see you," Sheila said.

"To see you nice," he replied. "Back to Thames House, please."

She didn't ask about Terry. Perhaps she thought the details were classified. They probably were. Or would have been, had they existed. He called Tariq.

"John, how lovely to hear from you. How can I help?"

"I've had an idea. I know there supposedly isn't much to see, but I'd like you to get the CCTV of the break-in to Broadcasting House last night. And, to the extent that the intruder does appear, compare his or her dimensions with those of the two men who killed Mobeen Dhanial."

"Sorry, John. Not possible. Not yet, anyway. Where are you now? Anywhere nearby?"

"On my way back to Thames House."

"I've got my hands completely full, that's all."

"What's going on?"

"You know Phyllis and Edna were going into Peterson's house today? Well, they struck gold. He didn't have the tape, but what he did have was a DVD, clearly marked 'Panorama'. At first, we thought it must be a trap – I mean, how clumsy is that? But no: according to Phyllis, it's Conservative Party policy to avoid MP4s where sensitive material's concerned: too easy to duplicate. Anyway, she inserted it into a CD-stroke-DVD drive, extracted the files, blah-de, blah-de, blah. We're analysing it now. And that's the fascinating story of why I'm so busy."

"Okay. But this is also important."

"You think we may be dealing with one of the same guys?"

"Maybe even both, I don't know."

"You're an expert on body-language. If I get you the two sections of footage, you could look at them on your computer, at your desk, with a nice relaxing cup of coffee. It should give you at least an idea. Then we can analyse it in more detail later. How does that sound?"

"It sounds lovely. Thank you."

"No, thank *you*, John. And, assuming that's everything, I sincerely hope you have a safe journey back. Maybe catch you later."

Tariq hung up just as the car stopped in front of Thames House. Mordred checked in at reception, went straight to his desk, turned on his PC and went to his Inbox.

There it was: *The two sections of footage. Good luck!* Tariq al-Banna,

Part of him was disappointed; he'd hoped to call Tariq – *I'm back now, when can you send me those files?*

But Tariq probably wouldn't be flustered. And anyway, when you were a top British spy and the security of the nation depended on you, wasn't it better sometimes to just get on with your job? He downloaded both files and watched them one after the other.

The disappointment of not being able to rile Tariq was compounded by the disappointment of having his hypothesis refuted. Whoever had broken into Broadcasting House – and there wasn't much to go on: a shoulder here, a six-inch diameter bit of back there, occasionally someone walking away in the distance – it didn't look like either of the two men who'd attacked Mobeen Dhanial.

A shame, partly because everything else had fitted so well. Those two guys had known Terry McNamara, so they'd have the requisite insider's knowledge. As GU men, they'd probably also have lock-picking, safe-cracking skills. Perfect... but the bloody stupid facts didn't support it.

He pulled himself up. Never disrespect the facts. He wrote up an account of the night's events for Ruby Parker, then hit send.

Still another nine hours till *Pano*-bloody-*rama* aired. He couldn't just sit on his hands, not after Terry McNamara and the two GU men. He should probably get back to Broadcasting House and find out if Terry was back. Carol would help him out.

Probably. Although she might think she'd already given him a golden opportunity.

How to explain he'd failed to grasp it?

He'd cross that bridge when he came to it.

His phone rang. *Alec.*

He picked up. "Hi."

"Hi," Alec said. "I hope you don't mind, but I'm ringing you for something incredibly trivial, on the face of it. A bit of moral advice. You're the only person I know who thinks about right and wrong before they enter a situation. Most people only think about it when there's a problem."

"Is that meant to be a compliment?"

"Not necessarily, no. A person's strengths and weaknesses are usually the same qualities seen in different circumstances. Sometimes it's a strength, sometimes not. Anyway, I need your help. But only if you have a moment."

"It just so happens that a lead I thought I had has turned out to be dud, so yes. Fire away. Although I'm not promising anything."

"Valentina Leontievna Morozova."

"What about her?"

"I mean – Okay, I'm not sure how to put this, so I'm just going to say the words, and if it comes out a bit mawkish, I want you to think of alternative ways the sentence could have been expressed, and evaluate every single one of them, yes? Here goes. Do you think it would be ethical for me to ask her out on a date? I mean, I know there are other considerations: I'm a spy, she once worked for the FSB, we don't actually know that they haven't something compromising on her, etcetera, but I'm leaving the practical matters to one side for now, because if it can't be morally justified?... I don't know. Do you get what I'm saying? Don't tell anyone else we had this conversation."

"I won't. If you like her, and she's not completely repulsed by you - "

"She isn't. That's the great thing. I know Pasha Domogarov was killed right in front of her eyes, and that's going to take a lot of getting over, although she'd stopped really loving him some time ago, so she says, she definitely liked him a lot. The age gap was too big, you see. I'm more or less exactly the same age as her. But even so, the amount of grief she's dealing with, well, it's not inconsiderable."

"She actually told you all this?"

"When I debriefed her in Orpington, yesterday, yes. We spoke at length about the case, and when she'd told me everything she knew, we got talking a bit more informally. She's very religious, and she's not very enamoured of western liberalism, but then neither am I. She didn't pretend to be something she's not. We really got on. And I'm religious. Cecily and I – that's my third wife, ex- now - never did get back together, but she got me going to church again. Occasionally. Not every week. Not every month, actually. But I do believe in it, Christianity, some bits."

"Is there any possibility Valentina Morozova could have been leading you on? And possibly all of us?"

"We found her bound and gagged in the back of a car. Her supposed boyfriend was killed in front of her. Kseniya Yumasheva and she are big friends, and they both tell completely different stories: Kseniya said the Russians are trying to take over the BBC; Valentina says it's all about weakening the government. If it had been a plot to mislead us, they'd have got their stories straight, and, if they hadn't, they'd be annoyed

with each other for going off-script. But they're not. And finally, we subjected her to a lie detector test."

"Okay, you win."

"So what do you think?"

"I don't think it would be immoral for you to ask her on a
date, Son."

"Thanks, Dad."

"You'll have to run it past Ruby Parker first, though. You
know that, don't you?"

"I'd factored that in, yes. And I'm not the only one. Disturb-
ingly, there's also Suki and Roman Shirokov, Jonathan and
Olga Pamfilova, Bruce and Kseniya Yumasheva. They're all...
I don't know, considering dating. Which, when I think about
it, does look suspiciously like an attempt to infiltrate the British secret services. Only, we're all adults, and we're intelligent
people. Anyway, I'm filing the possible infiltration under
'practical considerations' for now. I was only calling you for
ethical advice. Obviously, pragmatically, you're no use at all."

"Thanks. I better get off the phone now."

They hung up. His phone immediately rang again. *Unknown caller.*

The GU? Already? *Hello, John, we saw you looking at us today,
and we know you know about us and Terry and -*

"Hi," he said.

A woman's voice: "Hello, is this Mr Mordred? Hi, this is
Carol, the receptionist from Broadcasting House. I'm sorry,
you probably think it's a bit cheeky, me just calling you out of
the blue like this, but we've got your number on the system - "

"I was just thinking about you, actually. Sorry, I didn't
mean that in the chat-up sense. I simply meant -"

"It's okay. I've got a boyfriend, and I'm sure you have too. I
mean, or girlfriend. Or I mean... I don't know. The thing is,
the reason I'm calling - "

"Terry's come back? He wants to see me?"

"No."

"Sorry. You speak. I'll just shut up."

"It's very complicated. I shouldn't really be doing this. I've accessed your data without your permission."

"It's fine. I give you permission. Retrospective permission, if that helps. I can come over there and physically sign a form, if you like. What was it you wanted, Carol?"

"How did you know my name? Sorry, obviously I just told you. And it's written on my badge. Not that you can see it now, but you could earlier. Terry hasn't come back, no. I don't know where he is. But someone else in the building urgently wants to speak to you. He knows you were here earlier because he saw you. I don't know why he didn't come and speak to you then, but he didn't. Anyway, he's in a bit of a state, and I felt a bit sorry for him, and so I promised I'd call you. His name's Philip Toussaint-Molloy. He's a *Panorama* producer."

Bloody hell. "Where is he?"

"Here, in the building."

"Is he nearby where you are? Could you put him on?"

"He's gone upstairs, I think. I don't know why. He was here a few moments ago."

"Thanks, Carol. I'm coming over."

He took the lift down to Thames House reception. The stairs would probably have been quicker, but he didn't want to look as if he was in too much of a hurry.

"Where are you going?" Colin asked nervously as he filled in the book. "You can't leave on your own, John. I'm not allowed to let you."

"It's urgent," Mordred said. "I haven't time to arrange a bodyguard."

"But I'll get sacked."

"No, you won't. It doesn't work like that. You warned me; you tried to stop me; I made a dash for the exit. You - "

Annabel and Phyllis emerged from the lift behind and to one side of the desk. Colin turned to face them. He'd obviously donned his beseeching face because Phyllis immediately looked vaguely sorry for him. Annabel, as always, continued to look impassive.

"What's going on?" Phyllis said.

"I need a bodyguard, apparently," John replied.

"You *know* that, John," Annabel told him. "You're not stupid. You should have arranged it before you - "

"Something's just come up," he said. "Right this minute. I can't go into details here."

His phone rang. *Unknown caller.* Bloody hell.

"Hi," he said.

"Hello, John. Terry McNamara. Sorry I couldn't see you this morning: something really important came up. I've spent most of the morning dealing with lawyers, expecting an injunction. I'm here now if you want to see me. I hope you haven't gone off the idea of a *tête-à-tête.*"

"Absolutely not. Give me twenty minutes."

He hung up just as Annabel put her phone in her bag. "We're your bodyguards now," she said. "I've cleared it with Ruby Parker. She wants you to call her on the way over, obviously, explain what's going on. Have you called for a taxi?"

"Not yet." He needed to ring Carol back, find out about Terry. Something didn't feel right.

"Colin, could you see if Sheila or Kevin are available?" Phyllis said.

Colin looked like he could never repay her and Annabel. "Absolutely!"

"Hello," Carol's voice came. "Broadcasting House, how can I help?"

"Hi, Carol, John again. Sorry: Mr Mordred. You called me a few moments ago. Has Terry McNamara come back yet?"

"I haven't seen him, no. I'll just ask Sandra. Hold the line a minute, Mr Mordred."

"Kevin's outside the front door," Phyllis said.

They marched through the exit and got into the car, John and Annabel on the back seat, Phyllis in front. "I'll explain everything on the way," he said.

I'll explain on the way. The biggest cliché in cop history, inserted naturally into an unfolding chain of events. Minor cause for celebration.

Carol: "Hello, Mr Mordred? No, he definitely hasn't returned. I'm sorry."

"Thank you." He hung up. They were driving now. Rain fell. None of them had coats.

"Please could you ring Tariq?" he asked Annabel. "I need him to locate the Director General's mobile. Then I'll call Ruby Parker."

Annabel took out her phone without the slightest quibble, threw back her blonde hair to improve access to her left ear, and pressed call.

Had it been John on the phone, Tariq might well have claimed to be too busy, or cited some legal issue, or otherwise hummed and hawed, but he tended to stand rigidly to attention when his wife was around. Mind you, so did everyone. She was Annabel.

"Tariq, I need you to locate someone's mobile phone for me," she said. "Urgently. John, what's the number?"

"O775 676 4577," Mordred said. He showed her his screen. She repeated it. They waited a minute.

"He's in Claridge's," she said eventually. "Thank you, Tariq. I love you," she added matter-of-factly, and hung up. "Now, John, I think you'd better ring Ruby Parker, explain what's happening. She doesn't like surprises any more than Phyllis and I do, and we'll be there in roughly ten minutes."

Chapter 26: Annabel Sticks a Four Inch Pin into a Man's Bottom

"It sounds suspiciously like a trap," Ruby Parker said when he'd explained. "Although I can't imagine precisely how it might work. We're discovering some strange things about this *Panorama* video, incidentally. It contains significant holes in a way we assumed was impossible. Not obvious ones, but it can't hold up to sustained scrutiny. The problem is, as it's been throughout, we're the intelligence services. If we tell the BBC they'll be sunk if they screen it – *when*'s probably a better word, now – they'll assume we're merely doing the government's bidding. And that's compounded by the fact that, legally speaking, we're handling stolen goods. How long till you arrive at Broadcasting House?"

"Two or three minutes."

"Have you asked Tariq to check the location of Philip Toussaint-Molloy's phone? Because if he's no longer there, the three of you are off on a wild goose chase."

"Terry obviously wants me there, otherwise he wouldn't have phoned. I mean, despite the fact that he's possibly only pretending to be there."

"He might just want you *not* to be somewhere else. Obviously, he's probably got no idea where you could be, but he might be erring on the side of caution. Ask Annabel to call Tariq. I could do it, but I'd have to ask you to hold the line."

Annabel had already taken out her phone. "I'm on the case," she said. "John, show me the number."

He obliged. "I'll try to get Philip Toussaint-Molloy to stop *Panorama*," he said. "Send me some of the evidence you've dug up. I think he trusts me."

"He'll be 'in the zone', as they say, now," Ruby Parker replied. "So it's probably too late. He's probably totally focussed on getting it out of the way; he'll also be prey to the sort of understandable wishful thinking that takes a while to over-turn, even with the best evidence in the world, and finally, he probably doesn't have the authority to intervene in the sched-ule at this late stage. We need to get hold of the DG."

"Terry might be at Broadcasting House now. He probably knew it'd take me a while to get there. Maybe he was on his way."

"Stop here, please, Kevin," Annabel said, as they drove along Portland place, about fifty yards before their destina-tion, around the corner. "Phyllis and I will do a recce. We'll meet you round the corner, John. I've got a horrible feeling you're going to be attacked. When Kevin stops the car, count to ten, then get out, and make straight for the entrance."

She and Phyllis got out onto the pavement. They set off at a brisk pace.

Kevin pulled out again into the traffic. "I'll see you're all right, my friend," he said. "I've got a score or two to settle with those Russians."

"Er, thanks," Mordred said.

"Don't mention it. And no need to count to ten, either."

"I think when Annabel said that, it was more of an order than a request."

"Fair point. Probably safest then."

Bloody hell, even Kevin was scared of her.

The car pulled up next to the bollards dividing the forecourt from Langham Street. Mordred couldn't see Phyllis or Anna-bel. He looked at his watch, opened the door and stepped onto the pavement.

He had the advantage of suspecting he might be attacked, and he could handle himself in a fair fight, so he wasn't wor-ried.

But when someone was determined to get you, he or she didn't usually play fair.

As he strode towards the entrance, he was aware of a man standing directly in front of him, ten yards away, blocking his path. He adjusted his direction slightly. The man casually compensated, all the time appearing to look at the ground. Early thirties, burly, casually dressed, baseball cap with a long peak.

At the same time, another man appeared to be zeroing in from an angle, just to his rear.

As always in these sorts of situations, he found himself shut in faster than he'd have thought possible. Surrounded, effect-ively, though there were only two of them.

The guy in front smiled as he removed a long dagger from his zip-up hoodie – *this will hurt a bit, my friend, but it's nothing personal* – while the guy behind stood ready to perform a body-grip if things became awkward.

Confident that he had this, he feinted to the left slightly, but before he could roll, the man with the knife screamed. As An-nabel told it later, she'd fully inserted a four-inch pin into his left buttock. He lost control of everything, and since his grip on the knife was part of that, she was able to divest him of it without a struggle. To make sure he wasn't going anywhere, she thrust the knife deep into his thigh - careful, presumably, since she was Annabel and knew about these things – not to breach an artery.

The other man turned and began to run. Too eager. She kicked him forward, increasing his velocity to a fraction more than he could cope with, and he fell flat. He scrambled to his feet and sprinted away. Just before he reached Langham Street, Phyllis appeared from nowhere and expertly stuck out her foot, launching him head-first into a bollard. The crunch was audible even from where John was. He didn't get up.

Two police officers were approaching, a man and a woman. Annabel showed her ID. "Detective Inspector Elle Hadding-ton," she said furiously, "and you two useless jokers are?"

Mordred could see what was about to happen. He took several paces away, then discreetly called Thames House and requested urgent corroboration for DI Elle Haddington.

Before either officer could answer, Annabel cut in, louder. "Thank you so much for finally arriving, we really appreciate it. This guy here was nearly stabbed right in front of you, and you just stood there. Oh no, that's right: not exactly you didn't: you simply waited until the action was over, when you presumably thought you were safe, then you sauntered over like the kings of the proverbial parade. After I'd dealt with the whole thing entirely on my own. Well, absolutely magnificent, both of you. Take a bow. And some people say the Met's not what it used to be."

Something was wrong. They weren't looking at her in anything like the cowed, deferential way they should be. She'd paused, waiting for the inevitable lame excuse, but it didn't come. In response, she looked set to continue haranguing.

Mordred walked over. "I need to be inside," he told her. "Urgently."

"I will be putting this in my report," she said as a parting shot. If they'd attacked her at that point, he had no doubt she'd have floored them both, only not in her usual insouciant manner.

Phyllis caught up with them. They showed their IDs and entered Broadcasting House through the revolving doors. He kept an eye on the two police officers. They turned around and walked away through the Langham Street tunnel to his left. He stopped Annabel and Phyllis behind the glass frontage for a brief conference.

Annabel didn't look like she needed his dragging her away explaining – they really did have to be inside urgently, after all – but she obviously didn't know three-quarters of the true story. He needed to brief her. It might have serious repercussions later.

"I'm pretty sure they weren't real police officers," he said.

She laughed. "What on earth makes you say that?"

"I'm not completely certain. I'm only telling you because it might be worth remembering later. They didn't say anything at all, and you're right: they waited till the action was over, and they were in no hurry. And they didn't look particularly penitent, or even as if they understood a word you were saying. You paused for them to make an excuse. Nothing."

"I noticed that," she said. "It did seem peculiar. But then, the police can be like that sometimes. They're not necessarily helpful or even nice."

"Where are they now?" he asked.

Annabel looked through the window. "Gone. With their tails between their legs, I assume."

He smiled. "They walked away without talking to each other. Just as if they'd been recalled to the factory in a science-fiction film. Repeat: without talking to each other. That's got to be significant. No sense of, *We'd better get our story straight for when we get back to the station.* More like, *Cover blown, moving out. Over.*"

Annabel nodded. "Has it occurred to you that, since you were just almost killed, you might be in a rather strange place now? I mean, seeing threats where there aren't any? I'm not putting you down, John. That would be psychologically normal."

"It's possible," he said. "But it might be better to err on the side of caution."

"Do you think we should call for backup?" Phyllis asked him.

"We don't want to look silly," he said, after a moment's thought. "Maybe I really am imagining things."

"Agreed," Annabel said. "We can all handle ourselves in a fight. If we're outnumbered at any point, then we'll reconsider."

'Looking silly' was Annabel's worst nightmare, and thus an important component of her Achilles Heel. Everyone had one.

He'd never tested the amount of danger she considered acceptable as an alternative to mild humiliation, but he suspected it was considerable.

"Let's find Philip," he said.

They walked up to the front desk. Phyllis and Annabel showed their police ID cards and Carol immediately retired into a shell, as if she might be personally responsible for any wrongdoing they were here to address.

"Has Terry come back yet?" John asked.

"I haven't seen him, but I'll just check the system," she said self-consciously. She looked at her screen. "No... No, he's definitely not returned, I'm afraid."

"Because he called me on my mobile and told me our appointment was back on again, and I should come over."

"Oh, I'm really sorry about that." She blushed slightly. Maybe she did recreational drugs in her spare time, and she'd been brought up with the conviction that not only was it wrong, but it brought a visit from the police as surely as night follows day. "He *is* naughty," she added.

"Anyway, never mind. I'm partly here to see Philip Toussaint-Molloy, the *Panorama* man."

"Oh, yes. Well, I hope *he's* here. It would be like Monty Python if he wasn't, wouldn't it?"

"Correct."

"He did seem to go upstairs, like I said, when I was talking to you. And I haven't seen him check out at all. Let me just confirm." She did more screen-looking and mouse-moving. "No, he hasn't left!" she announced, as if it was the jackpot. "I mean, not officially, anyway. I don't know precisely where upstairs he went, so I don't know exactly where to send you. But I can give his mobile a ring. It's on the system, and I *am* allowed. Just give me a moment."

She walked off and turned her back to phone, presumably so Mordred wouldn't see what digits she was entering and data-protection rules would remain uncompromised.

"The obvious conclusion is that Terry set you up," Phyllis whispered. "He lured you here so you'd be killed."

"My thoughts exactly," Annabel said. "He's got questions to answer when we finally catch up with him."

"The problem will be in establishing that he knew those two guys," Mordred whispered. "Look outside again. Look at the forecourt."

Carol came back. "I've found him," she said. "He's on the top floor. He says you'll find him 'in the room you both had tea last time.' I don't know where that is. Does it make sense?"

"Completely," John said.

She handed over three lanyards. "If you could wear these, please. And, er, one other thing. He said please could you knock six times on the door before you go in. I don't know why. I said I'd ask you. I told him: *that's all I can do, Philip: ask them.* He was pretty insistent, though. Same when he was down here, earlier: *intense*, I'd call him. Like Van Gogh. You know: Vincent."

"Thank you."

John, Annabel and Phyllis walked to the lift. No one else got in and they ascended alone.

"I take it when you said, 'look at the forecourt'," Annabel said, "that you were talking about the absence of commotion."

"You've just put a knife into a man's thigh," he said, "and Phyllis, you knocked another man out. Not only are they both gone, but there's no sign they were ever there. And no police, no ambulance, no hubbub on the front desk – I admit, Carol's too far back to see, but you'd think someone would have called it in – and no sirens, at least not that I could hear."

"What I'd call eerie," Phyllis said. "John, you've been in the room we're apparently on our way to now, yes? Can you see the forecourt from there?"

"Unfortunately, it's at the rear of the building," he said.

"I'm still against calling for backup," Annabel said. "But we definitely need to inform base about what's happened, and maybe let them make the risk assessment."

"One of us needs to keep an eye on what's happening downstairs at ground level," Phyllis said. "It won't take three of us to interview Toussaint-Molloy."

"I'll scan the forecourt," Annabel said. "I'll call Ruby Parker while I'm there. I've got my police card, so I can access all areas and probably get them to bring me a pair of binoculars and a cup of freshly ground coffee. We'll split up when we get out the lift. Call me when you've finished with Philip Toussaint-Molloy."

The lift doors opened. Annabel took her phone out and went to Google Maps. They walked along the corridor together, and she branched off at the third intersection. She didn't say goodbye.

"Bloody hell, it's like Pan's Labyrinth in here," Phyllis said.

Finding their way was more difficult than Mordred remembered. There were staff about, and some of them stopped to ask if and how they could help, but given that even Carol hadn't known where Philip Toussaint-Molloy was, and they had no name or number for the room they were searching for, they didn't know how to phrase a request.

"I think this is it," Mordred said eventually. He knocked six times.

The door opened an inch. One of Philip Toussaint-Molloy's eyes appeared. "Who's with you?" he asked.

"My colleague," Mordred said. "Don't worry," he added, as if it was a spy film and he was talking to the stock paranoid character, "she's a friend."

Phyllis looked at him as if he was mad. "Thanks."

Philip Toussaint-Molloy opened the door and stood aside to let them in. It became clear as they entered the room that he'd had a table up against it.

"There are no locks on any of these doors," he said. He laughed. "You tell me: what's a guy got to do to get some privacy these days?"

"Put a piece of furniture up against the door," Phyllis said. "That's how I usually do it, anyway. Pleased to meet you, Mr Toussaint-Molloy. My name's Phyllis Robinson. Like John, I'm with Her Majesty's Spy Services. How can John and I help?"

"Pleased to meet you Ms Robinson," Toussaint-Molloy said, grabbing her hand and shaking it vigorously. "Thank God you're here. I've a story to tell."

"We thought you might have," John said.

"Don't just stand there," Toussaint-Molloy replied. "Help me get this table back under the handle."

Chapter 27: Inside the Cauldron that is Broadcasting House

Phyllis and John helped Philip Toussaint-Molloy get the table beneath the door handle, more by way of humouring him than a genuine desire to help, then sat down on two of the six chairs in the room, facing each other from opposite walls. Their host sat down beside the door, as if he simply had to keep an eye on it. As far as they could tell, he wasn't armed. His behaviour suggested he wished he was.

"Carol said you wanted to talk to me," John said, when the silence became oppressive.

"Who's Carol?" he asked. "No, sorry. Carol, of course. The receptionist on the front desk. Carol."

"Going by appearances," Phyllis said, "you're a little frightened someone might be trying to harm you."

Philip laughed. "I think that's an understatement. Look, I'm just going to talk, because we may not have much time, and I'm pretty sure that's how you'd prefer it anyway: me just talking, yes? Am I right? I'm an intelligent man. I don't usually behave like this, but I tried to get out of the building earlier and I swear someone tried to kill me. Then I tried it again and the same thing happened. Then I spoke to Carol and asked her to phone you, and he – my assailant - came inside. I could see what he wanted, so I ran away."

"I assume you've called the police?" Phyllis said.

"This is deeper than that," he replied. "The police could get me out of the building and into a taxi… maybe. If they believed me, and that's a big 'if'. They couldn't protect me at home."

"I don't understand," Phyllis said. "Why would anyone want to kill you?"

"Because they know what you did," John said. The insight arrived in almost the same moment he uttered the words.

Philip and Phyllis turned to look at him. "You stole the *Panorama* tape from Broadcasting House," he continued, "and gave it to Orville Peterson."

Toussaint-Molloy gulped. "How on earth did you know?"

"No one else fits the bill," John said, "You found out your programme is full of untruths. You took those findings to Terry. You weren't too worried at that stage, because you didn't think you'd be implicated. It was the fact-checkers, and ultimately Terry himself, who would get the flak. Normally, that sort of thing would have been done entirely in-house, but because of the special nature of this particular programme – its sensitivity, likely impact on government and susceptibility to leaks - Terry hired an outside company. Obviously, when you first learned that – oh, say six months ago? - you were concerned. But Terry reassured you. He told you it was his head on the chopping-block if it all went wrong, not yours, and he was even happy to put that in writing. Which he did, in front of several of the BBC's top lawyers. So however many mistakes there are in tonight's *Panorama*, and however egregious they might be, you could relax. It wasn't your problem. Or so you thought."

"Bloody hell," Toussaint-Molloy said. "That's exactly how it happened. And you got all that from – what? – deduction?" He grinned inanely. "My God."

"Once I realised you'd taken the video," John said, "the rest kind of fell into place. Anyway, two or three days ago, you began to get even more nervous. You'd been to Terry with your concerns. Terry didn't appear to have done anything, and then you realised: the thing about flak is it doesn't just take one person with it: it spreads. So you looked again at the evidence, deeper this time. You forensically fact-checked the fact-checkers checking. What you found horrified you. You went straight back to Terry, and once again, Terry promised to look into it. But Terry sat on his hands. All the indications now were that he wasn't remotely interested. By this time, you were panicking. You decided you had to tell someone – anyone - who could put the brakes on. So you broke into Broadcasting House – I use the term 'broke into' loosely – and took one of the master tapes and passed it anonymously to Orville Peterson."

"I passed it to Tom Ford," Toussaint-Molloy said. "If Peterson has it, he must have got it from Ford."

"But you had to give it to one of those two, because you thought that, since they've been kicking up such a fuss about it, they'd naturally look at it, audit it properly, probably in collaboration with a team of lawyers - in the way Terry should have - and then slap an injunction on it. Monday night, 8.30: no *Panorama*. Job done. Only it didn't work that way, because no injunction came."

"And I don't understand why!" Toussaint-Molloy exclaimed.

"Then you tried to leave the building, and someone tried to kill you – they'd worked out, just as I belatedly did, that only you could have taken that tape - and, well, Terry's now gone AWOL."

"I'm assuming part of the reason you know such a lot," Toussaint-Molloy said, "is that Peterson gave MI5 a copy instead of plumping for an injunction. Which, I must say, is very decent of him. More so than I expected."

"I wish you were right," John said. "It'd considerably improve my view of human nature. Unfortunately, someone – someone Russian, I imagine, though not presenting as such - seems to have reminded Ford and Peterson that their big ambition in life is to bring down the BBC. Ford wants to be the next Director General, and Peterson wants to scrap the licence fee and reconstruct the Corporation on the model of Fox News, or Russia Today or Al Jazeera, or all three. Both of them are idealists – not ideals that you or I share, but they're honest, well-intentioned men, in no one's pocket – and they decided an injunction wouldn't be in the interests of their ideals. No, it'd do far more damage to the BBC if the programme actually went out, and *then* they were able to show everyone what a travesty it was: that there never was a secret refugee centre in Aylesbury; that there were no refugees shipped back to Russia and Belarus; that the sweeping persecutions of white-slavers and their employees in Moscow and Minsk never happened; that everything, but everything, was fiction, and the BBC has slipped up big time. Worse, had no one seen through its mendacities, it would probably have brought down the government, which was plausibly its secret aim."

Phyllis nodded. "Because it slipped up so badly, it can only have been deliberate."

"And so we can already foresee the shape of public debate for the next few days," John said.

"Yes, indeed," Toussaint-Molloy put in. "*Many people have been saying for some time that the BBC is the ideological tool of a small, but powerful liberal elite, and, on this occasion, its aim was presumably to provide the pretext for what would be a left-wing coup in all but name. Regrettably, it must go.* Something like that."

"Thankfully from the conspirators' point of view," John continued, "Ford and Peterson will soon be in the perfect position to sink it. Peterson with his suddenly wildly popular Private Members Bill, Ford with the kind of insider's knowledge that history's very last Director General would need to carry out the difficult transition from public to private ownership. *Only by following their lead can we preserve a semblance of liberty in this country.*"

"I take it Terry McNamara's being blackmailed," Phyllis said.

"That's my view," Toussaint-Molloy replied. "I don't know what they've got on him – or even who 'they' are: right-wingers of some stripe, I suppose - but I can't see any other explanation for his behaviour."

"I think Terry's role was always to take full responsibility afterwards," John said, "then to cede all the points that the

BBC's critics are likely to level against it, and silence anyone within the Corporation who attempts to defend it. To steady the ship as it sinks, in other words, and ensure it sinks as quickly as possible. Then finally, in an excess of public contrition, to recommend exactly the measures Ford and Peterson propose."

Toussaint-Molloy hmm-ed. "He'll hang on as DG until the transition's complete. If you're right, he's the key person."

"We've got to find Annabel and get out of here," John said.

"Didn't she say she was calling Ruby Parker?" Phyllis asked. "Why haven't we heard from her?" She took her mobile out, pressed Call twice, then three times, then looked quizzically at the screen. "My phone's not working."

John and Philip looked anxiously at theirs and frowned. Ditto. They were on their feet now.

Should they leave the room? Were they safest here?

"That's why Terry called me from Claridge's," John said. "He'll have rung Carol to get my number, then double-checked it by ringing me. Then he'll have passed it to the Russians. The Russians presumably accessed my Contacts list. Then they put a blocker on all our phones. It can be done."

"But it would have to be done from within this building," Toussaint-Molloy said. "I know a little about these things."

"So Terry's got accomplices," Phyllis said.

"Bound to have," John replied. "The Russians wouldn't leave something like this entirely in the hands of one man. He'd need a support group, for psychological reasons as much as anything else."

"The IT department's on the third floor," Toussaint-Molloy said.

"So I should imagine the Russians will have it heavily guarded," John said.

Toussaint-Molloy laughed. "There aren't going to be any *Russians* in here! What are you talking about?"

"Just trust us, Philip," Phyllis said. "Though technically, you're right. They're almost certainly *not* Russians, just working for them. I'll explain in a moment."

"Oh, *shit*," Philip said. "Those are the guys who tried to kill me, yes?"

"Well... probably," John said. He turned to Phyllis. "I'm not sure whether it's better for us to stay here, or make some kind of break for it. Do you know how showing a programme like *Panorama* works? I mean, in detail?"

"Not really," Phyllis said.

"Even I don't really know," Toussaint-Molloy said. "I always imagine it's a bit like in films. Six or seven executives sitting in a row facing a wall covered with monitors, and a long, shared desk full of knobs and switches."

"Could be," Mordred said. "I don't know either."

"Was there a *point* to your question, John?" Phyllis asked.

"Whatever the truth of the matter," he continued, "there has to be some kind of override switch within the building that would allow a person – only with the DG's approval, I'd imagine – to cancel a programme at the last minute."

"Let's call it the big red button," Phyllis said. "What about it?"

"The Russians that attacked me outside were there to stop me getting into the building, because they thought once inside, I'd be able to access it. When I bypassed them, they'll have panicked. They'll have sent in as many bods as they can muster."

"But as far as we know," Phyllis said, "most of the 'Russians', in the sense we're talking about them now, were expelled after Bellingcat exposed the identity of Mobeen Dhanial's killers. So, these must be Brits, or at least non-Russians, working on Moscow's behalf, but probably unaware of the fact: private security employees, hired through fake companies, that sort of thing. In other words – and this is the important thing - they'll be indistinguishable from genuine BBC employ-

229

ees. Terry will have provided them with the means to fool Carol's scanner at the front desk. The whole building could be riddled with them."

"Oh, *shit*," Toussaint-Molloy said again.

"So the question is," John said, "are we safer just waiting here? Remember, they don't know exactly where we are. Even Carol didn't know."

"She knew we were on the top floor," Phyllis said. "Which narrows it down a bit. What about Annabel?"

"Annabel went off to call Ruby Parker," he replied. "She'll have seen her phone's blocked, and she'll probably have realised what's happened. The reason she hasn't come to find us is because she doesn't know where we are. She peeled off when we passed Andy Pandy and Looby Loo."

"The portrait picture?" Toussaint-Molloy said.

"Not the real-life," John confirmed. He turned to Phyllis. "Besides, the thought of us going to rescue Annabel is laughable. She could thrash all three of us with one hand tied behind her back."

"I vote we evacuate this room now," Phyllis said. "If they arrive here, we're fish in a barrel. They only need call for reinforcements, then we're cornered and possibly dead. After all, killing us might not be counterproductive. Whatever happens, *Panorama*'s the BBC's baby, broadcast by the BBC. And we've just been murdered by people unknown. And hey, we were probably working for the government anyway, so who cares?"

"Oh, *shit!*" Toussaint-Molloy said again.

"And go where?" John said. "Outside the building, they'll be waiting for us. Inside, they'll be searching for us."

"Here, we're dead," she said. "We can get disguises, cut our hair, I don't know. There must be a bloody costume department somewhere nearby. This is the BBC. And given that Annabel's Annabel, she'll be out there somewhere, looking for us, and probably our best hope of staying alive."

"Oh, *shit!*" Toussaint-Molloy said again.

"*Shut up!*" Phyllis told him. She pulled the table to one side and flung the door open. A middle aged man in a hi-vis jacket stood with a gun, apparently caught off guard while trying to listen. She kicked him in the stomach, wrenched his weapon from him, then punched his face as he tried to come back. "See what I mean?" she said, as he crumpled. "Come on, Philip, stop being a wuss. We need you to show us where the costumier is."

"I don't know," he said. "I'm in current affairs!"

"Well, *bloody find out!*" she said. "Go into an office or something! Flash your card! Use someone's phone, for God's sake!"

"A map of the building would be equally handy," John said. "Then we could find out where the big red button is." He stopped by a fire alarm button and punched it through. A siren blared.

"What are you doing?" she said, above the noise. "I mean, obviously I can see..." She grinned. "Aha."

"The real employees will go down into the forecourt, making it harder to kill someone down there, unnoticed. The fake employees will stay in the building, and so we know that, in about five minutes' time, anyone we meet's hostile."

"And if we can set a real fire going, we might be able to get Fireman Sam to rescue us," she said.

"I was thinking more about entering an empty office and calling Ruby Parker on a landline," he said.

"That too," she replied.

"More like instead. You'd be an easy target for a sniper at the top of a fireman's ladder."

"Oh, *shit!*" Toussaint-Molloy said again.

"No one would shoot us at the top of a fireman's ladder," she said. "Think about it: they only want to stop us accessing the big red button. Once we're on the ladder, that's no longer possible."

"But sometimes these guys hold grudges," John replied.

People were pouring from offices and side corridors and making for the emergency exits. Before Phyllis or John could intervene, Philip disappeared in the human river, slightly faster than everyone else, and hurtled through the doors to the stairs.

John grabbed Phyllis's hand. "Come on."

She resisted. "We can't join him, John. There'll be people downstairs, waiting for us. We'll be toast as soon as we're out of the building, crowd or no crowd."

"I wasn't thinking of leaving, just going down a floor or two. They're looking for us on the top floor, remember?"

She acceded. They descended two floors, then left the flow to enter a deserted corridor.

"If only you didn't have that hair," she told him. "It's like someone's highlighted your head. No offence. I mean, in normal circumstances - "

"None taken." He opened an office door and went in. Bingo: a nice big desk with a lovely landline. "Keep watch or ring base?"

"I've got a gun," she said, "and unlike you, I'm not afraid to use it. I'll keep watch, thank you."

"I wonder if they've all got guns."

"Gee, who knows? There's the phone. Pick up the receiver and press the little numbers."

They all knew Ruby Parker's number by heart. He keyed it in while Phyllis stood in the doorway, gun in both hands, looking both ways, like she was still in Afghanistan.

The phone picked up. He recited a code into a voice recognition system and another phone started ringing. Twice, then Ruby Parker picked up. "John? Where are you?"

"Inside Broadcasting House. Have you heard from Annabel?"

"A few moments ago. She's looking for you. We've got three armed response units on their way."

"How soon till they get here?"

"They're there now, just about to enter the building. Is Phyllis with you?"

"She's keeping watch."

"Was it your idea to set the fire alarm off?"

"Yep."

"Okay. Good thinking. Now, hide somewhere. Anywhere. It's a big building, and we estimate there's no more than ten of them. They won't have time to locate you."

"Do we still need to find Terry?"

"More than ever, I'm afraid. Strangely, this counts as a separate incident. We can show it's linked to Panorama, but not – as it stands right now - to an armed government attempt to stop it airing, which is very bad news indeed."

"We could just put Toussaint-Molloy on air, get him to fess up, as the Americans say."

"The conspiracy theorists would have a field day."

"I thought he was at Claridge's. Terry, I mean. Not Phil."

"His phone was. He's not."

"We need to flush him out from wherever he is."

"Thank you, John. I had realised that."

"Sorry. Thinking aloud, that's all. Look, he must be on his own. He's obviously *been* to Claridge's at some point, otherwise he couldn't have phoned me from there. If things go the way he wants, tomorrow morning there's going to be an almighty storm. Given that he's not at Broadcasting House now, when a possible terrorist incident's occurring, questions are going to be asked about his whereabouts. If he was in company with someone, that would come up on the CCTV. If he was out of public view, it would look suspicious. So he must be in London somewhere, but out of CCTV sight. Which means a restaurant or a gentleman's club, or – anywhere private. And he'll be banking on staying there till nine o'clock, when *Panorama's* over. At which point, he'll emerge and he'll have witnesses to the fact that he was doing something innocuous."

"I'm not sure how that helps."

"Think about the Web Brigades."

"Pardon?"

"We need to get Tariq on this. Put out an All Ports Alert sort of thing, but on social media, with a big picture of Terry and a caption. Something like, 'Broadcasting House is under terrorist attack, where is Terry?" the final clause in capitals. Tweet it to every BBC celebrity in existence, see if we can get it to go viral. If we haven't flushed him out in about an hour, offer a reward. In the meantime, get onto the Chair of the BBC board, get him to call a meeting. Find Philip Toussaint-Molloy, get him to make a statement to the police. Contact Peterson and Ford: tell them we know they're in receipt of stolen goods and we can proceed the hard way or the easy way. Find out who Terry hired to check facts, and see what they're really up to. I think we've got enough now to at least put *Panorama* on ice, with or without the DG."

A slight pause, as of relief. But also as if it was the sort of conclusion she'd have reached soon enough herself. "I do believe you're right, John," she said.

"The police are here, John," Phyllis said from the door. "The real police. If we don't want to be shot, we'd better get down on our knees and put our hands up."

He sighed and did as she suggested. The usual degrading end to a case solved.

Half an hour later, Terry McNamara was still sitting alone in Admiral's Choice, a five-star restaurant the size of a large suburban dining room, just off Wardour Street. The very centre of London, so no one could later accuse him of hiding out. He'd made his battered calamari starter last thirty minutes, probably a record for any customer. The steak was about to arrive. By the time he'd finished that, *Panorama* would have started. Then dessert, and maybe another drink or two. He needed to

234

make the most of the peace and quiet. He wouldn't be getting any more for a few weeks now, not till all this was over.

He felt his pocket out of habit and realised for the tenth time that he'd ditched his phone at Claridge's. People did forget their phones sometimes. Nothing suspicious about that. And there was nothing incriminating on there. His friends had checked it, just to make sure.

The only possible problem was Toussaint-Molloy. But he'd have been taken care of now: without a phone, of course, it was impossible to check. But Philip *and* John Mordred, *both dead:* it was horrific, utterly *horrific!* And obviously, the BBC accepted full responsibility for everything. No excuses. We'll do whatever's necessary now to make matters right. And so on and so forth. Lots of public hand-wringing.

The waiter, a clean-shaven young man with gangly limbs, appeared from nowhere.

"Enjoying your meal, sir?"

"Er, yes, thank you. Sorry, you startled me."

"Apologies, sir. Shall I take your plate?"

"Yes, please."

The waiter obliged, leaving Terry alone. But with a subtle sense of foreboding that hadn't been there before.

Because, although it had only lasted a couple of seconds, there'd been something off beam about the whole exchange. The way the waiter subtly seemed to be trying to see his face.

Could something have gone wrong? My God, what to do?

Stop panicking, that's what. Stay calm. Nervousness had this sort of effect: you started seeing things that just didn't exist.

He swept his eyes as casually as he could to the bar. The waiter, on his phone, looked across, and when their eyes met, looked hurriedly away.

Terry stood up. His heart pounded. He walked to the bar and slapped down four twenties. "Sorry, I've left my phone in Claridge's. Keep the change."

"Are you – sorry – are you Terry McNamara, sir?" the waiter called.

But he was through the double doors. He took the stairs two at a time and ran out onto the street.

Which way to Claridge's? He might just be able to retrieve the situation now, if it looked like he'd honestly suddenly missed his phone.

But – he laughed, hopelessly - he was so used to being driven everywhere, he didn't know which direction to go! He put his hand instinctively in his pocket for Google Maps.

But Google Maps was in bloody Claridge's! Oh my God, you couldn't make it up!

People were looking at him oddly. They really were. Not everyone though, just one or two.

Something had happened. He might just be able to wing it from here. Go into Leicester Square, just around the corner, ask for directions to Claridge's, then keep his head down. Later, someone might be able to verify *he'd asked for directions to Claridge's.*

Ask a policeman, even better.

He ran into Leicester Square, scanning for possible help. People were looking at him. Someone pointed. A policeman came over.

All the fight went out of him and he turned to water. This was it. Barring some miracle, the game was up.

Then he saw something surreal. Above the policeman's head. An illuminated billboard with his face on and the caption, 'WHERE IS TERRY?'

He laughed. There would be no miracle today.

Chapter 28: Alec Stands a Better Chance of Living Happily Ever After

By noon, the day after Terry McNamara's arrest and the last-minute replacement of *Panorama* with a repeat of *Fake or Fortune?* the media had more or less satisfied everyone's curiosity regarding most aspects of the case. Only a few people in MI7 knew the missing information, either from direct experience or from classified testimony, but what they had amounted almost to a complete picture. That afternoon's 'debrief' of Red Department's core members was therefore expected to be more a brisk Q&A than a narration, by Ruby Parker, of what had actually been going on, throughout, beneath the surface.

Annabel, Phyllis and John spent the morning writing their reports. At 10am, John decided he needed a break. He went up to the canteen for a coffee and a Twix, and sat alone by the window reading Jules Evans's *Philosophy for Life* blog on his phone.

Two minutes later, Alec joined him with a cup of tea. They hadn't planned a meeting and for a moment, John didn't know what to say. They weren't allowed to discuss his experience at Broadcasting House until he'd committed it to writing, and he was still only halfway through.

For once, though, Alec looked content to sit without talking. But they couldn't. "How's Valentina?" John said.

Alec sighed. "Much as it pains me, I've decided against pursuing it any further. A textbook case of hello, goodbye. Thank you for your advice the other day, though."

"Any particular reason?"

"I told you about Suki, Jonathan and Bruce. Since then, I've learned of three other quasi-romantic liaisons between MI7 staffers and the so-called Novelists. Something's going on, and I'm in my forties, about a decade older than all the budding lovebirds. I'll be expected to 'set an example'."

"You mean you think that, if there *is* something fishy going on, Ruby Parker will be harder on you than on them."

"Of course she will. I'd expect her to be. I wouldn't blame her."

"You're talking as if it's already happened."

"It hasn't. But it will. I do think there is something 'fishy' going on. It's too much of a coincidence. They just come in here, then they pair up with our guys. Immediately. Like someone in Moscow put them up to it. And they're all pretty right-wing."

"They're not 'right-wing'. They're religious. Specifically, they're Russian Orthodox. You can map that onto a grid of - "

"Precisely. It's the same thing, for all practical purposes."

"Which is just what a rabid liberal would say. Consign them all to the same bin. Forget diversity for the time being. They're all fascists."

"I mean, I don't even mind that sort of thing as a rule, but I'm not sure I'm up to being 'traditional' all the time. And I'm quite suspicious when someone like Suki, who's on every leftie bandwagon that's ever rolled along Brighton seafront on Pride Day, gets sucked in by one of them."

"Maybe she's open-minded. A lot of liberal folk are."

"Most of them are permanently outraged, in my experience. Mind you, so is everyone these days. Which is one way these Russians are different, I suppose. Right-wing but... nice."

"I don't think Suki belongs in the incensed camp. Maybe I could stick up for you all. I mean, put the case for the defence."

"Meaning?"

"I don't know how many of the Novelists we've rescued, but we're their first contact with friendly Britons. And they're quite attractive, and so are we - one or two of us - so why shouldn't there be some kind of attraction? Look at those photographs we saw of them in seminar room E17. They definitely didn't look like a bunch of spies. They looked like they were all in love with each other, even then. I mean, in a lower case way. And they're 'in love' with some of us now. And why shouldn't that be innocent? And where there's attraction, there's usually at least the possibility of a relationship."

"Yes, but you're not supposed to act on it. That's taking advantage of your professional status. It's crossing the line."

"Rubbish. Your professional relationship ends when you've interviewed them. How long's that take? Anywhere between five minutes and two days; very rarely more. It's hardly likely to inculcate a sense of dependency on their part. It's not like a doctor-patient thing, or a teacher-pupil thing. There, I admit, a romantic relationship's clearly wrong. I'm pretty sure this isn't the same."

"Even so, always play safe where Ruby Parker's concerned. I don't want to blot my copy book. I've my pension to think about."

"Perhaps you should be planning more deeply than that."

"Explain."

"Perhaps you should be thinking about your old age generally. You could accumulate a massive pension and end up with no one to share it with. Or you could take a chance on love, as Abba might have said, and have a loving companion in your twilight years."

"There's an old saying, John: when poverty comes in at the door, love flies out of the window. Rough translation: you can have your pension and you could conceivably have Valentina Morozova – in an ideal world – but there's no possible world in which you can just have Valentina Morozova. That wouldn't work."

"Do you know what I think this is really about?"

"Me being cowardly? Go on, say it. I expected we'd hit that particular rock sooner or later. I'll save you the bother of trying to prove it. Maybe I am. Maybe."

"I think it's about you, a man, having to go to Ruby Parker, a woman, and talk about your feelings, ask her permission to proceed. You think she'll somehow humiliate you."

"Obviously she will. She'll say no. But that would be even more humiliating coming from a man. So it's not about the gender-divide, no matter how great a headline it might make in *The Guardian*: 'Alec Cunningham behaves in sexist manner.'"

"Better to have loved and lost than never to have loved at all."

"Very helpful, John. Ta."

"There's nothing to stop you going to Ruby Parker with your concerns about the younger members of the department, and casually tossing in something like, 'I was almost sucked in myself. I got on really well with Valentina Morozova. I nearly considered asking her out, then I came to my senses. I thought, Hey, wait a minute, I'm the Grand Old Man of Red Department. I should be setting these young pups an example.' She can't humiliate you then. It's not a crime to be tempted. She might even say, 'Alec, you're being silly. If you really like Valentina Morozova so much, why not ask her out? We'll do a few more background checks, you can sign a few extra papers, and you take care you don't talk in your sleep when you're on a case, and let's take it from there.'"

Alec flicked his eyebrows. "When you strip all that of its obvious sarcasm, John, it's actually an incredibly good suggestion. I hadn't looked at it like that at all. I might even get credit for having spotted the problem."

"And it might not even *be* a problem, and you might get to date the lovely Valentina before some other MI7 bod gets in. I hear Carl has a bit of a thing for her."

Alec nearly spluttered into his tea. "*Carl? Carl Jacobsen?*"

"I just made that up. I didn't even know we had a Carl."

"I'm pretty sure we *have*. I'm not one hundred per cent sure his second name's Jacobsen, come to think of it, but there he is. Over there, with the chess players."

"That's Russell Crowe."

"*Russell Crowe?* Is that someone's idea of a joke? A nickname, right?"

"No, that's his actual name."

"Bloody hell, he looks exactly like him! I thought his name was Carl."

"To be fair, 'Carl' does sound a lot like 'Russell'." Mordred stood up and picked up his mug. He always took it back to the serving hatch, to save the staff the trouble. "Anyway, now I've solved your latest problem, I'd better get back to my desk. Have a good morning."

Alec raised his teacup. "Ciao."

At 2pm they joined Edna, Phyllis, Annabel and Ian in Seminar Room E14, around the usual square arrangement of tables. After Ruby Parker's short introduction, Alec asked the one question on everyone's lips:

"How, specifically, was Terry McNamara being blackmailed?"

"We don't yet know the answer to that," Ruby Parker replied. "And perhaps we never will. It may not even have involved lawbreaking. Sometimes people can be blackmailed with things they personally find embarrassing."

"You mean, maybe someone threatened to tell his wife about a prostitute he visited?" Edna asked. "For example?"

"That sort of thing, yes," Ruby Parker said. "And you're right: the too-acute personal embarrassments usually *are* of a sexual nature. In the last century, we might well have found out whatever it was before he became DG but, after the 1989 Security Service Act, the BBC asked MI7 to stop vetting its top appointments, except those involved in war bulletins and or with access to classified government information. In a sense, what the Russians had against him is irrelevant now. I doubt they'll tell us. Firstly, because McNamara did his best for them, and they appreciate that sort of thing in foreigners; he might even get a welcome in Russia when he gets out of prison, in probably about three or four years' time. Secondly, however, if they do leak it, we might trace the source – we're getting better and better at that – and right now, I believe they're trying to keep their heads down."

"There hasn't been any mention of Russia on the news," Annabel said.

"The Prime Minister's not eager for yet another diplomatic showdown," Ruby Parker said. "And if I'm perfectly honest, I'm sure certain elements in HM government are rather disappointed the whole thing failed. They'd have dearly liked to see the BBC dismantled."

"So we're keeping Russian involvement quiet partly as a kind of 'better luck next time' gesture," John said.

"You might well call it that," she replied.

"What about Ford and Peterson?" Phyllis asked.

"They're unlikely to be charged with anything," Ruby Parker said. "The most anyone could pin on them now would be receipt of stolen goods, but then, you'd have to prosecute Philip Toussaint-Molloy, and since he acted fairly heroically in defence of the truth, no one wants to go down that road. Besides, Peterson and Ford aren't bad men; quite the opposite. Some of us may not share their ideals, but that's how living in a democracy's supposed to work. It would be purely vindictive to ruin their careers."

Silence.

"I can't think of anything more I want to ask," Annabel said.

Ruby Parker looked around the table. "It probably hasn't escaped anyone's notice here," she said, "that this was a very sophisticated plan indeed. Its originator – and all the evidence points to Pasha Domogarov in that role – identified a set of values shared by the establishment in Moscow and by a significant proportion of people in this country. The plan didn't involve co-opting the two principals, Ford and Peterson. There were no trips to Moscow, no clandestine meetings with oligarchs on Washington's proscribed list, no third-party transfers of favours, nothing. Tom Ford is on record as saying he wouldn't trust Vladimir Putin as far as he could throw him, and I'm pretty sure Peterson feels the same. They never knew they were being used and, in a sense, they weren't: no untoward consequences would ever have followed for them from abroad had they succeeded. Yet their triumph would definitely have advanced Russian interests. I mention this because I think we'll see more and more of it in the future. The 'bad guys' won't necessarily be bad guys. They'll only be such in the rarefied sense that they're being used, for a specific purpose, by outside powers of whose existence they're not even aware. It may be their precise *role* in a particular set up we need to be looking at, not at their connections and personal motivations."

"So it was a friendly plot," John said.

Everyone turned to look at him.

"Novel use of the word 'friendly'," Alec said.

"Are you being serious, John?" Annabel asked. "Or is this another of your throwaway gnomic utterances?"

"We all believe in British values," John said. "Or at least what they should be. Tolerance of difference, multiculturalism, human rights, kindness to animals, the ability to laugh at yourself, compassion for the less well off. If we identified someone in another country – somewhere those values aren't respected – and tried to manipulate that country's political system so that individual got power – in other words, so both our countries could have a meaningful conversation - I'd call that friendly. Especially if we were just letting that person be that person, not bribing or blackmailing him or her. It's certainly friendlier than staging a violent coup, or trying to foment a revolution, or bombing the centres of power, which is how it's always been done in the past. All we want is a conversation. Yes, on our terms, but doesn't everyone want that in the first instance?"

Alec shook his head. "'I'll have a conversation with you when you're on your knees.' That's what 'on our terms' means. From Britain's perspective vis-à-vis Russia."

"Conversation still means conversation," John replied.

"No, it doesn't," Alec said. "Because words are defined by those who hold power. As a victim, your understanding of 'conversation' almost certainly isn't the same as your oppressor's. So there *is* no meaning, not in the sense of an agreed definition."

Edna grinned. "My, this has turned into a different sort of meeting!"

"Unless you mean the phrase 'on your knees' literally," John said, "which you can't do, because it's self-evidently a metaphor, then what counts as being 'on your knees' is also open to interpretation."

"You'll know what it means when you experience it," Alec said.

"I wouldn't call novichok 'friendly', John," Phyllis put in. "Nor torturing gay people in Chechnya."

Ruby Parker held her palms up. "Enough."

More silence. This time, of a different sort.

But then the silence ran on, as if Ruby Parker herself was wrestling with it. She put her palms flat on the table then looked at everyone in turn.

"I'm not going to take sides in your discussion," she said, "but what I am about to tell you – something I'd originally decided to keep to myself – may persuade you I already have. Shortly before Grey was ordered to give us the case, I had a meeting with its supposed head, Sir Harold Kelly. He'd learned that the Russian plot to undermine the BBC had another, recondite level, of which its putative originator, Stanislav Kuznetsov, was unaware, as were all the so-called Novelists, as was everyone in the Russian Embassy."

"Kind of mega-mega-top-secret?" Ian said.

"So how did he find out about it?" Edna asked.

"I'll come to that in a moment. I included it in my report for that day, and Black hasn't queried it, so I'm pretty sure it's not a fabrication. In any case, it wouldn't be unusual for Grey to get its hands on that sort of intelligence... when the Russians want us to have it."

"So what did Kelly say?" Alec asked.

"That, in fact, unbeknown to Kuznetsov, the Novelists were chosen partly on the basis of their looks, partly on the basis of their idealistic inclinations. A prerequisite of acceptance was what we might call a healthy degree of scepticism about politics in general. Rabid nationalists were strictly disbarred. Naturally, Kuznetsov believed he was in sole charge of the selection process from start to finish, but he was mistaken. He turned the vetting process over to FSB subordinates, and they were discreetly given a different spec. The term 'Novelists' came from this higher level. It was intended to give them a romantic aura, and of course, it was designed solely for our consumption. On one level, they really *were* meant to sabotage the BBC – at least, in the first instance - which is why the GU went after them with such gusto: it didn't know of any other agenda. But if, and when, that failed, they'd be in our hands. And then some of us would probably find ourselves 'attracted' to them, for want of a better word. Young, vulnerable, intelligent, good-looking, artistic: in the words of the modern phrase, what's not to like? Given enough time, so the thinking was, they might easily end up with deep, personal connections to members of the British intelligence services."

"Bloody hell," Alec said. Everyone looked at him. He'd turned pale.

"How many of the Novelists have we now apprehended?" Phyllis asked.

"All eight," Ruby Parker replied.

"So what are we going to do with them?" Annabel asked. "We can't send them back to Russia. That would effectively be murder."

"What do you think?" Ruby Parker said. "We're going to give them new identities and integrate them into British society."

Alec frowned. "But... But I take it we're not allowed any contact with them."

"On the contrary," Ruby Parker said. "You can have as much, or as little, as you like."

"I don't understand," he replied, after a moment. "They're potential Russian spies, aren't they?"

"That was Grey's position," she said, "and I agree up to a point. In the sense that everybody's a potential anything. They weren't trained as spies. Someone in Moscow – I think it probably *is* a single person: a high-ranking official with an inquisitive disposition – has decided to play a game with us. We only get to access it once we've defeated Kuznetsov's plot, which, of course, we now have. It's like a little satyr play at the end of the principal drama; a diversion, a bagatelle. Obviously, because it's only semi-serious, it doesn't matter if we know the details, which is how Grey got to know about it. But it wasn't designed for Grey, because it's not the sort of thing Grey would consider in a million years. We would. It's essentially a wager, and it runs like this: here are eight Russian citizens, poised finely on the ideological divide that separates Britain and Russia. They're yours if you want them, and we rather think you will, simply because, in many ways, they all embody attitudes both our cultures hold dear. However, we also know that our cultures are also deeply dissimilar in crucial ways. The question is, in the long run, all things being equal, will these eight gravitate more towards your way of thinking and behaving, or towards ours? You can decline our wager if you like, but that would be pusillanimous, and an implicit admission of your inferiority. Accept, therefore, and we'll see what happens.

"If I'm right," she went on, "then someone in Moscow does want a conversation. Of a very oblique kind, I admit, but a conversation none the less. And I've never been one to decline that sort of thing. So yes, Alec, to get back to your original question: you can have as much or as little contact with them as you like. And that goes for Suki and Bruce and Jonathan. You can tell them that when you next see them, if you think it'll help."

"You think we'll win the, er, 'wager'?" John said. "Assuming that's what it is. I mean, they're bound to get homesick. They'll all pine for Russia sooner or later. It's natural."

"And I expect them to see that it's natural," she said. "And deal with it accordingly. But do I think a state based on human rights and the rule of law is better than a kleptocracy? Yes, obviously. My only concern – and it's a serious one – is that Britain may deteriorate to the point where most people in our country cease to care about freedom or justice. In that case, the terms of my wager with Moscow would evaporate. Britain and Russia would have become as indistinguishable as Tweedledum and Tweedledee."

Silence.

"Even so," she added, "it's a risk I've decided to take."

No one said anything else. Paradoxically because there was too much to talk about. The meeting closed at 2.45pm and everyone returned to their desks.

That evening, Phyllis went out with Annabel and Edna to a Turkish restaurant in Highgate; John and Alec went to a mock-Tudor pub in Crouch End with a model biplane over the bar called The Railway Tavern. They couldn't go out in a bigger group, because MI7 protocols forbade it; single-sex groups were supposedly less conspicuous, and therefore just about acceptable. Alec and John sat at a table in the patio garden with a pint of real ale each.

"Do you think she's actually gone crazy?" Alec said. "Ruby Parker, I mean."

"She did say she got it from Grey."

"She got the fact that there's a nest of potential spies in our midst from them. Not that kooky business about a wager."

Mordred smiled. "I'm not sure she truly believes there's someone in Russia who's challenging her to a staring match."

"Just going by her own words this afternoon, I'd disagree."

"I think she's decided to act *as if* that's the case. It's a useful fiction."

Alec scoffed. "Useful for who?"

"For her. She's testing the limits of her own belief in the superiority of a rights-based democracy."

Alec took a sip of his beer. "A lot of people are doing that at the moment."

"I fully expect the better her to win."

"I thought you meant useful for me. For Alec Cunningham."

"How is Valentina?"

He grinned in an involuntary way. "I asked her for a coffee. This afternoon."

"I thought you might. How did she react?"

"I'd say, she looked pleased."

"Well, thank God. Thank God for common sense."

"Cheers to that."

"Na Zdorovie!"

They clinked glasses.

When Mordred got home that night, Phyllis was already in bed. She put her arm round him as he got in beside her. Whatever she and Edna and Annabel had concluded about Ruby Parker – and he had no doubt that was one of the things they'd discussed – she'd tell him about it in the morning.

He should go and see Ruby Parker first thing tomorrow, although he wasn't sure he would. He'd had a lot to drink. Although the alcohol-inspired Mordred was one of his better selves, it didn't always look that good, even to him, in the cold light of day.

But he'd had an idea about her Muscovite 'high-ranking official with an inquisitive disposition'. It had to be some religious evangelical. What the nine were now doing, if they were doing anything at all, was inadvertently spreading the ideals of the Russian Orthodox Church. If Alec wanted to get anywhere with Valentina, he'd have to convert. And he probably would. The others, too. No one believed in very much in the West any more: morals, yes; the deeper, supposedly 'spiritual' stuff, not really. And a church that had produced both Dostoevsky and Tolstoy ... well, it certainly couldn't be all bad.

That night, he dreamed he was a blonde-haired man – someone like Colonel Vorotyntsev in *August 1914:* young, patriotic, principled - sitting in a poky office, somewhere deep within the Lubyanka Building, discussing the prospects for the department's London wager with his superior, a small, grim-looking Afro-Russian woman.

Afterwards, he couldn't remember what she'd said. Nevertheless, he was overpowered by a sense of *who she was*. Feared and respected in equal amounts by government ministers, opposition members of the Duma and civil servants, cerebral, punctilious, charming up to a point, devoted as a medieval monk to higher (but to most outsiders, hopelessly arcane) ideals, ruthlessly observant, but, if you didn't happen to be in her good books that day, implacable.

He didn't get her name.

Acknowledgements

I used several books in the writing of this novel:

Roger Mosey *Getting Out Alive: News, Sport and Politics at the BBC* (Biteback 2015)

Robin Aitken *The Noble Liar: How and Why the BBC Distorts the News to Promote a Liberal Agenda* (Biteback 2018)

David Sedgwick *BBC: Brainwashing Britain?* (Sandgrounder 2018)

Tom Mills *The BBC: Myth of a Public Service* (Verso 2016)

Charlotte Higgins *This New Noise: The Extraordinary Birth and Troubled Life of the BBC* (Guardian Faber 2015)

My own view of the BBC (for the virtually nothing it is worth) is that it probably is guilty, in the words of John Humphrys, of 'liberal bias', but that, to a large extent, that is an unavoidable consequence of its public service remit. We would almost certainly be worse off as a nation without it.

As always, I would like to thank Lynn Hallbrooks for her careful proofreading of the text of this novel.

Books by James Ward

General Fiction
The House of Charles Swinter
The Weird Problem of Good
The Bright Fish
Hannah and Soraya's Fully Magic Generation-Y *Snowflake* Road Trip across America

The Original Tales of MI7
Our Woman in Jamaica
The Kramski Case
The Girl from Kandahar
The Vengeance of San Gennaro

The John Mordred Tales of MI7 books
The Eastern Ukraine Question
The Social Magus
Encounter with ISIS
World War O
The New Europeans
Libya Story
Little War in London
The Square Mile Murder
The Ultimate Londoner
Death in a Half Foreign Country
The BBC Hunters
The Seductive Scent of Empire
Humankind 2.0
Ruby Parker's Last Orders

Poetry
The Latest Noel
Metals of the Future

Short Stories
An Evening at the Beach

Philosophy
21st Century Philosophy
A New Theory of Justice and Other Essays